THE FIRST ONE TO DIE

ALSO BY VICTORIA JENKINS

The Girls in the Water

THE FIRST ONE TO DIE

VICTORIA JENKINS

bookouture

Published by Bookouture
An imprint of StoryFire Ltd.
Carmelite House
50 Victoria Embankment
London EC4Y 0DZ
www.bookouture.com

ISBN: 978-0-34913-244-0
eBook ISBN: 978-1-78681-313-8

Printed and bound in Great Britain by Clays Ltd, Elcograf S.p.A.

Papers used are from well-managed forests
and other responsible sources.

MIX
Paper from
responsible sources
FSC® C104740

NOW

She forgot that the other girl was holding a knife. For a moment, everything else was wiped away and she was back there, humiliated and with no one to fight her corner. Her arm flew out, her fist meeting the side of the girl's face. The girl with the knife recoiled, cried out in pain, and fell back against the kitchen door; a second blow was landed. The knife was dropped to the floor. She swung again and again, her anger with the world culminating in a torrent of violent rage. The other girl tried to fight back, but her attacker's strength overpowered her and she found herself cornered, helpless to do anything other than accept the repeated blows landing upon her. She slid to the floor, desperately trying to cover her face with her arms as her attacker continued like a madwoman; a creature possessed.

At last it stopped. The red mist faded, dropping to the floor like a fallen curtain, leaving her exposed. Then she saw what she'd done. She stopped, stood back; saw the bloody mess she had made of this person she didn't know. She saw the violence she was capable of; all those years of suffering and endurance built up into one seething outburst of uncontrollable rage. She leaned down and took the knife from the floor. The girl looked up at her, barely able to speak; desperate pleas leaving her mouth in an incoherent babble of pain and fear.

She drew the knife back before plunging it in.

CHAPTER ONE

All she'd been told was to pack a bag of overnight things and something she could wear out to dinner. Other than that, Chloe had no idea where they were going. Scott picked her up at just gone five o'clock after finishing work. Chloe had been off that day; a rare lazy Sunday spent idling away the hours in Alex's back garden, making the most of an uncharacteristically warm June. The air had felt so still those past few weeks, so peaceful, that to Chloe's young yet cynical mind it was inevitable there was something lurking around the corner to upset this alien calm.

In the meantime, she was making a concerted effort to try to enjoy the here and now.

'What's this mystery trip in aid of then?' she asked, as she put her bag in the back and got into the passenger seat of Scott's car. 'My birthday's not for another six weeks.'

He shot her a smile. 'Does there have to be an occasion?'

'Usually.'

'OK,' he said, stretching the letters in a drawl. 'It's Sunday.'

'And …?'

He gave a shrug as he pulled away from the kerb. 'Day ends with a y,' he suggested.

Chloe laughed. She knew it didn't sound as relaxed as she had hoped it would; if anything, there was something stilted and forced, which she knew he would pick up on. The truth was she'd been dreading this evening. Their six-month relationship had been so far a very calm and steady affair: dinner dates once a week, the occasional cinema trip at weekends (work permitting) and afternoons on mutual days off spent on the sofa at Scott's flat when his housemate was working and they had the place to themselves.

It had all been very polite.

Yet despite how well they'd been getting on and how much she liked him, Chloe was aware of the elephant in the room. They'd still not had sex. It was ridiculous, she thought – only adolescents and members of the kind of religious group she'd managed to escape from years ago dated someone for six months without having sex with that person, and yet regardless of how much she might have wanted to sleep with Scott, she could never find herself able to switch her mind off from the past. Until she found a way to do it, she felt she was destined to live the life of a nun.

The thought that most men would have given up by now often preyed on her mind. She glanced at Scott as he drove the car down the slip road and on to the M4 headed west. He looked impossibly handsome; even more handsome than the first time she had seen him, way back before Christmas, chatting with another member of staff at the poolside in the leisure centre where he worked. She had found herself unable to take her eyes off him then, like some lovesick teenager transfixed by the new boy at school. Now, she still couldn't believe that she was here, sitting in his car beside him.

Something had to go wrong. And yet, so far, there had been no well-concealed flaw let carelessly slip; no chip in the otherwise perfect exterior.

Chloe had lived a life that had repeatedly reminded her of the mantra that if something appeared too good to be true, it usually was. The thought wasn't helping her in her quest to move forward: a move Alex was constantly reminding her she needed to make.

When they arrived at the hotel, Chloe realised it must have cost a small fortune. She had never stayed in a hotel where a member of staff carried guests' bags to the room, and within moments of merely being in the lobby she found herself feeling horribly out of place.

'You OK?' Scott asked, sensing her anxiety.

Chloe took a glance at the clothes she was wearing – sandals, leggings and a thin cotton off-the-shoulder sweater – and felt a wave of relief at the thought of the dress in her suitcase. 'Yeah, fine,' she lied.

They went to their room to dress for dinner – Chloe changing in the bathroom in order to keep any glimpse of her body concealed from Scott – and went down to the hotel's restaurant. She felt mildly ridiculous in the dress she had chosen: an outfit that was so unlike her she wouldn't have blamed Scott for thinking an intruder had emerged from the en suite. She took pride in her appearance and in her day-to-day life liked to look smart, professional, yet now she was unable to shake off the feeling that she resembled a cast member of an MTV reality show. As they sat, she tugged at the hemline of the dress, wondering whether in her eagerness to look as though she'd made an obvious effort she had ended up appearing desperate.

'You look lovely,' Scott told her.

'I feel stupid.'

Scott opened the menu, using it as an excuse to ignore the comment. 'What do you fancy?' he asked, not looking up.

They were interrupted by a waitress, who took their drinks order. Chloe studied the menu without really looking at it, self-consciously pushing a short strand of fading blonde behind her ear. Until recently, her hair had always been long. It had also been bottle-blonde, but she was now allowing the colour to grow out.

When the waitress left, Scott put his menu on the table. 'Do you want to go?'

'No,' Chloe said, too quickly.

'You just don't look like you want to be here. We can go and get a bag of chips, order a takeaway … We don't have to eat here.'

'It's fine,' she said, the words snapping from her more abruptly than she'd intended. Her gaze fell to her left, and to the couple on the next table. The woman was looking over at them, making no attempt to hide her interest in their conversation.

'I'll have the beetroot salad,' Chloe said, choosing the first vegetarian option she'd seen.

Scott returned his attention to the menu. When the waitress came back with their drinks, he ordered food. They sat in silence, the awkwardness punctuated by the occasional comment about the restaurant's unusual decor and then, later, the food.

'Is it OK?' Scott asked. Chloe had been pushing her salad around the plate with her fork, unaware she'd been doing it until she was interrupted. What was wrong with her? she wondered. She was in a lovely restaurant with a lovely man; someone who paid her enough attention to care how her food was. Wasn't this what she'd wanted?

'It's great.'

'Tell your face then.' It was said with a smile, but Chloe realised she was proving a disappointment.

'Come on,' Scott said, trying to catch the attention of the waitress. 'I'll get the bill.'

Back up in their room, Scott was quick to apologise. 'This was a stupid idea. I'm so sorry.'

Chloe sat on the edge of the bed. 'Don't be silly, it's not you …' She cut herself short, aware of what she'd almost said. Of course it wasn't him – they both knew that much already. It was her and all her stupid insecurities: her reluctance to let anyone too close, her inability to shut off her memories, her apparently incessant need to continue punishing herself for past mistakes.

'I just, you know … You mentioned feeling guilty about being at Alex's so much, and Ben's always at mine, so …' Scott covered his face with his hands and sighed. 'Sorry.'

'Stop saying sorry.'

She patted the duvet beside her, realising as soon as she'd done so that she was like a pet owner beckoning a faithful dog. She wondered how the situation could possibly become any more embarrassing. 'It's OK. Honestly.'

He sat beside her. 'I've just gauged this all wrong. It's a bit too much, isn't it?'

Chloe nodded. 'Can I put my other clothes back on?'

'Course you can. You do look lovely, though.'

She laughed. 'Don't be nice. I'm just a fake tan away from *Geordie Shore*.'

She made to stand from the bed, but Scott took her hand in his, holding her back. 'I didn't bring you with the intention of ... you know. That's not what this is about.'

'Well of course it is.'

She spoke the words before she had time to consider their possible reception. Scott looked as though she'd just thrown something at him: a sort of wounded, shocked expression that evidenced the fact he hadn't expected her to be quite so blunt about it.

'Come on, Scott,' she said, desperate now to make light of the increasingly awkward situation. 'Dinner, hotel room ... You weren't really planning on us coming back here for a game of Scrabble, were you?'

His eyes remained fixed on her, whether in surprise or disappointment Chloe couldn't be sure. 'Actually, I did ask the manager if I could borrow the Scrabble board, but she's already loaned it out to room twelve.'

Chloe's face softened and she jabbed him in the ribs with an elbow. 'I'm sorry. This is lovely, it really is. It's just ... I want to, but ...' She looked away, embarrassed by the words that hadn't even been spoken.

'You don't have to explain anything.'

I do, she thought. She already had, several times over – to the point at which she'd become bored of the sound of her own voice – and yet no matter how often she tried to explain to him why physical intimacy had become such an issue, the words always sounded ridiculous and her reasoning seemed more and more absurd.

Scott squeezed her hand and leaned in to kiss her. 'The seafront's just a few streets away,' he said. 'Fancy going for a walk?'

She smiled. 'Love to.'

CHAPTER TWO

It was a warm, clear night and the party had hours earlier spilled from the house and into the yard at the back of the row of terraces. The air felt electric that evening, alive with the excitement and relief of exam season closure. The last exam had taken place two days earlier, and Friday night's party had gone on right through into Sunday, stopping only for people to catch a few hours' sleep and restock on supplies before starting again. A dull thud of bass throbbed through the building like an irregular heartbeat, stifling the senses of those people who remained within the four walls of the house. Outside, drinking games were being played around a plastic garden table, its surface barely visible amid the array of bottles and glasses that adorned it. Joints were being passed between friends, bad jokes shared, sexual innuendo thrown into every conversation.

A train rattled past, noisy and fast: the 23.14 from Cardiff Central to Ystrad Rhondda, at this point midway through its hour-long journey; stopping just further up the track in Pontypridd. From the second floor of the terraced house in Treforest, from the bedroom at the back, the students who lived there often watched the trains go past – sometimes on sun-bleached afternoons, sometimes on nights like this, when the orange glow of the carriages would whizz past in a hazy blur of light. They could escape the noise of the world up on the ledge that jutted out over the first-floor bathroom. Up there, secrets had been shared and promises made. They were young – they knew those promises would likely be futile against the weight of time – but some had been made with good intentions.

Jamie Bateman was standing in the kitchen, watching through the window as an unfamiliar group of people laughed exaggeratedly over something that had just been said. He wondered if any of his housemates actually knew these people, or if they'd just heard evidence of a weekend-long party and gravitated towards the nearest available alcohol. Sidestepping the other people who lingered in the kitchen, Jamie moved to the back door. He could see Leah sitting on the stone wall at the end of the yard, her head resting against the side of the wooden shed in the corner. She was watching a drinking game unfold at the table, her face impassive as the people around her grew increasingly animated. Her long hair fell over the side of her face, managing to exaggerate her drunkenness.

He wondered where Tom and Keira had got to. The more he thought about them, the more he realised he didn't want to know.

A girl fell into him as she passed, steadying herself with a grip on his elbow and a giggled apology. He studied her as she straightened: pale face, pink lips; eyes wide and slightly too far apart. He wondered what she saw when she looked at him. He wondered what any of them saw. Women seemed to look through him as though he wasn't really there. Everyone seemed to look at him that way. The girl's apologetic expression quickly changed; she eyed him with curiosity now, wondering why his stare was so prolonged.

When Jamie glanced back out at the yard, Leah had looked up, her eyes now fixed on him. Her dark hair had been swept to one side and her legs were pulled up on to the wall, hugged to her chest as though protecting her. She looked away and turned her attention back to the table.

Jamie went back into the house.

*

Upstairs, in the back room of the second floor, Tom and Keira were sitting on the ledge outside her bedroom window. She was agitated, annoyed by his refusal to ever see things from anyone else's point of view. The roof was usually a place for quiet and calm; that evening, it was the only place they could escape the prying eyes and ears of others.

'How did you think people wouldn't find out?' she snapped.

Tom took a deep drag from his cigarette and exhaled slowly, losing the smoke to the summer evening breeze that was more noticeable up there than down in the yard below.

'Jamie knows as well,' she told him.

Tom rolled his eyes. 'Jamie doesn't know anything. He doesn't know what day of the week it is most of the time.'

Keira sighed, exasperated. 'And get that out of my face.' She gave his arm a shove, redirecting the clouds of smoke that trailed from his cigarette.

He turned sharply to her, alcohol fuelling his already short temper. 'What is the matter with you tonight?'

'Jesus.' Keira turned to the window, swung her slim legs through the gap and went back inside the bedroom. 'I just thought you were different, that's all.'

'Why?' Tom followed her back into the bedroom, having to duck lower to get his tall frame through the open window.

'What?'

'Why would you think I'm any different? Different to what?' It was said with a smirk that was intended to be noticed. It was intended to provoke a response.

God, he was annoying. She had thought for a while she was beginning to like him – he had grown on her during the past eighteen months, although in much the same way as the verruca she'd once needed to have removed – but when he was behaving like this, like his usual stubborn, ignorant self, she could feel nothing but contempt towards him.

'I just thought you were a bit more intelligent, that's all. Obviously I was wrong.'

'Never got caught, have I?'

'That's luck, Tom, not cleverness. It's only a matter of time before your luck runs out. Especially if people are starting to talk.'

He leaned against the wall and took a long drink from the bottle of beer he was holding. 'I'm going home at the end of the week. It'll all be forgotten. By September, people will have found someone else to gossip about.'

Keira sighed and sat on the bed. She pushed a length of dark hair from her face and studied him, standing there so casually as though everything was fine. In that moment, she thought she might hate him. She didn't think she had ever hated anyone before, not really – it wasn't in her nature to feel anger or bitterness towards other people. But Tom knew how to push people's buttons.

And recent events had changed everything.

'I don't even understand why you're doing it.'

He smirked again; the look infuriated Keira. 'You wouldn't. I mean, look around you, Keira.' He raised the hand that held the bottle and moved his arm in an exaggerated semicircle in front of him. 'Look at your life.'

'I don't know what you mean,' she said defensively.

'Of course you don't,' he scoffed, taking another mouthful of beer. 'All this stuff … it's so normal to you.'

It was the drink talking, Keira thought. She had seen Tom behave like a pig before, had seen him sarcastic and arrogant and full of himself. But she had never seen him cruel, not like this. Did he mean it? If he did, it hurt more than she might ever have anticipated it would.

'Whatever you think about me, it doesn't give you the right to do what you've been doing. Have you even bothered to think about the people this might affect?'

Tom's expression changed, something dulling behind the pale grey of his eyes. 'You're so fucking sanctimonious, do you know that, Keira? It must be fucking perfect living in your little princess world.'

'Oooh,' she said, retaliating against his spite. 'Big word there – well done.'

She recoiled on the bed as he threw the bottle he'd been holding against the wall. It smashed into tiny shards and stained the paintwork with an abstract shock of cheap lager. 'That's exactly the kind of patronising shit I'm talking about. You make everyone feel this fucking big.' He moved towards her and waved his hand in her face to demonstrate his meaning.

For the first time, Keira felt afraid of him. She'd found out things about him she would never have thought possible. She didn't want to be living with someone like this. What else was he capable of?

'I'm fed up of always being made out to be the bad guy.' The words were spat in her face, showering her with his anger. 'You want to know what's really going on … ask your little friend downstairs.'

Keira's brow furrowed questioningly. 'What's that supposed to mean?'

He shook his head. 'Open your eyes, Keira. Life isn't one giant Disney movie. Oh … and everyone thinks the same as me, by the way. Spoilt little rich bitch.'

Tom stood back and stormed from the room. Keira got up from the bed and stared at the wall on which the thrown drink was already beginning to dry in trails that ran like thick teardrops. They were supposed to be coming back to this house after the summer holiday, returning in September for their final year. They'd got on well together, at the start.

Before they'd known each other, she thought.

She considered what he'd just said. Was that really what he thought of her? Was that what they all thought of her?

She went back to the window and pushed it wide open. Climbing back out, she sat on the ledge they had come to treat as a makeshift balcony and reached for the drink she'd left there. She glanced down at the narrow stretch of yard beneath her, hearing voices and laughter drift up towards her; feeling so much further than just two floors from the people scattered below. She didn't belong here any more.

There were things she wished she didn't know; things she wished she'd never been made aware of. She had already signed a contract for the following year's rental agreement, but there must be some way of getting out of it. She couldn't come back here now, not with things as complicated as they were.

She felt tears catch at the corners of her eyes. She thought of her mum and dad. She thought of her sister. She wanted to go home.

The bedroom door sounded behind her and Keira sighed, wiping the back of her hand across her eyes in an attempt to conceal her tears. She didn't want a repeat performance of the argument they'd already had. Tom had said everything there was to say; she didn't need to hear any more. She felt so upset, she didn't even want to look at him.

She wondered again whether what he'd said was true, if that was how other people perceived her. She was lucky, she knew that, but she'd never tried to rub anyone's face in her good fortune. If she had, she'd never meant to. She'd never tried to belittle anyone; she had thought they were her friends. If she really did make people feel that way, she'd never been aware she was doing it.

She felt him behind her, then everything happened so quickly. A hand touched her back for the briefest of moments before a firm shove sent her flailing from the ledge. She tried to break her fall, twisting desperately through the air, but there was nothing to catch hold of, nothing with which she could stop herself.

A single scream cut through the night air.

CHAPTER THREE

The call woke Detective Inspector Alex King at twenty past two in the morning. Uniform had been called to a house in Treforest, where it was reported a young woman had fallen from a rooftop. When Alex got there, the street was eerily quiet. The majority of the partygoers had already been sent home, though by all accounts clearing the scene had been pretty shambolic. Some had fled; others had stayed to gawp. Incidents such as this usually generated crowds of rubberneckers, people who longed for a glimpse of misery as an interlude in their lacklustre lives; a reminder that no matter how disappointing their own existence might be, some poor sod's had just got a whole lot worse.

According to the call she'd received, there had been an outbreak of panic at the house on Railway Terrace, with many revellers fleeing as soon as they became aware of what had happened, while others gathered around the victim, arguing over what to do. The neighbours in the adjoining houses had been woken by the screams of eyewitnesses.

'How many people were here?' Alex asked the first of the two uniformed officers already at the house. He looked barely old enough to be out of school, and the sheepish expression that preceded his response was enough to answer the question.

'We can't be certain.'

'Why not?'

The officer shrugged, which managed to irritate Alex more than any words might have done. 'There was a houseful, apparently.'

The paramedics had pronounced Keira North dead at the scene. Her housemates were sitting in the living room, a girl and two boys, the three of them side by side on the sofa, stunned into silence. Alex glanced into the room as she passed, unable to ignore the chaos that surrounded the three students. A drink so blue it bordered on fluorescent had been spilled over the end of the beige sofa. Empty bottles and dirty glasses littered the flimsy self-assembly coffee table in the middle of the room. Evidently the party had been an eventful one long before its traumatic ending.

The girl had been crying; there were telltale signs of mascara smudged down her cheek and her skin was flushed with an assault of raw emotion. She was sitting nearest the door, her body turned at an awkward angle from the two boys beside her as though she was trying to block them out and pretend neither of them was present.

'What sort of state are they in?' Alex asked the officer, nodding towards the living room.

'Not too bad now. The girl was pretty drunk when we first arrived, but the accident seems to have sobered her up.'

Alex followed the young officer through to the kitchen. The back door was open, leading out on to a small L-shaped area that passed as garden space. Like the inside of the house, the place was a mess. Smashed glass lay strewn on the patio slabs and cigarette butts adorned every available surface. There was evidence of drug use on the garden table.

She stepped into the yard. It was still warm out, despite the unearthly hour. Another man – the second of the two attending officers – was waiting there for her.

'Scene-of-crime officers are on their way,' she told him.

She studied the fallen body. The girl's head was snapped back at an angle, her eyes still open. They stared past Alex's shoes, unseeing, the life drained from the pupils. She was wearing a pair of black leggings and a short-sleeved checked shirt that had risen to her waist during the fall. Her long hair was tangled in messy tendrils across her back and face.

'Why the hell has everything taken so long?' Alex said, directing her impatience at the officers. 'The call was made at just before midnight. Almost two and a half hours ago.'

She didn't need to say any more; the unspoken accusation hung in the air between them. She stood with her hands on her narrow hips, her unnerving focus switching between the two men as she waited for some sort of response.

The second officer shot the first an uneasy glance. 'It was chaos here. They had a houseful – we tried to get it cleared as quickly as we could.'

'Cleared? Of what … witnesses?' Alex shook her head and bit her tongue, saving the reprimand for later. 'Show me the room.'

She and the first officer went back into the house. The young man showed her upstairs, to the bedroom that had been Keira's and from which she had fallen. The room was neat and tidy, everything organised and in place. History textbooks lined the shelves above the closed laptop that sat on the desk. A dressing table stood to the side of it, make-up and hair products in orderly rows beneath the mirror. The bed was made, though indentations in the duvet suggested that more than one person had recently sat there.

Hanging above the bed was a photo collage; an array of images protected by clear plastic envelopes. Alex moved to the head of the bed and studied them closely. Many of the photographs had captured moments that had taken place in this house, and the faces she had seen downstairs in the living room were instantly recognisable. Then there were others: family, school friends; an accumulation of a young life's worth of memories.

The word 'accident' echoed in Alex's brain. Accidents could happen so easily, she thought. Misplaced footing, attention distracted by something or someone; it was easy to be caught off guard and end up suffering the consequences of a moment's carelessness.

'Anyone know what's gone on here?' she asked.

The broken glass on the carpet near the window indicated that something had happened in this room before Keira North had fallen to her death. It was a beer bottle, thrown against the wall; a splash of stains ran in streaks down the paintwork. Alex went to the window. She could feel the eyes of the young officer behind her, watching her every movement. If the looks that had been passing between him and his colleague were anything to go by, they both realised themselves guilty of a catalogue of errors.

'We're not sure. The three downstairs said they don't know anything about it.'

Alex turned sharply. 'Did you come up here?' she asked. 'When you got here?'

The officer hesitated on a response, which gave her the answer she needed.

'How long did it take for one of you to get up here?'

The officer looked past her, to the still-open window. 'Ten minutes,' he mumbled. 'Maybe fifteen.'

Alex's reaction stamped itself on her face. Ten minutes was more than sufficient time for the scene to have been contaminated or altered. What had they been doing during that time, other than chasing off potential witnesses? She pursed her lips, trying to hold in her frustration. She would deal with the two of them later.

She turned back to the window. It was a large single pane of glass, side-opening. It swung into the room, allowing anyone inside to climb out on to what the students had apparently used as a makeshift balcony. It was clearly a breach of some sort of health-and-safety law. How tragic that it would take a young woman's death for the landlord to do something about it. He or she would probably be facing charges too.

Careful not to touch the window, she leaned out to assess the space. The air was like stepping from a plane into a Mediterranean summer's evening. There was a stillness; a stark contrast to the reported chaos of events just hours earlier. The cruelty of time, thought Alex. The world kept spinning, clocks kept ticking: time didn't stop for anyone's tragedy. Tomorrow the world would carry on as though Keira North had never existed.

There was a concrete ledge that ran the width of Keira's bedroom, about nine feet long and a foot and a half wide. It led on to the sloping roof of the first-floor bathroom. It was from the ledge that Keira was reported to have fallen. What had she been doing there? It didn't look obviously dangerous, although Alex imagined that any thoughts of safety had been easily abandoned under the fuggy influence of alcohol. The ledge was not wide enough to comfortably stand on, not without consideration of the drop below; at most, it could be used as a step between the window ledge and the bathroom roof. Partygoers reported having seen Keira sitting on the ledge earlier in the evening, and if that had been the case, Alex wondered how she had come to fall. Losing balance while drunk and standing was one thing; losing balance while sitting down seemed far less plausible, particularly given the angle and placement at which she had landed.

Alex drew back from the window. 'Anyone with her when she fell?'

'Her housemates say no.'

'The three downstairs?'

The young officer nodded. They heard a noise at the front door. 'SOCOs,' Alex said. She gave the officer a nod and headed back out onto the landing. As she made her way to the first floor, she could hear the housemates talking downstairs in the living room, whispers that couldn't be deciphered from her listening spot at the top of the staircase. When she went down further, her footsteps caused creaks on the stairs and the conversation came to a sudden stop.

She stopped at the living room. 'You've all provided statements?' she asked.

The three nodded, their movements so in sync that it looked almost as though they had been rehearsed.

Back out in the yard, a SOCO was crouched on the ground near Keira North's body, tracking the area for clues. 'Broken neck, you think?' Alex said, as the woman looked up to greet her.

The woman nodded. 'Good chance.' She pointed to the roof of the first-floor bathroom. 'Looks as though she hit the roof there before landing here. Must have been horrific to see.'

More horrific for the poor girl who was now lying at her feet, Alex thought.

She glanced at the yard around them and thought about the bedroom upstairs. Almost three hours had passed before this place had been properly treated as a crime scene. Potential witnesses had been left to walk away. If this turned out not to be a tragic accident, how much crucial evidence had been lost during that time? She looked back at the girl on the ground, and then at the scene-of-crime officers, trying to hold back the thought that this was all too little, too late.

CHAPTER FOUR

Chloe and Alex made their way to Interview Room 2, where Tom Stoddard, one of Keira North's housemates, was sitting waiting. Alex looked tired, dark shadows circling her eyes, the yawn she attempted to stifle behind the back of her hand made obvious by the unintended exhalation that escaped with it.

'I'm sorry I wasn't there last night,' Chloe said, noting her colleague's efforts to appear more alert than she was. 'I'd have been able to attend the call with you.'

She had been living at Alex's house for months now and was worried about outstaying her welcome. Though Alex had done nothing to make her feel in the way, Chloe wasn't sure that living and working together was always a good idea. She liked their partnership. She liked the friendship they'd developed. She didn't want Alex to reassess either based on the fact that she had grown sick of finding Chloe's used make-up wipes left on the bathroom windowsill.

'You're allowed a night off,' Alex told her. 'How was it, anyway?'

'It was good.'

'Good ... that's all you're giving me?'

Chloe smiled. 'Yep.'

Alex rolled her eyes. Chloe knew exactly what she fishing for and she would likely make sure she got it later – little though there was to tell – when they were both back at the house. Chloe had been denying herself the chance of happiness for too long; Alex had kept reminding her of the fact. It was about time the habit got cut loose.

Alex pushed open the door to the interview room and held it aside so Chloe could enter first. The young man sitting with his back to them stood hurriedly when he heard them come in, his sudden movement in contrast with the lazy expression his face wore. He stared at them, impassive, his eyes watery behind the telltale sheen of a hangover.

Tom Stoddard was twenty years old and came from Leeds, according to the background check that had now been completed. He was studying architectural engineering at the University of South Wales and claimed to have known Keira North since early in the previous academic year.

'You can sit down, please, Mr Stoddard.'

The young man slumped back into his chair, his resentment at having to be there already obvious. None of his behaviour seemed normal for someone whose housemate had just the night before fallen to her death.

Alex pressed the button on the tape recorder that sat to the side of the desk against the wall. The boy studied it with scepticism, as though expecting it to spontaneously combust.

'Interview with Tom Stoddard commencing 11.03, Monday 12th June. Present in the room are Detective Inspector Alex King and Detective Constable Chloe Lane.'

'Am I under arrest?' Tom asked, his eyes still fixed on the tape recorder.

'No. We record every interview in case any detail needs to be returned to. How long had you known Keira North, Mr Stoddard?'

Tom's eyes finally met Alex's. They were a pale grey, made even more muted by the alcohol that clearly still flooded his system. When he moved, every action was slowed with the lingering effects of the weekend that had gone before. 'We met early on in the first year of uni, so October before last, roughly.'

'How did you meet her?'

'On a night out with friends. She was with Leah – that's how I met them both.'

'Leah Cross? Another of the people you share the house with?'

Tom nodded. Remembering the recording, he said, 'Yes.'

'So you got on well, developed a friendship ... decided to live together in your second year.'

'Yeah.'

'How did that work out?' Chloe asked.

'Good. Yeah ... it worked out well.'

'What about Jamie? Did you already know Jamie too?'

Tom shook his head. 'There are four bedrooms at the house and there were only three of us, so we advertised for someone and chose Jamie.'

'He's not a student like the rest of you, is he?'

Tom shook his head. 'He works for an insurance company.'

'Did you ever have any involvement with Keira North other than just as friends?'

'No.'

Alex glanced at Chloe. The answer had come too quickly; it was clearly planned, as though the young man had been waiting for the question. If he had been involved with Keira as anything more than a friend, why lie about it now? It seemed a fair assumption that anyone who had nothing to hide would have no objection to sharing the truth of a relationship.

'Is there anything you want to tell us about last night, Tom?' Chloe asked.

The young man was clearly not as calm as he wanted them to think he was. Despite the relaxed posture – the slouched shoulders and the arms that dangled lazily at his sides like a lethargic ape's – his face betrayed his unease.

'Someone who was at the party says they saw you going into Keira's room at approximately half past eleven, about twenty minutes before she fell from the roof,' Alex said. 'Was this person mistaken?'

Tom's arms moved from his sides to his chest, where he folded them in a barricade against the two women sitting opposite him. 'No. I did go in there.'

'Was this person right about the time at which they saw you going into the room?'

He shrugged. 'I don't know. I suppose so. You lose track of time at parties.'

Alex sat back, mirroring his pose. He was aware of it and it seemed to unsettle him.

'There was arguing heard coming from the bedroom. What were you and Keira arguing about, Tom?'

He sat forward and put his arms on the desk. 'Who was it?' he asked. 'This person,' he added, mimicking Alex's phrasing.

The comment was met with Alex's trademark curled lip. She'd seen enough of this young man to decide she didn't like him: too sure of himself, too arrogant, too ready with his excuses. One of his housemates had died, yet he was behaving as though she had just popped out for a while and would be returning later, as usual. His only concern seemed to be centred on the inconvenience her demise was causing him.

'You had a houseful last night, Tom. Safe to say more than one person saw you go into or come out of Keira's room. So let's try again ... What were the two of you arguing about?'

'Keira fell from the roof,' Tom stated. 'It was an accident, wasn't it? Why are you asking me all these questions?'

'We need to speak with everyone who was at the party last night to build a picture of the events that led up to Miss North's death. What were you arguing with her about?'

'I was downstairs when she fell,' he said, ignoring Alex's question yet again. 'I was in the kitchen. There are people who'll tell you that's where I was. I didn't see her fall. I don't know what happened.'

'Thank you for that,' Alex said, 'but it wasn't what I asked.'

The young man glanced at Chloe before looking back at Alex. If he thought he was going to get any reassurance from her, Alex thought, he was looking in the wrong place. Chloe had a particular dislike of liars.

'Look,' Tom eventually said, 'Keira was a bit uptight, all right? She wasn't happy about how many people turned up over the weekend and she was freaking out about the mess. It was just a silly argument, that's all. Just drink talking.'

Alex nodded. 'Drink talking. You or her?'

'Both,' Tom said with a shrug.

Alex sat back in her chair and let her eye dark eyes rest on him for longer than was intended to be comfortable. 'If you think of anything else, Mr Stoddard, please let us know. I assume you'll be going home for the summer?'

'Yeah. Few days' time.'

The young man stood, having already taken his cue that he was free to leave. There was something so arrogant about him, Alex thought again; something overly confident in his manner, despite the nerves so apparent during the interview.

Had this man – little more than a boy – taken the life of his housemate? And if so, why had he done it?

CHAPTER FIVE

Leah heard voices in Leighton's office, so she waited outside and managed to resist the urge to pace the corridor. She hadn't got a minute's sleep. They had spent half the night in the waiting room at the police station and the other half on sofas at friends' houses. Keira's death persisted in playing over in her mind, that ear-splintering scream still ringing in her head like the replaying of a nightmare. She had seen her fall, and now she couldn't erase that sight from her mind. Keira had bounced like a rag doll from the bathroom roof to the yard below, her body landing with a thud that had seemed to echo into the night.

When she closed her eyes, she could see her friend lying lifeless on the patio slabs. She wondered whether the image would ever fade.

The department was quiet. The exams were finished and a majority of students were now thinking about heading home for the summer, if they hadn't already done so. Leah wasn't going home, she'd decided months earlier. There were too many things she could be doing in South Wales – productive ways in which her time could be spent, rather than whiling away the summer months back in Devon – and going home had never really been an option anyway.

But in the aftermath of Keira's death, she wondered whether leaving for a while wouldn't be such a bad thing. The house would be filled with the memory of her friend, each room consumed by the echoes of her voice and her laughter. She already felt haunted; she didn't know whether she'd be able to stay here on her own.

The door to the office opened abruptly, startling Leah from her thoughts. A male member of staff – one of the tutors who'd taught her on a modern European fiction module – emerged from the office and gave her a second look as he made his way past.

'Hi,' Leah said.

The man nodded but said nothing.

Leighton was sitting at his desk, a half-eaten sandwich and a cup of tea in front of him. He looked up at her, his face unable to disguise his response to seeing her yet again in his office. He had apparently assumed that the end of the exams would mean the end of her too.

'I might get to finish these papers this side of Christmas,' he said with a sigh. He put his pen down on the desk and held her stare, his expression reading like a question mark.

Leah hovered by the door. 'Sorry … shall I leave you?'

'No, it's fine,' he said, pushing his chair back from the desk. It was clearly far from fine. 'What do you want?'

Leah's face fell. She didn't like him when he was like this – cold, unwelcoming, as he was most of the time. Yet the more distant he became, the closer she wanted to get. He seemed to treat all his students this way, and she wondered what he was even doing there. He didn't seem to like lecturing; he didn't seem to like the students – not the majority of them, at least. Perhaps he was bitter, she thought. Not for the first time, she noticed the titles that sat on the bookshelves that lined his office. There were the classics, the texts that featured on the various modules he must have taught over the years; there were theoretical studies on the authors who were at the top of his list of apparent preferences. Among them, almost hidden if you weren't looking for them, lurked his own titles – his brief foray into novel-writing that had resulted in lacklustre sales and what must clearly have been a disappointment for him after such obvious faith in his own creative abilities.

'I take it you've heard about last night? Everyone seems to know already.'

Leighton pushed his sandwich aside and ran a hand through his dark hair. 'Yeah, bad news always travels quickly. It's terrible. Do they know what happened?'

Leah sat in the chair opposite him. If she waited for an invitation to sit, she'd be there all afternoon. She studied his face, trying to find the signs of the softer him she knew existed somewhere behind the stern exterior.

'I know what happened,' she told him. 'I saw her fall.'

She didn't think for a moment that Leighton was interested in any of this, but she didn't have anyone else to talk to about it. Jamie had gone to work after speaking to the police, and Tom had been called to the station later that morning. She didn't really want to talk to either of them anyway. The atmosphere had been frosty in the house for a while before Keira's death; now, it had turned to ice between them.

Leah herself was due at the station within the next hour. Although they'd given statements the night before, the fact that they'd all been drinking meant the police were asking for them again, sober this time. She had known they would all be reinterviewed. She supposed it was part of the procedure, under the circumstances.

What were the circumstances, though? Keira had fallen, hadn't she?

'That must have been awful.'

She hated the sound of his insincerity. In fact, it made her angry; a pulsing sensation that she felt in the depths of her stomach, churning like acid burn. He didn't really care about her. He didn't care about any of them. He hadn't cared when she'd been upset before … why would he start now?

'It was. I haven't slept all night … I can't get her out of my head. You know when people talk about things happening in slow motion, like in a film, or an out-of-body experience? That's what it was like. I saw her fall, and I couldn't do anything to stop it. I felt so helpless.' She paused. 'Have you ever felt like that?'

Leighton's eyes narrowed. He had no sympathy for her – that much was obvious. He just wanted her out of his office. Men like him took what they wanted, when they wanted, and they could never see why they should be held accountable for their choices. Their actions.

She wanted him to hold her, but she realised they'd gone beyond that long ago.

'Term's over,' he said, as though she needed reminding. 'You shouldn't be here.'

She leaned on the desk, disturbing the paperwork waiting for him. 'It's like that, is it?' she asked, unable to keep the disappointment from her voice. 'So I do what over the summer, exactly? Wait for you to contact me?'

The photograph of Leighton's wife and two daughters that sat at the corner of the desk had been disturbed with the rest of his things, so that it was turned towards Leah as though to taunt her. She had seen it before: his wife, blonde and glamorous; his two daughters, Isobel and Olivia, younger versions of their mother, both of them picture-perfect. How could he keep that image there, Leah wondered, facing him every day – their beautiful faces looking out at him, watching him – when he knew what he was guilty of?

'I think that's probably for the best, don't you?'

She figured it was a rhetorical question, but she wasn't going to just accept it. 'So we go about things on your terms then, when you say so?'

Leighton's jaw flexed. 'Leah, these buildings are a ghost town during the summer. You keep showing up here, people are going to get suspicious. Is that what you want?'

She bit her lip. To be honest, she wasn't sure the idea of people finding out the truth really bothered her too much. He was the one with a family. He was the one who had to go home every evening to his wife and get into bed with her knowing he was lying to her. It was his neck on the line, not hers. When she thought about it – which she had, often – she realised she really didn't have much to lose.

'No,' she said. 'It's not.' She stood from the chair and made a point of reaching for the photograph to turn it back to where it had originally faced. Leighton watched her do it. He might have had the good grace to at least look ashamed, embarrassed – something – but no, he was far too self-assured for that.

'You'll be in touch then?'

Leighton nodded. There was a knock at the door; not waiting for a response, the person on the other side clattered into the room, almost falling into Leah.

Anna Stapleton, the creative writing tutor, was dressed in her standard faux-boho fashion, all floor-length floral skirt and more cheap jewellery than an Argos catalogue. She seemed to exist in a haze of perfume, suffocating anyone who had the misfortune to get too close. 'Oh, sorry – I didn't realise you had company.'

'Actually, Leah's just leaving.'

Anna gave her a smile, which Leah returned.

'I'll leave you to it then,' Leah said reluctantly.

She left the office and pulled the door shut behind her. She waited a moment in the corridor, absorbing the promise that had been made. She knew Leighton had been telling the truth when he said he'd be in touch.

He was always back in touch.

CHAPTER SIX

Alex glanced through the open doorway at the couple waiting for her in the family room. It was one of the supposedly nicer rooms at the station; carpeted, as though soft flooring might in some way lessen the hard truths delivered within those four walls.

'I can do this with you if you want me to,' Chloe offered.

Alex shook her head, her focus still fixed on Keira North's parents. Of course she didn't have to deliver the news that Keira was dead; the family's local constabulary had been informed of the tragedy, and it had been left to a couple of their officers to relay the news to the young woman's parents.

'This is the worst part of the job,' she said, thinking aloud. 'Well … one of them.'

The physical reactions of loved ones in the immediate aftermath of such news, the expressions on their faces, was something Alex found difficult to forget. The sounds that accompanied them were often even more harrowing and persistent; those guttural reactions, those low moans that emanated from the depths of a person would stay with her for long afterwards, their echoes haunting her.

'Someone's going to have to accompany them to the hospital. I'd rather you stayed here. Leah Cross is due in soon. Find out everything you can.'

'You really don't believe this was an accident, do you?'

'No,' Alex said, reaching for the door handle. 'I really don't.'

Chloe put a hand on her arm. 'I'll be upstairs if you need me.'

Knowing she could no longer delay the inevitable, Alex stepped into the family room and closed the door behind her, leaving Chloe to head back upstairs. David North stood from his chair, his wife's hand still clutched tightly in his.

'Mr North,' Alex said, shaking his free hand. 'Mrs North. I'm Detective Inspector King.'

She didn't get any further: Louisa North's sob filled the room in a burst of noise and emotion. David North sat back quickly, putting a comforting arm around his wife's shoulder.

'I told you,' Louisa said to him, concealing her face behind a hand as though ashamed to have anyone else see her tears. 'I said this would happen.'

Alex took a free chair to the side of David and gave him a look that was intended to be supportive. Whether or not it would have the desired effect was impossible to tell. How on earth could she offer any useful support to a couple who had just lost one of their children?

'Said what would happen?' she asked gently.

Louisa North – a petite woman who looked younger than her forty-seven years – wiped her fingertips beneath each eye in turn before lowering her hand and looking at Alex for the first time. 'We were told there'd been an accident. That Keira had fallen. So why are we here, speaking with you? Detective inspectors work on crimes, don't they? Not accidents.'

Her previous single sob now escalated into a full-blown bout of tears, and Alex reached for the box of tissues that sat on one of the shelves, offering it to David. She watched as he pulled one from the box and pressed it into Louisa's hand.

'What are we going to tell Natasha?' the woman sobbed.

Natasha was the couple's younger daughter, eighteen and in her final year of sixth form. The sisters were apparently close; so close that Natasha had been considering studying in Cardiff that September so that she could be near to Keira.

'We don't yet know the exact circumstances surrounding your daughter's death,' Alex told them, 'but we do know that an argument took place in her bedroom shortly before the fall. Until we've established what happened, we don't want to come to any conclusions. You've been assigned a family liaison officer. She's here in the station – I'll introduce you. Any questions you may have, or concerns, please speak with her. She's here to help you in any way she can.'

'Keira was murdered, then – that's what you're saying, isn't it?'

David North's hand tightened around his wife's. 'That's not what's being said, love.' His own voice was shaking now, weighted down with the force of a grief that was likely not yet fully realised. How long would it take for the impact of what had happened to this family to take its full effect? A month? A year? Alex suspected that in many cases no amount of time was enough to absorb the shock of such a loss. People just found – somehow – a way to adapt; their bodies continued to function, yet their minds would never exist in the same way again. Life went on, but lives stopped.

'I appreciate that this must be incredibly difficult for you, but we will need one of you to make a formal identification.' She paused, knowing that what was to come next would only add further suffering to an already harrowing situation. 'Due to the circumstances surrounding your daughter's death, it has been necessary for a post-mortem to be carried out.'

David North looked at her with confusion, his eyes narrowing in an expression of unreserved accusation. His wife lowered her hands from her face. Her eyes were red and bloodshot and her mouth was set in a scowl, ready for attack.

'No one told us,' David said. His voice was calm, for now, almost disbelieving. The repercussions of Alex's words hadn't quite sunk in, that much was obvious.

'Post-mortems need to be carried out quickly, within the first couple of days after death.' Particularly where a crime is suspected, Alex thought.

'We didn't give permission,' Louisa said. 'No one asked us. We didn't give permission.'

Alex leaned forward in her chair. 'The decision is never taken lightly, Mrs North. We have reason to consider misadventure, and carrying out the post-mortem was the first step in giving us the best possible chance of finding out what happened to Keira, and why.'

'You cut her up,' Louisa said slowly, looking at Alex yet through her. 'You cut up my little girl.'

At her side, Alex could see Keira's father visibly react to his wife's choice of words. His shoulders stiffened as though he was fighting to keep himself upright and his face contorted in a pained grimace, holding back his own tears.

'I know this is incredibly difficult, but we will need a formal identification of the body.'

Louisa North clung to her husband's hand, her face buried in his chest and her wails muffled by his clothing.

'Was she drunk when she fell?' David asked.

She looked up sharply at him, a look of horror on her face. 'Why would you ask that?' She snatched her hand away from his, holding it in a fist in her lap. 'Whose side are you on?'

David sighed. The sound was tired – exhausted – and it seemed to fill the room, sending a further surge of anger through his wife. Alex didn't want to play audience to the scene about to unfold, but it was sadly part of her job.

'This isn't about sides,' David said, fighting to keep his emotions in check.

Louisa stood suddenly and turned to the wall, her arms folded across her stomach. From behind her, Alex could see the woman's shoulders shaking. David North was looking up at his wife pleadingly, but she refused to meet his eyes.

Alex stood. 'Keira wasn't drunk,' she told them.

'You see,' Louisa snapped, turning back to her husband. 'She was a good girl, a sensible girl. She wasn't some idiot who got so drunk she couldn't stand – she was never like that. Why would you even start to think that?' She turned her focus to Alex. 'So what now?' she asked, anger spilling from her every word. 'You cut her open just so you could tell us what we already knew. My daughter is dead and all you can do is sit here talking about whether or not she was drunk. If you think there was more to it, why aren't you doing something about it? Why aren't you looking for whoever did this to my daughter?'

David North reached out and put his hand on the sleeve of his wife's jacket, but it was quickly knocked away.

'Mrs North, I know this is an awful time for you and I appreciate that all this has come as a shock, but—'

The laugh that cut Alex's words short was harsh and brittle, and in that moment Louisa North looked nothing like the woman who had walked into the station an hour earlier. All pretence at composure had been lost; now she was merely an embodiment of her emotions, raw and visceral, every nerve and scar visible.

'You know, do you?' she said accusingly. 'You know what it's like to lose a child and then have some stupid woman who's doing nothing tell you she appreciates what you're going through?'

The words might have hurt her, but the look Louisa North gave her was far more painful. Alex wanted to take the woman's suffering, hold it in her hands, discard it for her, leave it somewhere it could be safely forgotten; somewhere from where it would never be able to make a return. She wanted to bring Keira back, undo everything that had happened to this family. Instead she stood there, as Louisa had said, doing nothing.

She thought the woman was going to hit her. Louisa's hand was still balled into a fist, tensed and ready at her side, her face set in a look of such anger it seemed to have cast itself as permanent.

Judging by David North's reaction, he had also had the same thought. He put a hand out to his wife again, taking her by the arm. His fingers wrapped around her wrist and he pulled her gently back to the chair beside him.

'Come on, love,' he coaxed. 'Come on.'

At once all the anger seemed to leave her; in its place, an overwhelming grief. Louisa North sank into the chair, her body collapsing as though her bones had been reduced to foam. She pressed her head against her husband's shoulder. When she wailed – a guttural, piercing, animal noise – the sound was stifled by his sleeve. He put both arms around her, rocking her like a child.

Alex's eyes met his, and in that moment she felt they at least understood one another, even if she could never know what they were going through.

She reached for the door handle and left the room, closing the door softly behind her.

She would give them some time alone before she told them their daughter had been pregnant.

CHAPTER SEVEN

You never know what you are capable of until you do it.

Bad thoughts have travelled with me for a long time now, but that's all they ever were. They were only thoughts, and there was no one to tell me whether they were wrong or right. There was *no wrong or right*. They were only thoughts. The thought isn't a crime: the deed is. When you take the thought and put it into action, that's when everything changes. I've *changed*. I should probably fear it, but there is something about it that is empowering.

I waited behind her, but not for long. I didn't want to allow myself time to change my mind. Waiting would lead to deliberation and I've already done too much of that, for far too long. Too many people have got away with what they've done. But not this time.

Approaching her, I could smell her perfume, thick and expensive – so strong she might have bathed in it. It seems strange to describe a scent as smug, but that's exactly what it was.

I hate her. I hate all of them.

It is so easy to blend in and go unnoticed. Hate can be kept well hidden: if you want it to, it can remain without colour, taste, sound. I have chewed it up and swallowed it down for so long now, digesting it for the sake of others, when all I've really wanted to do was spit it out and let everyone see it in all its disgusting truth.

The sound of her scream has stayed with me. It replays in my brain, disturbing yet somehow satisfying. It sounds like helplessness. Like despair. It sounds exactly like the things I have felt but have kept *locked inside for all this time. I have transferred my pain to someone else, and it feels good to finally be rid of it.*

　　Had I thought myself capable of it, really? No.
　　Did she deserve it? Yes.

CHAPTER EIGHT

Alex stood at the side of the table upon which Keira North's body lay beneath a sheet, trying not to let her focus linger for too long on the girl's parents. Nothing could have prepared them for seeing their daughter as she was now. The wail that had ripped from Louisa North's throat was even more disturbing than the one that had filled the station when Alex had informed the couple that Keira had been pregnant.

'She was raped.' Louisa turned sharply to Alex now, her eyes red and expression defiant. 'She must have been. She wouldn't have let this happen.'

David moved from his wife, recoiling as though the suggestion had caused him physical injury. 'I doubt that's what happened,' he said quietly.

Louisa turned her attention to him. 'How would you know?' she snapped. 'None of us know anything.'

'She wouldn't have kept it, would she? And she'd have told someone, surely? I don't know.' David turned away from them both, no longer able to look at the shape of his daughter's form beneath the mortuary sheet. Alex could still see the girl's dead eyes staring past her as she had lain on the cold ground of the backyard at the house where she had died, though she had tried to fight the image from her mind. She could see the stitches that had sewn up Keira's abdomen; a crude attempt to mask the cuts that had been made to remove the baby from her womb. A girl, the pathologist had said.

'We may be able to tell more once Keira's laptop has been examined,' she told them.

'You've taken her laptop?' Louisa's anger flared, redirecting itself at Alex. Her face reddened and her jaw tightened, trying to hold back the torrent of fury Alex knew still lay behind it.

'It might give us an idea of what happened leading up to the party,' Alex explained. 'We need to know who she'd been in contact with.'

'So her privacy is violated for a second time?' Louisa snapped, stepping towards Alex. 'It's not enough for you that she's been cut up, that she's …' She glanced back to her daughter, unable to look for too long. She still couldn't bring herself to speak about or acknowledge the baby.

'They're just trying to find out the truth,' David said, trying to pacify his wife.

'The truth,' Louisa spat, 'is that our daughter has been treated like a piece of meat, and you're happy with that, are you? You're OK to let it happen, just standing there and doing nothing?'

She pushed past him as she left the room, her tears audible as she fell out into the corridor. Rather than go after her, David moved closer to his daughter.

'I'm sorry,' he said.

Alex wasn't sure whether he was apologising to her or to Keira.

Chloe sat with DC Daniel Mason in one of the station's interview rooms. Opposite them, Leah Cross was already crying. Chloe had fetched a box of tissues, one of which the girl now held to her face as though trying to conceal her tears behind it.

'I'm sorry,' she said.

'No need to apologise,' Chloe told her. 'We need to talk to everyone who was at the party last night,' she explained, 'so thank you for coming in. You were in the back garden when Keira fell, is that correct?'

Leah nodded. A loud sob was followed by a sharp intake of breath as she attempted to regain her composure. 'Sorry,' she said again, 'it's just been such a shock.'

'Of course. Take your time.'

Leah sat back in her seat, lowering the tissue from her face. She held it in her lap between both hands, tearing fine strips into it. 'I was in the yard, sitting on the back wall. Everyone was laughing, drinking … you know, just normal stuff. There was a scream …' She hesitated for a moment to catch her breath again. 'Keira was suddenly just there, on the ground, not moving. I can't stop picturing her lying there.'

Dan looked to Chloe. He always seemed uneasy around crying, she thought, despite the fact that he had two young daughters. She'd have thought he would be well versed in dealing with emotional outbursts.

'Were you and Keira close friends?' he asked Leah.

The young woman nodded. 'Yeah. We got on well. She was a really nice girl. I can't believe what's happened.'

'This is going to be a difficult thing to consider, Leah,' Chloe said, 'but do you know of anyone Keira might have had a disagreement with recently? A falling-out over anything?'

The girl looked at her, her face caught by surprise. 'No. I mean … Keira got on with everyone. Why would you ask that?'

'An argument was heard coming from Keira's room just before she died,' Dan told her. 'Tom has admitted he argued with her. Any idea what it might have been about?'

Leah shook her head. 'I was outside for most of the evening. I only popped back in a couple of times to use the bathroom, and I went to the one on the first floor – the boys' one. I didn't see Keira much last night.'

'Why was that?' Chloe asked.

Leah shrugged. 'She'd been a bit quiet over the past couple of weeks. I don't know … she just wasn't herself. I think she was tired after the exams and was looking forward to going home. I didn't think too much of it really.'

'Did Keira have a boyfriend?'

Leah shook her head.

'But you'd have known if she did?'

'Of course. I mean … yeah, I'm pretty sure she'd have told me. She was seeing someone for a bit last year, over the summer, but she'd met him back home and they decided it couldn't really go anywhere, not with them both going back to different universities. Since then, she'd not been seeing anyone.'

She stopped and studied them critically for a moment, suspicious now. 'Why are you asking about all this?'

'Keira was pregnant,' Chloe told her quietly. Leah's reaction was enough to confirm she'd known nothing about this. She moved her hands from her lap, resting them on the table in front of her before gripping its edges as though it was the only thing keeping her upright.

'She didn't tell you?' Chloe said.

Leah shook her head. 'No. No, she didn't tell me. How far gone was she?'

'Five months. Any idea who the father might have been?'

She shook her head again. 'She never said anything to me. I mean, I thought we were close, I thought she used to tell me things, but obviously not.' She stopped for a moment, her face crestfallen. She had taken the news of the pregnancy personally, reading Keira's silence as a question mark over the friendship she had thought they'd shared.

'Why are you asking me this?' she said again. 'You don't think …' Her words trailed into silence and her face fell as she realised the implications of the questions. 'I thought this was an accident?'

'We don't know anything yet,' Chloe admitted. 'That's why we need to gain as many facts as possible. You've been really helpful, Leah, thank you. If you think of anything else, no matter how small it might seem, please let us know.'

CHAPTER NINE

It was obvious why Jamie was home late from work that evening. He stumbled into the house at around 8.15, falling into the hallway and sending Tom's bike clattering to the tiled floor with a noise that would have woken the others if they hadn't still been up. They had been allowed to return to the house that afternoon. Leah was in the makeshift dining room, a narrow space that was a thoroughfare between the kitchen at the back of the house and the long hallway. It was barely wide enough for the table she was sitting at, but she didn't like to eat upstairs and the living room was always taken over by Tom, who was usually watching TV while wearing little more than a pair of boxers.

He was in there now, sprawled on the sofa in front of some mind-numbing crap that Leah would only sit through if someone paid her for her wasted time. She was trying to make a plan. A long fourteen weeks lay ahead of her, quiet time in which she wouldn't have the distractions of her university course or anything else. Or at least so she'd thought. After what had happened, it was difficult to focus on anything else.

She was determined, now more than ever, to do something productive. Everything suddenly seemed even more urgent. More fragile. She didn't want to waste the time she had. Life was precious – social media was always reminding her as much: *Seize the moment*, *Today is a gift, that's why they call it the present*, and all those other crappy, supposedly motivational quotations that filled her newsfeed every time she caught up with the internet. They had a point, she supposed, no matter how simpering some of them were in their execution.

And planning was keeping her mind from the memory of Keira's body lying lifeless on the patio slabs in the yard. It was keeping the echoes of that scream at bay.

'Jesus Christ, watch it.'

Leah leaned back in her chair to look through the open dining room door and down the hallway. Tom had emerged from the living room – for once, he'd been considerate enough to put on a T-shirt – and was assessing the damage to his bike. At his side, Jamie was propping himself up with a shoulder against the wall and eyeing Tom with a silent, simmering contempt.

'You know something, don't you?'

At the sound of Jamie's words, Leah pushed back her chair and headed out into the hall. Tom had rested his bike back against the wall and was trying to go back into the living room, but Jamie was blocking the doorway.

'You're drunk, Jay,' Tom said. 'Get out of the way.'

Jamie's face was pink, flushed with alcohol. He was a terrible drinker. The others had found out not long after he'd moved in that just a couple of drinks was enough to send him silly, and too many could prove disastrous, which had happened on several occasions. He'd had a pretty sheltered background from what Leah knew of him: strict parents who had made a point of never allowing him to get away with normal teenage antics and had been keen for him to follow in the family farming business, regardless of what he wanted to do with his own life. He'd moved from Carmarthen to South Wales in an attempt to get away from them, but it seemed to everyone else that independence was something Jamie struggled with.

'Get your fucking hands off me,' he said now, as Tom tried to push him aside from the living room doorway.

'Jamie, come on. I'll make you a cuppa.' Leah looked at him imploringly, not wanting the scene to escalate. There were tears in Jamie's eyes.

'Why did the police want to speak to you about Keira?' he asked, still looking at Tom.

Tom's sigh was audible. 'They spoke to everyone. That's what they do.'

'You were in there longer than the rest of us. Why?' Jamie's voice was shaking, tripping across the words. For a moment, Leah felt almost sorry for him.

'For fuck's sake, just leave it.' Tom barged Jamie with his shoulder, but didn't expect the retaliation that met him. Jamie was tall and strong, but Leah had never seen him use his size to particular effect before. The first blow hit Tom in the stomach, winding him. He staggered and stumbled back out into the hallway, falling into Leah. She knew it wouldn't end there. There was no way Tom was going to take a punch without fighting back, if only for the sake of defending his wounded pride. Regaining his balance, he lunged at Jamie.

Leah moved between them, but her efforts to put an end to the fight before it got started were rewarded with a punch, meant for Tom, to the side of her face. She was momentarily numbed, as though her head had been submerged in ice; almost as though there was no feeling at all. It didn't last long: within seconds, a searing, burning sensation was setting fire to her skin. She put a hand to her cheek, pressing lightly. She could already feel it bruising.

Jamie seemed to sober up immediately. 'God, Leah, I am so sorry. I didn't mean ...'

She raised a hand to him, accepting his apology. She didn't blame him; she blamed Tom. He was always trying to stir up trouble; always trying to goad Jamie. Even now, her face swelling and her expression betraying obvious pain, he was standing there smirking, oblivious to everything but yet another opportunity to belittle his housemate.

'Nice one, Jay,' he said. 'Punching girls. Tell you what, you want to be careful when the police show up looking for you. They'll have you down as prime suspect.'

Jamie's face twisted into a grimace. Leah had never seen him like this, so pent up, so aggressive. She couldn't bring herself to look at Tom. Jamie had a point: what *had* the police wanted to speak to Tom about? Yes, they'd spoken to all of them, but neither she nor Jamie had been kept as long as Tom had. Leah had never trusted him. Now she was beginning to wonder whether she was safe under the same roof.

She put a hand on Jamie's arm, ignoring Tom. 'Go to the kitchen. Please. I'll be there in a second.'

Jamie peeled his eyes from Tom, mumbled something beneath his breath and headed down the hallway and into the dining room, leaving Leah and Tom alone in the hallway.

'How can you stand there smirking after what's happened?' she said.

'Look at you, doing your best friend act,' he replied with a sneer.

Leah looked him up and down, her expression laced with contempt. For a moment she felt like blurting out what the police had told her that afternoon. Tom hadn't mentioned it, so she doubted he knew. If he had known, he would have used it as yet another way to wind Jamie up. She decided to save it, storing the information for a time when it could do the greatest damage. If anyone deserved it, it was Tom.

'You slept with her, didn't you?'

Tom said nothing.

'Was it just to get at him?' Leah gestured towards the door through which Jamie had disappeared. When she didn't get an answer, she took her assumption as accurate. 'I think we all need a break from each other. When are you going home?'

'Wednesday,' Tom said. He pushed past her and headed up the stairs, leaving Leah in the hallway staring at the empty space his arrogance had moments earlier filled.

As far as she was concerned, Wednesday couldn't come quickly enough.

She made her way back through the dining room to the kitchen, where Jamie was waiting as instructed. He cut a pathetic sight, she thought, his pale blue eyes blurry with the weight of alcohol and his blond hair a mess, as though he'd just got out of bed rather than having just arrived home. His work clothes were creased; his shirt was hanging out from his trousers and was buttoned up wrong, making him look like a schoolboy who still needed his mum to dress him in the morning.

'I am so sorry,' he slurred.

Leah shook away the apology, although the heat in her face was still burning like a flame. 'It's fine. It wasn't your fault.'

'I can't get my head around what's happened.' Jamie stumbled to the sink and reached for a glass from the draining board. He filled it with cold water from the tap and drained it in a series of noisy gulps.

'I know. None of us can.'

'*He* doesn't seem too bothered.'

'Ignore him. He's not as cool and calm as he likes people to think. Anyway, he'll be gone in a couple of days.'

Jamie turned back to her, using the worktop to steady himself. 'Just you and me, then.'

Leah watched him for a moment, uncertain whether this was a good or a bad thing. 'Just you and me.'

They heard the sound of Tom's footsteps hurrying back down the stairs; moments later, there was the slam of the front door as he left the house.

Jamie finished his water and put the glass into the sink. 'How come you're not going home for the summer?'

Leah shrugged. 'Not much to go home for. Anyway … you should probably go to bed. Try to get some sleep … things will look better in the morning.'

Even to her own ears, her words sounded hollow. Nothing ever looked better in the morning. In Leah's experience, things only ever looked worse.

CHAPTER TEN

Alex stood in Superintendent Harry Blake's office trying to maintain her composure. It was difficult when she knew he doubted everything she believed about Keira North's death. He had already made it clear he thought it was simply an accident.

'You've heard what happened last night, I take it?' he said. 'A sixteen-year-old girl's in a coma after taking something at a nightclub.'

'I know, sir. Chloe and Dan are heading over to the hospital soon to speak with the girl's mother.'

'Her condition is critical,' Blake said. 'This needs our focus. By all accounts, the girl took one of those so-called party smarties that have been doing the rounds. The drugs squad in Cardiff has been working on this stuff for months. Whatever scum sold her that poison, I want him caught.'

The drug was a combination of Ecstasy mixed with a high volume of caffeine, intended to give users enough energy to see them through a night and into the next morning. They'd been given their nickname due to their bright pink colour, as well as the fact that they were apparently being distributed mostly among teenagers. What hadn't been so clear, yet was becoming increasingly evident, was their possible side effects.

'Yes, sir,' Alex muttered, speaking more to herself than to Blake. 'And I realise it needs our focus – of course it does. But just as this girl isn't less important than Keira North, Keira isn't less important than her either.'

The superintendent sighed and sat back in his chair. Not for the first time, Alex found herself thinking he shouldn't be there. He should have been gone months ago; he was supposed to be in remission, but his coming back to work had only proven a hindrance to his recovery. He looked pale and exhausted and she wished he would start looking after himself. She respected the fact that he hadn't wanted to leave before a suitable replacement had been found, yet at the same time she couldn't condone the way in which he seemed to want things neatly wrapped up for an easy ending to his career.

If only life was that simple, she thought.

'I don't need to remind you that what happened to that girl is a serious crime,' Blake said, and for a moment Alex was unsure which girl he was referring to. 'These bastards are obviously targeting teens, and it's our responsibility to make sure no one else's daughter or son ends up in intensive care. She's the third teenager in less than four months to be hospitalised. Now I appreciate that what happened to Keira North is tragic, but there is nothing concrete to suggest it was anything more than an accident.'

Alex held his gaze, trying to stop her top lip from curling. She could feel her frustrations coming to a bubble, ready to hit boiling point. 'Only because the attending officers made a complete balls-up of things.'

The superintendent raised his eyebrows, waiting for further explanation. Alex was more than happy to provide it for him.

'They took over an hour to clear the house of people, during which time every possible piece of evidence had plenty of time in which to become contaminated. They took contact details for an estimated fifty per cent of the people there, leaving us with now-unknown witnesses who might have been able to shed some light on what happened up in that bedroom. So yes, sir, we have nothing concrete at the moment, but I think it's fair to say it's evident why not.'

She paused for breath. She had already reprimanded the attending officers, though it had been far less polite than this.

'There was an argument in that bedroom not long before Keira died. There was evidence of violence, and, according to the pathologist, it was unlikely she would have landed where she did, in the position she did, if it had been a simple fall. I'd like to go public with this now. We need to speak with as many of the people who left that party without providing a statement as possible. Perhaps news of Keira's pregnancy might prompt a few more to come forward.' She paused again, briefly mulling over her next words. 'I respect you, sir, you know that, but are you sure you're not letting your own situation colour your judgement of this case?'

Blake's face tightened. 'Meaning?'

'Meaning it would be the easy option to consider this an accident. Quiet last few weeks.'

A couple of years ago, Alex would never have thought to speak this bluntly to her superior. Things were different now. There was so much behind them and so little time left. He was taking early retirement following a cancer diagnosis, a course of chemotherapy and a reconsideration of his life's priorities. The job didn't come first any more, and Alex appreciated that. He had two children still young enough for him to play more of a role in their lives than his career had previously allowed for. She got it, all of it.

Yet he also had to understand that she didn't have those things. Seeking the truth was her priority.

'That's what you think of me?' he said, his words steeped in a genuine sadness that made her feel instantly guilty for her choice of phrasing. 'After all this time, you think I'm just opting for the easy route?'

Alex sighed. 'That's not what I meant,' she said, knowing her words had made it sound as though that was exactly what she thought.

'I think you're becoming too involved in this one, Alex. Your attitude towards this case changed completely once you knew that young woman had been pregnant.'

Alex held his gaze, her jaw tensed in defiance. 'Keira,' she said, although she knew the superintendent was well aware of this. 'Her name's Keira.'

'You asked for a chance to prove this was more than an accident. So far, we've got nothing more than supposition and hearsay. I need something concrete to justify keeping this open as a case.'

Alex rolled her eyes. 'Money. Of course. We'd better consider the budget, hadn't we? More important than anyone's life, obviously.'

'I've asked you for evidence,' Blake said, ignoring her reaction. 'Find it.'

Keira North's face stared down at Alex from the evidence board in the incident room at the station. She had been a small girl, slim in build and with a face that looked like so many other young female faces these days, Alex thought: pencilled-in eyebrows, kohl eyeliner; pouting, gloss-stained smile. Young women were so heavily made-up these days that it was becoming impossible to tell what any individual actually looked like. It seemed strange to Alex – and curiously sad – that everyone should want to look the same.

Or maybe she was just getting old.

The team had assembled for a meeting regarding the investigation. The argument heard not long before Keira fell from the window and the smashed bottle that lay strewn in shards on the young woman's bedroom carpet implied that her death had been more than a tragic accident. Interviews with her housemates had subsequently aroused further suspicion, particularly in the case of Tom Stoddard. A theory of suicide had been bandied about by a couple of officers, but the post-mortem report that rested on the table beneath Alex's hand was about to put an end to further talk of that.

'OK,' she said, addressing the team. 'Let's get started. A few of you haven't had much involvement with this case until today, so I'll get you up to speed.' She raised a hand and pointed to the image on the evidence board. 'Keira North. Turned twenty last month. Studied history at the University of South Wales, second year. Her family is from Monmouthshire – they've already arrived in Pontypridd and are understandably distraught at their daughter's death.'

She paused to clear her throat. She was conscious of the envelope that still lay beneath her hand; of the pregnancy that had now been shared with the dead girl's parents. Louisa North's reaction to the news was something she was not going to be able to forget in a hurry.

'According to people who knew her, Keira was bright, friendly and happy. Her coursework grades were all good and she was predicted to do well in her end-of-year exams. She was supposed to be heading home to Monmouthshire this coming weekend, where she had a job lined up for the summer months.'

'Which would seem to rule out a possible suicide,' said DC Daniel Mason. He was sitting at the front of the group, just along from Chloe. The station's resident IT expert, he had proved his worth on a number of recent cases.

Alex raised her hand in agreement. 'Makes it seem increasingly unlikely. And as I said, Keira was reportedly a happy young woman. She'd made plans. None of these things suggest a person intending to take her own life. It's nonsensical.'

Her tone had changed, and with it her expression. It was obvious that her words were aimed at a couple of individuals among the group, and those people knew who they were. Those who had been suggesting suicide as a possibility despite the evidence stacking up against its likelihood were exactly the same people who broke out into a rash at the first glimpse of paperwork. They didn't want the hassle, and if hassle-free meant truth-free, then so be it.

Alex glanced at Chloe. Her eyes were somewhere else, averted from the photograph of Keira on the evidence board. She wondered if the young woman's thoughts in that moment were close to her own. Chloe knew better than anyone how devastating a false suicide conclusion could be.

'There are a number of reasons why this death is being considered suspicious. First, an argument was overheard between Keira and a man a short time before she fell from the window. We now know that the man in question was Tom Stoddard.'

'Her housemate?' one of the DCs asked.

Alex nodded. 'One of them. Tom Stoddard, Leah Cross, Jamie Bateman. All living in the same house as Keira since September last year. All at the party on Sunday night. There was also broken glass on the carpet in Keira's bedroom,' Alex continued, gesturing to the other images that adorned the evidence board. 'If you look at the stains on the wall here, it's obvious this bottle wasn't dropped accidentally. It was thrown against the wall. Tom Stoddard denies having done it. He said the argument heard between them was just about the number of people who'd turned up to the party over the weekend.'

Alex paused and slid the envelope that held the post-mortem result from the table. 'The most important update at the moment is the fact that Keira was five months pregnant when she died. It perhaps gives us a motive. The rest of the post-mortem findings,' she continued. 'Her neck was broken in the fall. And despite what we all might have assumed, Keira wasn't drunk. The toxicology report states there was no alcohol detected.'

'Drugs?'

Alex shook her head. 'We'll need to look into this further – check out whether she'd been seeing a doctor or a midwife. Also, had she told anyone else about the pregnancy?'

'Did her parents know?' one of the DCs at the back of the room asked.

Alex shook her head. Louisa North's reaction to the news that her daughter had been pregnant had been one of complete denial. She had continued in her insistence that her daughter had been 'a sensible girl'. Sensible or not, Keira had only been twenty years old. Thinking back to herself and her friends at that age, it occurred to Alex that even the most sensible of twenty-year-olds didn't really have a clue.

'She was barely showing, so she'd obviously been able to disguise the pregnancy from others,' she continued. 'None of her housemates mentioned it, so unless they were hiding the fact, it would seem they didn't know. Keira was due home soon – perhaps it was her intention to tell her parents then. We'll never know. But it seems unlikely there was no one she'd have confided in. It's a huge knowledge to carry alone, particularly at her age and away from home. I find it hard to believe that no one else knew her secret.

'I don't believe Keira North fell from that window accidentally. She was seen by several eyewitnesses sitting on the ledge during the time leading up to her death – something she and the other people living in that house had apparently done countless times before. Having been up there, it's difficult to see how someone sitting could have fallen. She was sober. Also, the trajectory at which she fell – the placement of her body upon landing – makes it seem unlikely that she simply lost her balance. She hit the roof of the first-floor bathroom in a way that could only have been achieved through force from behind.'

Alex scanned the room, knowing that half her colleagues were as sceptical of her suspicions as Harry Blake was. Most of them would have written this off as an accident and forgotten about Keira North and her unborn daughter. There was a reason why the police treated everything as suspicious until proven otherwise, but Alex knew she'd take no satisfaction in using Keira's death as the case with which to highlight the point.

Chloe caught her eye and gave her a reassuring nod. Alex needed it. It was confirmation that at least one person in the room didn't think she was overreacting and reading more into this situation than there was.

'There'll be a statement going out in a press release later today. Right, things to do,' Alex said, looking back at the images on the board. 'Eyewitness accounts need to be chased up from the people who've not yet already been spoken to. Dan, I know you're going to the hospital with Chloe shortly, but once we've got Keira's laptop and phone, we'll need a check on her recent emails, contacts – in particular, anything we can find relating to the pregnancy.'

'You think it's got something to do with her death?'

'Too soon to say,' Alex admitted. 'But like I said, it's given us a motive. Maybe someone knew about it and wasn't too happy. Until we find evidence to the contrary, we're all working on a murder investigation. Let's please not forget that.'

CHAPTER ELEVEN

Chloe and Dan stood in the intensive care unit, outside the girl's private room. They could see into the room, could see the shape beneath the blanket on the bed, but Amy Barker's face was obscured by a mass of bandages and wires. Her mother was sitting in a chair beside her, both hands wrapped around one of her daughter's. Janet Barker's head was dipped forward, her face partially obscured by the straggly mess of her hair. She looked sleep-deprived; distraught. She didn't notice the two officers for a while, her attention fixed on her child's face and on the horrifying damage one tiny tablet and a momentary lapse in judgement had caused.

The doctor treating Amy was looking at his notes. He ushered Chloe and Dan away from the window and out of view of the girl's mother. 'She's still in a critical condition,' he told them. 'At the moment, her chances of survival are fifty-fifty. The next twenty-four hours will be crucial.'

'You're pretty certain it was one of these party smarties she took?' Dan asked.

'We are now, yes. Amy has shown classic symptoms of an extreme reaction to the Ecstasy in the tablet. The initial fever reported by the people around her at the club was followed by hypothermia, which caused the kidney failure we're now treating. What isn't so clear is the effect on Amy's brain. That's where the next twenty-four hours come in.'

Chloe's attention remained with the scene she had just witnessed, her concentration momentarily stolen by the thought of

Janet Barker and her unconscious daughter. She couldn't begin to imagine what must have been going through the woman's mind.

'Why the hell do these kids want to take this shit?' Dan muttered, as the doctor left them.

'It's sold on the basis of its caffeine content, apparently. They think they're going to get a six-hour high from it. The dealers don't promote the Ecstasy side effects, obviously. Far less appealing.'

They stopped talking as Amy's mother appeared at the doorway, eyeing the two of them with uncertainty. She had been expecting them; she had already spoken with officers the night before, when her daughter had been rushed to hospital from the club in which she had taken the drug, but she had been in such an emotional state that they hadn't been able to gather much information from her.

Chloe introduced herself and Dan before leading Janet Barker to the relatives' room along the corridor. It was sparse and brightly lit, headache-inducing.

'The doctor has informed us of Amy's current condition,' she said as Janet took a seat beside her, 'so we appreciate what a difficult time this is. We do need a bit more information about last night, though, to help us build a picture of what happened to Amy before she took the drug. I'm sorry to have to ask this, but have you known your daughter to ever do something like this before?'

She had expected indignation from the woman – anger, maybe – but instead the question was met with a reluctant and tired shrug of the shoulders. 'Maybe … I don't know. I'd like to be able to say no, but how well does anyone know what their teenager is up to? She's sixteen – I can't follow her round all her life.' Janet's tone had become increasingly defensive, as though she thought the police held her responsible for what had happened to her daughter. Chloe wondered if, at some subconscious level, she might have automatically formed an opinion of this woman based on her daughter's actions.

'We're not here to pass judgement, Mrs Barker.'

'Ms,' Janet quickly corrected her.

'Ms … sorry. Our concern is with finding whoever supplied your daughter with the drugs and making sure that person can't cause anyone else harm. You might be aware of the media coverage this particular drug has received in recent months?'

Janet nodded. She twisted her hands in her lap. 'I've seen it on the news. Amy's not the first, is she? Probably won't be the last, either. They never bloody learn.' She sighed and sat back in her chair, leaning her head back and gazing up at the ceiling. She exhaled slowly, as if releasing all the tension accumulated over the past twelve hours. 'They're everywhere,' she said, almost talking to herself. 'Ask any of the kids – if they want them, they're easy enough to come by.'

'Amy's mentioned this to you before?'

'I've heard her and her friends talking. I always thought she'd have a bit more sense.'

'Which friends were with her last night, Ms Barker? It was an under-eighteens night, wasn't it?'

Janet Barker nodded. It had already occurred to Chloe that given the circumstances, the person who had supplied Amy Barker with the drugs that had landed her in the ICU was likely to have been either a fellow teenager or a member of staff at the nightclub. Was there someone working at the club who was selling drugs to sixteen-year-olds? What sort of person did that?

They had already requested CCTV footage from the club's manager. Dan had offered to trawl through it when they got back to the station.

'She went with her friend Jade,' Janet told them. 'She's here somewhere.'

'At the hospital?'

'Yeah.'

'Do you have her number?' Dan asked. 'If you could get her up here, we could do with having a chat with her.'

'Probably best not to mention us over the phone, though,' Chloe added. 'Might scare her off.'

Janet nodded and reached for her mobile phone from her pocket. A moment later, she was talking to her daughter's friend, asking her if she could return to the unit. Chloe wondered whether Jade too had taken something the night before. Had both girls tried what they'd been sold or given, and Amy been the unlucky one?

'How has Jade been towards you?' Chloe asked once the call was ended. 'Must be difficult for her to be here. She might be blaming herself.'

Janet gave an audible tut. 'Doubt it. They're all the same these days, aren't they? Me, me, me. I don't think Jade would know guilt if it strolled up and slapped her in the face.' She looked away for a moment in an apparent attempt to conceal the bitterness she felt towards her daughter's friend. 'She's here, though, I suppose,' she said, seeming to momentarily regret the anger of her words. 'That's something, at least.'

They spoke a while longer, as Janet filled the room with stories of her daughter's behaviour at school – not a bad girl, as she put it, but not an angel either. She liked to see how far she could push the boundaries any adult set around her; she had been the same as a young child. She stopped talking after a while, as though worried she had said too much and might have inadvertently incriminated Amy by telling them how she had tested her teachers' patience.

The door sounded and Jade entered the room. A small girl for her age, she had an array of piercings in her ears and looked as though she was still wearing the make-up she'd applied to go out the evening before. She had obviously been home at some point to get changed, and was now wearing a pair of leggings and an oversized T-shirt that swallowed her tiny frame.

'They said you were in—'

She stopped mid-sentence as she registered Chloe and Dan sitting with Janet. Chloe had barely had time to stand before the girl shot from the room, yanking the door shut behind her.

'Damn,' she muttered.

She ran after her, following her as she pushed through the double doors that led out of the ICU. She called out the girl's name in the corridor, but Jade only quickened her pace, the trainers she was wearing obviously coming in handy. It was almost as though she'd worn them with this exact purpose in mind, Chloe thought, as she panted behind her.

Chloe hated to run, and the girl was much faster. She seemed to fly down the stairwell, and within seconds she was gone. Chloe stood looking down at the empty flight of steps. It seemed everyone they wanted to speak to preferred not to speak to them.

CHAPTER TWELVE

Alex pulled up outside the student house on Railway Terrace. The street looked different in daylight: wider and dirtier, the buildings neglected and the air permeated with a tinge of grey despite the burst of summer sunshine fighting through the clouds overhead. She glanced in the rear-view mirror. David and Louisa North had parked up behind her. She could see Louisa in the passenger seat, staring blankly at the house in which her daughter had died just two days earlier.

'Here goes,' Alex said to herself, reaching for the door handle.

She was still disappointed by Harry Blake's response to the case. Scene-of-crime officers had attended the house in the early hours of Monday morning, but only after hours had already passed. The mistakes made by the first attending officers meant the building hadn't been searched thoroughly. Before the first signs of daylight, the young woman's death had been all but pronounced an accident by most. Superintendent Blake agreed, and Alex wasn't sure he would allow her sufficient time to prove otherwise.

She only hoped the others living there had had the common sense not to go into Keira's room and touch any of her things. The girl's parents had already endured enough. Tom Stoddard hadn't struck Alex as the most sensitive of individuals, although why he'd want to go into Keira's room following her death, she didn't know. Unless there was something he was trying to hide.

The three housemates had been told when the police and Keira's parents would be visiting the house and had been asked to make sure they were out before they arrived. The last thing David and

Louisa needed was the reminder that other young people – people whose everyday existences had intertwined with that of their daughter – were continuing their lives without disturbance.

As Alex got out of the car, Louisa and David stepped from their BMW and waited tentatively at the kerbside, as though reluctant to go any nearer the house.

'I've got some suitcases in the boot,' David said. 'Can I bring them in?' His voice was uneven, trembling.

Alex nodded.

'We'll just collect her clothes and things,' he added unnecessarily, seemingly desperate to break the unnerving silence. 'Someone will need to sort through them.'

Louisa North's top teeth were clamped on to her bottom lip, fighting back an onslaught of angry tears. She looked at the pavement, avoiding eye contact. Whatever was to come next, Alex thought, was going to be noisy and ugly and cruel. Grief was relentless but unpredictable. Though some sort of reaction was inevitable, how it would manifest itself could never be anticipated. Once they got inside the house, they were going to have to go through it with her.

She took one of the suitcases from David and led the way to the front door. It was quiet inside, almost unnaturally so. She noticed something else: it was a different house to the one she had visited in the early hours of Monday morning. The place was spotlessly clean and the air smelled of some kind of plug-in fragrance. The carpets had been vacuumed and the junk that had littered the stairs – piles of envelopes and discarded bags and jackets – had all been cleared away.

When she glanced into the living room, it was barely recognisable as the room in which she had interviewed Keira's three housemates. The lurid blue stain on the sofa had disappeared – either cleaned away or concealed by turning the cushion over – and there was no trace of the debris that had cluttered the room. As everywhere else, the place had been polished and vacuumed.

They had gone to quite an effort, Alex thought. For whose benefit?

David North was standing at the foot of the stairs, clutching the second suitcase to his chest. Louisa had hung back, still lingering by the door as though uncertain of whether or not she really wanted to go any further.

'Have you been here before?' Alex asked.

David nodded. 'September, when she moved in.'

'Let's take these to her room.'

She led the way soundlessly up the stairs, David and Louisa following. On the second floor, they went to the bedroom at the back of the house. It was as though time had stopped there. Though officers had since searched the room, things were still exactly as Keira had left them: a pair of pyjamas folded and placed on the pillows at the head of the bed; the book she had been reading still resting on the bedside table, its spine bent at the last page she'd seen.

Alex considered the nature of Keira's room and her possessions. They weren't those of an average student. There was a multitude of clothes in her wardrobe, all fashionable and with labels from the pricier end of the high street. If her parents' car was anything to go by, the North family wasn't short of money.

David North moved into the room like a ghost, his face fixed with an expression of hopelessness. Alex placed her suitcase on the floor, careful not to disturb anything.

'If you need me,' she said, 'I'll be downstairs.'

When she turned, she saw Louisa staring at the window. The woman didn't acknowledge her as she passed.

She headed down to the first floor and stood in the open doorway of one of the boys' bedrooms. Something wasn't right. She had never seen this room before, but she very much doubted that this was its usual state. There were no dirty clothes on the floor, no mugs or plates left lying around: all things she might have expected from the bedroom of a student. It was too tidy; too organised.

She moved further into the room, browsing the few textbooks that lined a shelf on the far wall. This room was Tom's rather than Jamie's: there were neat piles of university work, and Alex recognised the trainers he'd been wearing when they'd interviewed him the day before.

Anything that might be used as evidence had already been collected, so there was now no reason why the students shouldn't have tidied up. Maybe they had done it out of respect for Keira's parents. She raised an eyebrow at the thought. She'd been fairly cynical as a younger woman; now, at the age of forty-four, Alex looked for the ulterior motive in everything and everyone. It wasn't the best way to live, she knew, but life had done little to discourage the habit.

She stood with her arms folded across her chest, taking in the orderliness of the room. She felt a weight of pressure upon her. Someone had pushed Keira from that window ledge, she felt certain of it. There were two people upstairs who deserved the truth. At this moment, the responsibility to unearth that truth seemed to be hers and hers alone.

There was something about Tom Stoddard she didn't like and didn't trust. His housemate had died, yet he had seemed so nonchalant when he had been interviewed; so uninterested in finding out what had happened to Keira. Leah and Jamie had both cried during their interviews with the police, in mourning for the young woman they had considered a friend as well as a housemate. Tom's removal from what had happened seemed alien to Alex; she suspected that either he was emotionally defunct, or there was another more incriminating reason for his strange behaviour.

Her thoughts were interrupted by the sound of raised voices from the floor above. She went back out onto the landing, heading back up to Keira's room. When she got there, she found Louisa North outside the window, sitting on the ledge where her daughter had spent her final moments. Her husband was leaning out of the window, trying to coax her back into the room.

'Louisa, stop this, please.'

Alex raised a hand, signalling for him to stay calm. She had no idea what Louisa was doing, but anything was possible. They'd only seen the edges of her grief. There would be stages now – awful, seemingly relentless stages of sorrow that would drag this couple through the worst times their lives would ever likely have to endure – and what they were witnessing was merely the beginning.

'Louisa,' she said quietly, careful not to sound panicked by the woman's erratic behaviour. 'Can you come back in so we can talk?'

Louisa batted her husband's hand away before turning to come back through the window. 'You think I'm going to throw myself off the roof?' she said, her voice laced with scorn. 'Now? With my daughter's killer to find?'

The words were like a slap to David North's face. Tears sprang forth, his watery eyes contrasting with the pale lifelessness that had fixed itself upon his wife's face.

'She didn't fall from the ledge, did she?' Louisa said through gritted teeth, avoiding eye contact with them both. 'Someone killed my daughter.'

CHAPTER THIRTEEN

Leah stood at the doorway of Keira's room, looking at the blank spaces left by the absence of her belongings. The wall on which her collage of photographs had hung seemed strangely big with the images now gone, the wallpaper there brighter than the rest: an odd square of inappropriate optimism. Keira's desk and shelves looked soulless, their character now lost with all the possessions that had been taken.

What might Keira's parents do with her things? Leah wondered. They couldn't cling on to them all – that would be weird. Creepy, even.

Her eyes were drawn to the chest of drawers that now stood empty, all the make-up and perfume that had once been lined up on it in rows now gone. There was something left there, though. She picked it up and turned it over. It was a small gold pendant in the shape of two stars, one overlapping the other. She hadn't seen it before. Leaving it where she'd found it, she crossed the room and went to the window.

Had Keira really been pushed from that ledge? They'd sat there countless times over the past nine months and none of them had ever found it dangerous. If it had been, Keira wouldn't have gone out there. She had been a play-by-the-rules sort of girl, never taking risks or doing anything reckless. Once they'd found what they'd later come to call their balcony, Keira had requested that room. She had liked to sit up there at night and watch the world go by below her. No one objected, because she was just so nice. The rest of them could argue over anything – who'd left the milk out, who'd dragged mud up the stair carpet, which of the boys had used the bathroom on the girls' floor – but no one ever had cross words with Keira. She had been Leah's friend, or so Leah had assumed.

But obviously they hadn't been quite as close as she'd thought.

Why hadn't Keira told her she was pregnant?

It seemed so unlikely, but there was now no denying it as fact. If it was going to happen to anyone, most people would probably have assumed it would be Leah who would get herself knocked up while still at university. Even Leah would have believed that likely. No one would ever have suspected that Little Miss Sensible would go and do it. Leah hadn't even known Keira was sleeping with anyone.

She wondered why Keira hadn't taken the morning-after pill. Had she been on the pill and hadn't worried about the possibility it might not work? It wouldn't be the first time it had failed to do its job. Leah realised that trying to second-guess was useless now; she had thought she'd known Keira, but she had obviously known nothing.

She heard the sound of footsteps on the ground-floor stairs and went out onto the landing. A moment later, Tom appeared below. He stopped at his bedroom door, looked up and noticed her.

'They've been?' he asked.

Leah nodded and headed down the stairs. Tom looked even more tired than usual, with dark circles hanging beneath his eyes. His unruly hair was matted against his forehead, as though he'd been running. He looked as though he needed a shower, a decent meal and a week's sleep.

'Were you here when they came?'

'No.'

He pushed open the door to his bedroom and looked inside without entering. 'So you don't know if they've been in here?'

'Her parents or the police?'

Tom looked back at her with a sarcastic sneer. 'The police, obviously.'

Leah shrugged. 'I don't know. Did you move everything?'

'Obviously.'

He went into the bedroom and kicked off his trainers. Leah followed, uninvited. She stood near the doorway, taking in the unusual tidiness of his room.

'Where did you go last night?'

He turned to her sharply, his eyes narrowed. 'What the fuck's it to you?'

She held his gaze for a moment, wondering why he was so angry with everyone all the time. She didn't think someone like Tom was capable of feeling guilt, but perhaps it had snuck up on him gradually, taking him by surprise. She'd thought she'd known him pretty well; she had thought she'd known his boundaries. Now she realised she might not know anything. The thought sent a shiver through her body, chilling her.

The knowledge that Keira – her supposed best friend – had been pregnant yet hadn't thought to confide in Leah about it was gnawing at her. She wanted to know who the father was. She wanted to know if it was Tom. She couldn't stand the thought that he might have been closer to Keira than she'd been. That wasn't how things were supposed to work.

'She was pregnant.'

'Was she?'

Leah felt her heart pounding. 'How can you be so casual about everything? Don't you care about anyone but yourself?'

Tom rolled his eyes. 'I don't need all this drama. I'm sorry about what's happened, of course I am, but it was an accident, Leah. Just accept it.'

Leah felt anger boil within her. She lunged at him and slammed her fists into his chest. The unexpected assault sent him staggering backwards and he fell against the bed as he tried to maintain his balance. 'If you fucking hurt her …'

She didn't get to finish the sentence. Tom grabbed her by the wrists and flung her backwards, sending her flailing across the room. He followed, reaching for her shoulders this time before pinning her against the wall.

'You'll what, Leah?' he spat. 'If I hurt her, you'll what?' He smirked as he waited for a reply they both knew wouldn't come. She felt his fingertips digging into her skin, bruising her. 'That's right … you'll nothing. And we both know why, don't we?' He pushed her back against the wall before letting her go. 'I didn't touch her.'

Leah tried to catch her breath as her earlier anger was replaced by fear. How well did she know Tom, really?

How well did any of them know one another?

CHAPTER FOURTEEN

DC Daniel Mason was sitting in the main incident room, Keira North's laptop open on his desk. So far he had accessed her social media profiles and her email account. There hadn't been much of interest in either: countless automated messages about assignment criteria and deadlines; junk mail that had never been deleted; social media profiles that held generic content in the form of night-out selfies and 'my life is so hectic' status updates.

There were aspects of Keira's internet search history that had, however, proven of interest. Dan called Alex from her office to show her what he had found. She stopped at the coffee machine on her way to the incident room and handed him a black coffee with two sugars.

'Well spotted,' he said, taking a sip. 'How did you know I take two?'

Alex pulled up a chair alongside him. 'I'm not a detective for nothing. And you've been working here long enough now.'

'You seen this?' Dan asked, gesturing to Keira's laptop. 'It's a Microsoft Surface Book. They don't come cheap.'

'How much?'

'Fifteen hundred on a sale day. Parents must have a bit of money.'

'Found anything on there?'

'One thing's pretty certain,' Dan said, turning the laptop towards Alex. 'Keira North definitely knew she was pregnant. Searches for prams, advice on which foods to avoid during pregnancy ... even baby names.'

Alex looked down at her coffee, needing a moment's distraction. 'What else?'

Dan exhaled. 'Research into benefits for student parents. Forums offering advice on raising a baby while continuing to study. You think there's a link, don't you? Between her death and the pregnancy?'

'I don't know.' It was the truth: she still wasn't sure. The only thing she felt positive about was that Keira's death hadn't been an accident. Everything else remained a mystery; the longer it remained so, the less likely they were to find out the truth of what had happened.

'I wish I could be more help,' Dan said, sitting back in his chair and linking his hands behind his head. 'There's nothing here yet that looks likely to help us find out what happened to her – or more to the point, why it happened.'

Alex looked at the computer screen with an inescapable sadness. A young life had been lost, and another had been ended before it had even begun. Yet another – that of Amy Barker – was hanging in the balance in the intensive care unit of the hospital just a few miles away. Life was precious, though Alex realised she hadn't always known it. She wished she'd learned it sooner, although she knew enough to know that regret was also futile.

Her attention was stolen from the computer screen by the photograph on Dan's desk: his two children. He kept the photo just next to his computer, where his daughters could always keep an eye on him. Alex wondered how much of his wife's pregnancies Dan was able to remember, particularly those early months when worries seemed to gather like long-lost enemies returned to taunt the parents-to-be with their what-ifs. Had he and his wife shared the countdown to every scan, the sleepless nights when irrational fears became heightened, keeping them awake until the early hours; the nagging doubts that something would go wrong and bring all their hopes and excitement crashing to a sudden and brutal halt.

Keira had seemingly gone through all that by herself.

'Seems she was determined to do the best she could,' Alex said, looking through the notes Dan had taken.

'You know I don't like to get into the politics of this place,' Dan said, turning in his swivel chair, 'but I want you to know I'm behind you.'

Alex smiled sadly. It was good to know that not all her colleagues thought she was overreacting to the circumstances surrounding Keira North's death. It was reassuring to have other people's support, and yet she realised that if Dan knew what Harry Blake did, he too might not be so confident about her motivations.

She was finding it difficult to move past the superintendent's words.

'Look at this,' she said, gesturing to the dead girl's laptop. 'She cared about this child – all this internet history is evidence of that. She didn't fall from that ledge. She was sober, and being up there was something she'd apparently done countless times before. If she had thought sitting up there was in any way dangerous, I really don't believe she'd have been doing it.'

'You still think Tom might have had something to do with it?'

Alex shrugged. 'Seems the likeliest possibility at this stage, don't you think? They were heard arguing, and he was obviously lying when he told us he'd never been involved with her. Think he'd have taken the news he was going to be a father well? Seems pretty obvious what they might have been arguing about.'

She could never admit this to anyone, but the superintendent was right: finding out about Keira North's pregnancy had made this case almost personal for her. As far as she was concerned, whoever had pushed the girl from that ledge was guilty of a double murder. The law wouldn't see it that way, but Alex certainly did. And while she continued to carry that knowledge, she would remain determined to find out the truth of what had happened on Sunday night.

'We need to find out who else was at that party,' she said, trying to drag herself from her thoughts. 'Someone must know something. How did it go at the hospital?'

Dan took his focus from the computer screen. 'Amy Barker's still critical. Fifty-fifty, the doctor said. I don't think it's really hit her mother yet. One of the girl's friends was there – she did a runner when she saw us.'

'Something to hide?'

'Don't know. She was at the club last night with Amy when she collapsed. She's probably scared. Maybe she thinks she's going to end up on a drugs charge.'

'Or be held responsible for what's happened to Amy,' Alex suggested. 'Did you get hold of her?'

Dan shook his head. 'Stopped at her father's house on the way back here – her mother thought she might have gone there. He said he hadn't seen her. Her mobile keeps going straight to answerphone. I've asked her father to contact us as soon as she turns up.'

'Let me know when he does. Has the CCTV footage from the club been sent over yet?'

'Just got it,' Dan told her. 'It's next on my list.'

'Get Jake to help you.'

DC Jake Sullivan was one of the team's youngest officers, pale-faced, with a smattering of freckles that stretched across the bridge of his nose, patterning his cheeks, and a laugh that escaped him in short, sharp bursts, sometimes at inappropriate moments. He was recently promoted and had proven overly enthusiastic at times, following at Dan's heel like an excitable, untrained puppy.

Dan needed the help. He still had the rest of Keira's laptop to search, plus the call and text results from her mobile phone. He was the best they had when it came to technology, but this was too much for one person to undertake, especially with the time pressures they were under.

Alex stood to leave.

'Boss?'

'Yeah.'

Dan gave her a half-smile. 'I said there's nothing here yet. Doesn't mean there won't be.'

Alex returned the smile, though she was unable to conceal her doubt. She found it difficult to imagine what might possibly lead them closer to what had happened to Keira North.

CHAPTER FIFTEEN

Alex eased the door of her mother's room closed and stood in the corridor for a moment, trying to make sense of the day that lay behind her. She could never bring herself to look back before closing the door, despite the guilt her reluctance brought. Death was already in the room. It had been there with them for months now, settling itself in the corner and overseeing every hour Alex and her mother had shared together. It had a certain smell, a grey colour; a sound she could hear like a high-pitched ringing in her head, refusing to let its presence be forgotten.

She leaned against the wall and exhaled slowly, closing her eyes to press back the swell of headache that had formed at her temples. There was a buzzer sounding somewhere further along the corridor, and Alex found that if she focused hard enough on the white noise of her brain the buzzing became distant, as though she was no longer inside the building. She felt light-headed, her whole body made somehow weightless by the exhaustion that had been building over the previous few weeks, all leading to what she knew would be inevitable.

'Alex?'

Her eyes snapped open. The nurse on duty was standing alongside her, a forced smile spread on her face.

'You OK?'

Alex nodded and straightened. She pushed back her hair, awkwardly attempting to make herself more presentable. 'Did the doctor come this morning?'

The nurse nodded. 'Shall we go to the office?'

Alex followed, but her heart had sunk at the words. Going to the office never meant anything but bad news, yet she knew that nothing else could be expected. Bad news lingered in every corner.

She had been watching her mother die for over a year now. Her brain was shutting down in sections, like a glass office block in which the lights were turned off one by one before the close of day. It was cruelly painful to watch. Although they had had a difficult relationship at the best of times, she was all the family Alex had left. Losing her meant losing her only link to the past. Once she was gone, what would be left?

She followed the nurse down the corridor to the office, already knowing what would be said once the door was closed. Knowing didn't make it any easier. She had heard the words before – there had been previous scares in which she had been told to prepare herself – and yet this time something already felt altered. They had been offered extra lives, but they had all been used up.

As with every other time, she wished they could go back and undo the things they'd said years earlier; try and do things differently, better this time.

'The chest infection isn't clearing up in the way we'd hoped,' the nurse said, closing the door behind them.

Alex nodded. She wasn't sure what else she could do. The nurse gestured to a chair and Alex sat silently.

'You know your mother's medication was altered a fortnight ago.'

She nodded again. She had seen the doctor that week and he had prepared her for what was coming. He hadn't sugar-coated anything, and Alex had been grateful for that. She didn't need the softness of lies, no matter how well intentioned they might be.

Her mother wasn't living; this couldn't be called a life. She slept much of the time now, and when she was awake, she was mostly distressed. Her dementia brought with it a whole range of hallucinations: strange people in the bed beside her; children watching from the windowsill; animals on top of the television. They were alarming and confusing, and she spent most of her waking hours arguing with people who weren't there. She ate, occasionally, but recently she had stopped deriving any kind of pleasure from even that. What sort of life was this to cling on to?

'An infection always makes the dementia symptoms worse,' the nurse continued. 'You've seen this for yourself over the past couple of weeks. The anxiety, the confusion … these have all been exacerbated by it.'

'You're not expecting her to pull through this one, are you?'

The nurse opened her mouth to say something, then seemed to think better of it. She shook her head. 'I'm sorry. We've really done everything we can. The doctors have been altering her medications for a while now, but the deterioration in her condition has been so rapid since Easter. Antibiotics just aren't having an effect any more.'

'You don't have to apologise.'

For the first time, Alex meant it. Acceptance had been difficult. Watching her mother's decline had been slow and painful: the worst thing she had ever had to witness. It had been degrading and relentless, and she wouldn't have wished it upon anyone. For months she had been searching for someone to blame, someone she could hold responsible for what was happening, as though finding fault might somehow ease the pain. But it wouldn't, she realised that now.

And for the first time, she realised that letting her mother go would be the kindest thing they could all do for her.

'How long are we talking?' she asked.

The nurse hesitated. Alex caught her eye, willing an honest response.

'The doctor thinks maybe days … a couple of weeks at the most. I really am so sorry.'

Alex stood. There was nothing else to talk about, and staying there was only making things more difficult for both of them. She thanked the nurse – listening without really hearing when the woman offered her time and support should she ever need it – and left the office, making her way straight to the exit. She pressed a code into the keypad at the door and let herself out into the car park, driving away from the building without looking back.

It was only when she stopped the car a couple of streets away that Alex allowed the tears to flow. It was something she rarely did – something she hadn't done for months – but occasionally the need to cry overwhelmed her, as though everything she had kept inside her was permitted a moment of victory that she found herself unwilling to fight against. And she realised even before the tears came that she was mourning something that had never truly existed. She and her mother had never been particularly close; there had been times when they hadn't even liked one another, and when both had openly admitted it. Her mother had never forgiven Alex for giving up on her marriage. Alex had never forgiven her mother for doing all she could to help that marriage meet its final demise. The two of them had spent their last years together bitterly resenting the other, dancing awkward circles around one another in order to avoid having to confront the truth.

Yet for that past year she had been mourning her mother; mourning, she realised now, the relationship she wished she'd once had with her.

CHAPTER SIXTEEN

It was early evening. They had been basking in a week of unfamiliar sunshine and the warmth of the day was still such that Leah had forgotten to take a jacket with her when she left to go out. She hadn't really been thinking straight when she'd shut the door on the house in Treforest. Her mind was a meld of Keira, Leighton, Tom: of all the things she was losing any sense of control over. Everything was falling to pieces around her and she felt powerless to stop it. She didn't like feeling powerless.

She caught a train to Llandaff in Cardiff and walked from the station through the park. It was busy that day, packed with families and groups of friends whiling away the last warm hours of the summer evening. Cyclists, joggers, dog-walkers, parents pushing prams … She passed countless faces, and yet she had never felt so lonely. She wondered how any of them might react if she was to say to them, 'My friend died on Sunday. Murdered, they think. I miss her.' She wondered if anyone would care.

This was the thing: no one did care. Everyone was living their busy lives with their busy careers and their busy families, and no one really had much time for anyone else even if they pretended the opposite. Leah was on her own, yet no one else appeared to be. Everyone else seemed to form part of a unit. Everyone else seemed to be connected somehow, while Leah could feel herself isolated, floating. She didn't belong anywhere, to anyone.

She had always believed she didn't want to, but she had been lying to herself.

She left the park and headed out onto the main road, busy with slow-moving evening traffic. She had purposely taken the long route round, hoping to build courage before reaching her destination. She had known where he lived for a while now – she had checked the driver's licence in his wallet when he'd been out of the room once – but she had never yet felt the need to go to his house, not in the way she felt it now.

She'd searched for the house on Google Maps. It had been pretty much what she'd expected: a large semi with a driveway and a neatly tended garden that looked as though someone else was paid to manage it. From what she'd seen of Leighton's wife, Melissa, Leah didn't think she was the type to get her hands dirty. And she knew they had money, presumably plenty of it. Enough to hire a gardener. Probably a cleaner too. Leighton earned a good salary as a lecturer at the university, and he'd made a bit from his novels, though likely nowhere near the amount Leah imagined he'd hoped for. She didn't think he'd still be at the university if he had.

Then there were the other houses he owned: the ones he rented out to students just like her. She'd heard him talking about it to his wife once, the pair of them arguing over the phone about unpaid rent and a door that needed replacing after a drunken argument between two housemates resulted in the police being called. Leighton hadn't heard Leah at the door of his office; he didn't know she'd been standing there listening. Leah had wondered then if Leighton loved his wife. She still wondered about it now.

Melissa ran a beauty salon in the city centre, one of a small chain dotted around South Wales. Between them, she and Leighton must be worth a bit. Leah had been to the salon once, had booked in for a haircut. Once inside, she had changed her mind at the last moment. Melissa had been there, talking with another customer behind her as Leah had sat and watched them in the mirror. Designer clothes, nice make-up, expensive perfume that lingered in the air long after the person was gone … What did these women have to worry about? she thought. Nothing. One day, she was going to be just like them.

She recognised the house when she was still some distance away: its red-brick facade and its old-fashioned tiled roof. This area of Llandaff was like another world: no graffitied walls and upturned wheelie bins here, just expensive sports cars and pointless 4x4s that no one who lived in a city really needed. She felt it in her gut, a familiar twisting, burning sensation; the same one she could remember experiencing throughout most of her life.

She wondered whether both of Leighton and Melissa's daughters lived with them. The younger of the two was sixteen, so presumably still at school. The older was about Leah's own age, which made what Leighton had done all the more despicable.

Approaching the house, she felt a chill. She had never before been this close to his home, this close to his family. There was a faint flurry of excitement intermingled with the anxiety she felt in the pit of her stomach, but mostly just a nauseous feeling: a sick-to-the-stomach, no-turning-back-now sensation.

She crossed the road so that she'd be on the same side of the street as the house. She imagined herself for a moment trying the front door, finding it unlocked; walking through the hallway and into the kitchen, where the family would be at the table eating dinner. She would take a seat next to Leighton's wife and introduce herself; say, 'You don't know me, but …' Wait to see the look on all their faces – his in particular – when she exposed him to his family. The thought warmed her; she forgot the previous chill of nerves that had spread through her.

She stopped as she saw a car pull onto the driveway. A woman was driving; a pretty, blonde-haired woman whose face she was already familiar with. Melissa Matthews. Leah slowed her pace, giving the other woman time to get out of the car. She watched as

Melissa went to the boot and opened it, then she reached for her mobile phone from her pocket and hurried her step again.

She lingered at the entrance of the driveway, looking up at the house and then back to her phone. As she'd hoped, Melissa sensed her there and turned. She was struggling with the heavy bag of shopping she was unloading, but persevered, yanking it onto the edge of the boot before lowering it to the ground. When she turned to look again, Leah was still there.

'Can I help you?'

'Is this number sixty-three?' Leah asked.

Melissa nodded. She left the shopping where it was and took a couple of steps down the driveway. Leah felt her heart begin to thump beneath her T-shirt.

'I'm looking for Sarah Davies,' she lied, glancing back at her phone as though to check the non-existent address her recently invented friend had sent her. She hoped there was no one who went by the same name living in either of the houses next door, thinking now that she might have been better off picking a less generic name. She could feel Melissa's focus fixed on her face, presumably on the bruising on her cheek that had been left by Jamie's drunken punch. 'Sixty-three Acorn Drive,' she said, looking up to meet the woman's eye.

Melissa smiled. She was pretty, Leah thought again; very pretty. She had one of those faces people turned to look at, men and women alike. Why wasn't this woman enough for him? It didn't seem to matter what some people had. They always wanted more. Leighton Matthews was obviously one of those people.

She felt jealousy rip through her, clenching her gut in a way that had become so familiar.

I'm outside your house, she texted, returning her concentration to her phone as though messaging the friend who didn't exist. *Your wife is nice.*

'This is Acorn Way,' Melissa said, looking almost apologetic, as though she felt somehow responsible for Leah's wasted trip.

Leah rolled her eyes. 'What an idiot I am,' she said. She gestured to the phone still in her hand. 'I'll give her a call now – find out where I've gone wrong.'

She looked up and past Melissa's shoulder. There on the doorstep, frozen by the sight of her, was Leighton. His tall frame filled the doorway. His eyes were fixed to them, watching the exchange taking place. Leah gave him a smile before redirecting it to Melissa.

'Thanks,' she said. 'Sorry I interrupted you.'

She turned and headed back the way she had come, her step now energised by a new-found confidence. She was capable of so much more than people thought. She was underestimated. She had spent her whole life being underestimated.

Whatever else she might be, Leah thought, she wasn't going to be forgotten easily.

Once she was far enough away from the house, she stopped and returned her attention to her phone.

Tell her, or I'm going to.

CHAPTER SEVENTEEN

They arrived back at Alex's house at around nine o'clock that evening. Scott had met Chloe for dinner, insisting that regardless of her workload, she should make time to eat. Alex's car wasn't in its usual spot at the kerbside, and Chloe felt a flutter of anticipation in the pit of her stomach, knowing that time alone with Scott that evening was likely to end only one way. She had spent so much of her twenty-six years looking behind her and focusing on the things that were gone that she had missed what was happening around her. Thinking of how she'd reacted to the night at the hotel on Friday filled her with regret. Chloe wondered where Alex might be, already knowing the answer. One day I will be an old lady, she thought. If she was lucky enough to make it there, she didn't want to spend her old age consumed with regret for all the things she hadn't done.

In the house, she offered Scott a cup of tea, realising he was unlikely to accept. Their evening together had been short, yet they both knew where it had been headed, and tea-drinking was going to be a waste of what little uninterrupted time they might have.

She took him by the hand and led him upstairs to her bedroom, shoving her previous doubts to the back of her brain. She pulled the curtains shut, swallowing the last light of the evening, and held his face in her hands, pulling him towards her. She kissed him urgently, pressing her body to his. Already she could feel him hardening against her, and for the first time she found herself able to focus on him without the past infiltrating the moment and ruining it.

She gave him a gentle shove towards the bed and he sank back on to it willingly. She straddled him, kissed him again and moved down the length of his body, reaching to undo the buttons on his shorts. She felt his hand on her shoulder, squeezing it gently.

'You sure about this?'

Ignoring him, she pulled down his shorts. Thoughts nagged at the back of her mind, but she moved them aside one by one, obliterating them with the overriding desire she felt. The things she had done; the things she had once been: none of those mattered any more. She wanted this man. She hadn't told him yet – would keep it to herself a while longer – but she was pretty sure she was in love with him, and if this wasn't it, she doubted she would ever know it.

She wished she hadn't let her insecurities mar the time she'd had with him when they'd gone away at the weekend, but she was going to put all that behind her now.

Scott's head pressed against the pillows and an involuntary groan passed his lips. 'Jesus … what was in that pasta?' He sat up and slipped an arm around her waist. The other hand moved to the back of her head, his fingers grasping a length of her hair. 'God, you're lovely.' He kissed her, then pushed her from him and laid her on the bed, covering her body with his.

When they heard the front door open an hour later and Alex's voice calling to see whether Chloe was home, she pulled the duvet over their heads and the two of them lay giggling beneath it like a couple of wayward teenagers almost caught in the act. She didn't want to get up from the bed. It felt safe, it was warm, and for the past hour she had been able to shed her life along with her clothing, stripping herself of the responsibilities that came with her career and lifestyle choices.

'You should go and see her,' Scott said as he reached for his shorts from the carpet. 'Be rude to stay up here.'

She pulled him back for one last kiss before letting him go. She didn't want to see him leave, but he was right: it would be wrong for them to stay in bed when Alex was downstairs. This was one of the things she had grown to love about him: how considerate he was; how mindful of other people's feelings.

She watched him dress, then reluctantly got up from the warmth of the bed and retrieved her own clothes from the carpet, checking her appearance in the mirror on the inside of the wardrobe door. Scott reached his arms around her and turned her for a last kiss.

'Right,' he said, moving to the bedroom door. 'It's the left side that's less creaky, isn't it?'

She smiled and followed him out on to the landing and down the stairs. He snuck from the house like a burglar and Chloe straightened her clothes before heading to the back of the house and into the kitchen. Alex was standing at the sink washing dishes, her back to the door.

'Hey.'

'Hey.' Alex gestured to a saucepan on the cooker top. 'I've got some soup on if you want it.' She shook excess water from her hands and turned to Chloe, her expression altering on eye contact. Chloe realised why: it had been hard to conceal. Although she'd pulled her hair back in a makeshift style, her cheeks were flushed.

'I've had dinner. Thanks, though.'

Alex raised an eyebrow. 'Scott gone, then?'

Chloe might have blushed if she hadn't already realised Alex was trying to wind her up. 'Yeah, he's gone.'

Alex continued smiling to herself as she began to ladle soup from the saucepan into a bowl. 'You still haven't told me what happened at the weekend,' she reminded Chloe.

Chloe smiled as she took a seat at the kitchen table. She didn't mind the fact that Alex wanted to know more than she would normally be comfortable sharing. It was nice to have somebody care; reassuring to have somebody who showed a bit of interest in her happiness. It had been odd at first. Kindness wasn't something Chloe was accustomed to being on the receiving end of, although all that had changed in the previous six months. For the first time in a long time, she felt as though she had some form of family. She had Alex and Scott to thank for that.

'I don't want the sordid details, by the way,' Alex added, sitting opposite Chloe and placing her bowl on the table. 'Just a yes or no will do.'

'Yes,' Chloe said, rolling her eyes.

'Bloody hell, thank God for that! Good. Excellent. Right, change the subject.'

Chloe felt an inescapable twinge of guilt. She had been careful to keep her new-found happiness concealed where possible from Alex, although she knew Alex would never have expected – or wanted – her to do so. The previous year, Alex had become re-involved with her ex-husband. It had gone on for a few months before eventually leading to disaster. Then there was the issue of her mother's rapidly deteriorating health, something Alex rarely spoke of and had only recently made Chloe aware of. Until then, she had managed expertly to keep her professional life and her personal life separate. She was under an enormous amount of pressure, although Chloe realised she would never admit it. Hearing about Scott and how well things were going between them was the last thing she needed.

'Have you been to visit your mother tonight?'

Alex nodded.

'How is she?'

Alex let go of her spoon, leaving it to rest in the soup. Perhaps she might have chosen a better topic with which to change the subject, Chloe thought, silently reprimanding herself.

'She's OK. Well, not OK, obviously. She's as well as can be expected.'

Chloe watched her push the spoon through her soup, purposely avoiding eye contact. And with that, she knew the conversation was already over.

CHAPTER EIGHTEEN

The following morning, Alex and Chloe managed to catch up with Jade Richards, the girl who had been with Amy Barker at the nightclub on Monday evening. Jade hadn't been home since then, although her father hadn't seemed particularly unsettled by his daughter's absence. It didn't take long to determine that he was used to her independent ways. If anything, he seemed relieved to have her out of the way.

'You'd better stand either end of the hall,' he suggested, heading for the foot of the stairs. 'If she sees you here, she'll do another runner.'

Chloe shot Alex a look. She didn't fancy another sprint session in pursuit of the girl. Being with Scott had done wonders for her happiness but very little for her fitness levels. She was eating too much good food and staying too long in one place, something she was unused to. At the rate she was going, none of her clothes would fit her by Christmas. The irony of Scott being a trainee fitness instructor hadn't escaped her.

Alex gave her a nod, silently recommending she take the front door. She herself went down the hallway to the kitchen and waited impatiently, glancing behind her at the clock on the far wall.

'Dad!' There were a few thumps from upstairs, a couple of expletives, then the sound of footsteps padding reluctantly across the landing. Jade's father followed her as she started down the stairs, presumably satisfied that they now had her well and truly cornered.

Both Alex and Chloe had considered the possibility that Jade's disappearing act at the hospital had been an indication that she might have been guilty of supplying the drugs to her friend herself, but the more Alex thought about it, the more implausible it seemed. The girl was only fifteen, and although fifteen was old enough to get up to all sorts, she just didn't believe that this particular fifteen-year-old was capable of it. Would she really have been able to visit Amy in the hospital – to see her in that way, comatose and hooked up to all those machines – if she had been the one responsible for putting her there?

And even if she had provided the drugs, someone was responsible for dealing to her. Alex hoped the chain of suppliers wasn't going to prove too long.

'Dad!' the girl shouted again, louder this time, when she saw Chloe standing at the front door. She made a strange noise, the dejected howl of a caged animal, before continuing reluctantly down the stairs, knowing this time that there was no escape.

'Why did you run from me at the hospital yesterday, Jade?'

Chloe followed the girl into the living room. Jade threw herself onto the sofa and folded her arms across her chest with such aggression that she almost managed to hit herself in the face.

'Jade,' her father said, in what Alex imagined was intended to be a warning tone. It was pretty ineffectual. His daughter simply shot him a look that said she wished he'd go away and leave them to it. Her father responded with a look that spoke a similar message.

'You're not in any trouble, if that's what you're worried about,' Alex said.

The girl turned her head and rolled her eyes. It was times such as this that occasionally reassured Alex – if only for the briefest of moments – that not having children needn't necessarily be regarded as a personal tragedy. Teenagers seemed to exist as a whole species of their own: rude, ungrateful, insolent. Maybe she'd been spared.

Yet even in the face of Jade Richards' angst, she still doubted it. She felt a knot twist in her stomach, tight and familiar, and tried to empty her mind in an attempt to be freed from it.

'I don't know anything.'

'You were there, Jade,' Alex reminded her. 'Of course you do.'

This time, the girl didn't look at her. She leaned forward on the sofa and moved her arms from her chest, resting her elbows on her knees and covering her face with her hands, as though she was boiling up inside with anger.

But then they heard the sound of stifled sobs. Alex sat on the sofa, at the opposite end to Jade, where she could keep a cautious distance and avoid the risk of scaring her off once again. 'We're not interested in blaming anyone … no one except the person who supplied Amy with those drugs. Do you know who it was, Jade?'

Behind her hands, Jade shook her head.

'Amy's very unwell, you know that. If anything happens to her, someone is responsible. Someone's already responsible. I know you care about your friend – you wouldn't have been at the hospital yesterday if you didn't. Just think about what happens if another person takes what Amy took. No one deserves what's happened to her. You don't want that, do you?'

Alex glanced at Chloe, hopeful that they were about to break through the girl's barriers. Maybe Jade wasn't so bad after all. Maybe most teenagers weren't. She remembered herself at the same age. There had been times she had been angry at the world without really knowing why, despite the fact that she had come from a comfortable home and had a steady, relatively uneventful upbringing. Perhaps it was just a by-product of growing up.

'I don't know who he was,' the girl said eventually. 'I've never seen him before. He came up to us outside when we were in the queue. Amy was flirting with him.' She glanced awkwardly at her father, enough of a look for Alex to decipher that it was perhaps Jade and not Amy who had been doing the flirting.

'Did he give you the drugs when you were outside?'

Jade shook her head. 'Not in the queue, no.' She looked up at Alex; for the first time, the confrontational defiance was lost from her face. 'He mentioned them, but there were too many people about. Amy went back outside later to get them. I was supposed to take it first. I agreed to do it if she went out to get them. I thought it would be a laugh.' The girl's voice began to break. 'But I didn't swallow mine – I put it under my tongue and spat it out when she wasn't looking. A few minutes later, she was on the floor.' She had started crying fully now, this time not bothering to attempt to hide her tears.

Alex looked up at Jade's father. He was red in the face, either a display of embarrassment at his daughter's admission or a flush of anger that she had been so naïve. Probably both, she imagined.

'You said she went outside,' Chloe said, 'yet he didn't sell them to you in the queue when you were waiting to go in. So where was outside, Jade?'

'By the toilets,' she told her. 'There's a fire exit at the back of the club – it leads out on to this, like, yard bit where you can go for a smoke or whatever. One of the boys from school scored there last week – he told us that if you go there, you can usually find someone selling.'

Chloe shot Alex a look. Their thoughts were mirrored: these drugs had been targeted at teenagers, part of the sudden influx of party smarties being distributed at Cardiff's under-18 club nights. They had found their way out of the city and were heading further up the valleys, having now made their way to Pontypridd. So who was responsible for bringing them there?

'How old was he?' Alex asked. 'Same age as you? Older?'

'A bit older,' Jade said through snivels. 'Probably not much, though. Late teens, twenties … I don't know.'

'OK,' Alex said. 'We're going to need a full description – do you think you can do that for us?'

Jade glanced at her father, who was still standing in the doorway, still looking at his daughter as though he wanted to wipe the floor with her as soon as the detectives left. She nodded reluctantly. 'Yeah,' she agreed. 'Yeah, I'll give you a description.'

CHAPTER NINETEEN

DC Daniel Mason's desk was its usual orderly self, although a small stack of paper cups had formed at the side of his computer; the remnants of the caffeine-fuelled hours that had enabled him to sit through seemingly endless footage from the club in which Amy Barker had collapsed. Nightclub footage was always tricky to analyse, with the bright lights causing distortion and making it difficult to distinguish individual faces. He had been given the description Jade Richards had supplied, although it could have matched countless faces. There was nothing to make it individual in any way – no scars or tattoos that would have been unique to the man who had sold Amy the drugs. The only decent footage of Amy he'd been able to find didn't include anyone other than her friend Jade and countless nameless fellow partygoers. He wasn't sure whether it would be enough.

Chloe pulled up a chair alongside him. The footage was paused on a dark corner, half a female just in view towards the left edge of the shot.

'There's a fire exit here,' Dan told her, gesturing to the screen. 'It's just past the toilets at the back of the ground floor. Watch.'

He pressed the recording. The girl in the shot moved fully into the picture, gripping the arm of another girl.

'Amy and Jade?' Chloe confirmed.

Dan nodded. They watched as the two girls shared a brief exchange, one seeming to push the other closer to the fire exit. Then one of the girls – it was difficult to determine which, but from the lighter shade of hair Chloe assumed it was Amy – opened the fire exit door and disappeared from view.

It matched with the version of events provided by Jade.

No wonder the girl had run from police, Chloe thought. Jade was dealing with a guilty conscience: she had encouraged her friend to go outside to buy the drugs and had then watched her take them, too scared – or too clever, perhaps – to do it herself. She hadn't been prepared to take the risk of buying or taking, yet she had been ready to watch Amy suffer whatever consequences might befall her in doing so.

Amy re-entered the club and reappeared within the footage, visibly passing something to her waiting friend. She closed the fire door behind her and they left the shot.

'They went into the toilets,' Chloe explained. 'Amy thought Jade had taken hers, so she did the same.' She shook her head. 'Some friend. Any footage from outside the club?'

Dan shook his head. 'There's a camera at the door that picks people up as they're being security-checked, but by the time the girls got there, they must have already met this mystery bloke. Nothing.'

'What about Keira North? Find anything else in the emails?'

Dan tapped a pile of paperwork on the desk. 'Not the emails, but the phone records are a bit more interesting. This is what's been keeping me really busy,' he said. 'Alex might want to get our friend Tom Stoddard back in for another chat.'

'Yeah? How come?'

Dan flipped through the top few sheets of paperwork and retrieved a couple that were now strewn with highlighter markings. 'Read this,' he said. 'Looks like we may have found the father of Keira's baby.'

Chloe brought Alex up to speed on the exchange of text messages as they headed in Alex's Audi to the student house in Treforest. The messages had been sent between Keira's mobile number and Tom's six weeks earlier, just a few weeks before Keira had died.

'*Don't tell anyone about last night,*' she read.

'Is that Keira or Tom?'

'Keira. Tom then asked, *Are you ashamed of me?* Wink emoji to end. There's quite a gap until her response. *I just don't want anyone to know.*'

'What did he say to that?'

'*OK. Dirty secrets are always the best kind.* To which she replied, *I'm serious. Please.*'

Alex rolled her eyes. 'He's a charmer, isn't he?' She shook her head. 'I don't know … sounds like a one-night stand to me. Keira was already nearly four months pregnant by this point. Doesn't prove anything, does it? If anything, it makes it even less likely that Tom's the baby's father and therefore even less likely that he was the one who pushed her from that roof.' She sighed. 'Too many people claim to have seen him downstairs when Keira fell.'

'Doesn't mean he wasn't responsible.'

'How do you mean?'

Chloe shrugged. 'Might have got someone else to do his dirty work for him.'

Alex managed a smile. 'You and Scott are watching too many box sets.'

Chloe grinned. 'There's something else, though. A few days before Keira died, Tom sent her this. *Promise you won't tell anyone. I just need a bit more time to sort myself out.*'

'Weird choice of phrasing,' Alex said, slowing for a set of traffic lights. 'What's he referring to there? Won't tell anyone about what? Was there a reply from Keira?'

'No. Perhaps whatever it was, the conversation about it continued on the night she died. Maybe that's what they were heard arguing about.'

'He's definitely lied to us,' Alex said. 'I think where Tom Stoddard's concerned it might be a default setting.'

She pulled up outside the terraced house and the two women got out of the car. The front door was already open. As they approached, they heard shouting coming from inside the house, a male and female engrossed in a bitter exchange.

'You need to calm down,' the female voice could be heard yelling.

'Since when did you get to dictate?' the male voice shouted back. 'You don't tell me what to do. No one tells me what to do.'

The sound of Tom's anger was easily recognisable. He seemed to be making a habit of arguing with everyone he came into contact with.

Alex stuck out a foot and pushed the door further open. A large sports bag rested just inside. She pressed the doorbell, bringing the shouting to an abrupt end. Tom Stoddard appeared at the end of the hallway, his angry red face falling when he saw Alex and Chloe there.

'Going somewhere?' Alex asked, gesturing to the bag.

Tom sighed, his eyes rolling up to the ceiling then staying there so he wouldn't have to make eye contact with either detective.

'You're going to have to delay your trip, I'm afraid.'

Behind her, Alex felt Chloe's fingers press gently into her lower spine. She turned to her and Chloe nodded in Tom's direction, gesturing to his feet. Alex looked back and glanced down at the trainers Tom was wearing. It took a moment before she realised what Chloe was referring to and where her thoughts had taken her.

She remembered Jade Richards' statement.

They had wanted to talk to him about Keira, but it seemed that was not all they needed to discuss with Tom Stoddard.

CHAPTER TWENTY

It wasn't supposed to be like this. When I saw her there at the party, sitting on that ledge with her back to me, I couldn't believe my luck. I could get it done with little effort: nothing too strenuous; nothing that would get my hands dirty. I would be able to walk away from it without recrimination. At worst, it would look like an accident; at best, someone else would take the blame for her death.

This doesn't feel like it did in those initial moments any more. There was a rush of adrenalin, a surge of victory; the resounding sense that, for once, someone's sins had caught up with them. A wrong would be made right. I felt almost euphoric. A burning resentment that had simmered away for so long had been left to hit boiling point. When I pushed her, the lid was lifted; the pressure I had felt subsided. It felt liberating.

Now that moment has passed, I can feel the surge of hatred once again. It comes in waves, hitting me at moments I might not have been expecting it. It comes at night-time especially. Standing at my bedside, hatred visits me like a long-lost friend, taunting me with its refusal to be forgotten.

Sometimes panic takes its place. There is a horrible imbalance, a sense that the world has tipped to one side again and I don't have the strength to push it back. Only now I know I do. I've done it once before: I can do it again.

This wasn't how it was supposed to be. Everything has gone wrong, and there is only one way to put it right.

And only I can put it right.

Someone else needs to die.

CHAPTER TWENTY-ONE

If Leah had known it was him, she wouldn't have answered the door. She had presumed it would be Tom; he was supposed to have headed home to Leeds earlier that day, but his things were still by the door and he hadn't returned since the police had taken him for questioning again. Surely he hadn't been kept at the station all this time? The longer he'd been there, the more suspicious of him she'd become.

She wasn't able to push the door closed in time, and before she was able to hold him back he was already inside the hallway, shoving the door shut behind him.

'Jamie's upstairs,' she said cautiously, as though this might in some way deter him. She realised the attempt was futile. Leighton's face was reddened with anger. She'd seen him angry before, but never like this.

'Good,' he snapped. 'He can hear what a scheming little bitch you are.'

She opened her mouth to call to Jamie, but Leighton was too fast. He grabbed her by the arm and forced his other hand over her mouth, stifling her attempts to speak. She staggered backwards and hit the newel post, sending a flare of pain shooting up her spine. His other hand tightened around her arm, cutting off her circulation. She had seen enough of him to realise he had a temper, but she had never seen him like this. For the first time, Leah felt afraid of him. His hand was pressing against her mouth, his fingertips digging into her face.

'You're not going to call him. You're going to come with me,' he said, gesturing along the hallway, 'and you're going to listen to everything I have to say. Understood?'

She nodded, not really seeing any other option. He pulled her along the hallway, although there was no need; she would have gone willingly with him. She didn't really want Jamie to see any of this, though Leighton had no reason to know that.

In the dining room, he used his foot to push the door closed behind them, his hands still occupied with holding her arm and covering her mouth. They moved to the kitchen and he did the same there. She thought he'd let her go once they were in the kitchen, but he obviously didn't trust her not to cry out. He moved his hand from her arm and she felt the blood rush back to her wrist and hand. The pain was relocated when he grabbed her hair by its ponytail and snapped her head back.

'Listen to me, you devious little bitch,' he said, shoving her against the kitchen worktop. 'You stay away from my family. You don't go anywhere near my wife and you don't go anywhere near my kids. Got that?'

Leah nodded as much as she was able, though his hand holding her hair back made it difficult. She tried to speak, begging him to let go of her.

'You're not going to scream?'

She shook her head. He let her go abruptly and Leah reached for her neck, rubbing at the ache that had started there. 'What the fuck is wrong with you?' she said, swallowing gulps of air as she tried to catch her breath.

'Wrong with *me*?' He still looked as though he wanted to hit her, and Leah still wasn't certain he wouldn't. 'What the hell was that all about, coming to my house like that?'

'I just wanted to see where you lived.'

He looked at her incredulously. 'And that's any of your business because …?'

She could feel tears spiking at the corners of her eyes and she hated them. She hated how pathetic they made her look – how weak and needy – and yet she had already known that at some point they would make an appearance, betraying her. He didn't understand any of this, yet she had always thought it was obvious. She just wanted to be with him. She wanted to be a part of what he had.

'You've made it my business.'

'No I haven't,' Leighton snapped back. 'You're the one refusing to leave me alone.'

'So none of this is your fault? You've not done anything wrong?'

He flinched at the challenge, knowing there was no way he could possibly consider himself blameless. He'd had choices. He'd made them. All Leah was doing was making sure he faced up to the consequences.

He reached into his back pocket and pulled out a thick envelope. He put it on the kitchen worktop beside her. 'This is the end of it.'

Leah glanced at the envelope. 'You're paying me off?'

'Why not? That's what you wanted, isn't it?'

She started crying then, unable to hold back the tears any longer. She didn't bother to try to hide them and he didn't bother to pretend he couldn't see. He looked as if her sadness disgusted him.

'Don't do that,' he said, looking away from her and back to the envelope. 'Just take the money and stay the hell away from me.'

He moved to leave the kitchen, but she grabbed the envelope and stepped in front of the door, blocking his exit.

'Move.'

'Please don't,' she said. She reached for his arm, gripping him tightly. 'Don't shut me out, please.'

'Get out of the way, Leah.'

She stood her ground, staring at him defiantly. 'You can't pay me off. I'm not going anywhere.' She reached for the top of his jacket and shoved the envelope down inside it. She didn't care any more. He might have thought he knew her, knew what she wanted, but that wasn't it at all. Not any more.

'Take it and that's the end of it,' he said, reaching into his jacket to retrieve the money. He put it back on to the worktop. 'It's over. Say it.'

She held his stare, refusing to back down. She wasn't going to do what he said. Everything had been on his terms and now she was just expected to disappear at his command. It wasn't going to happen.

'No.'

His anger was tangible. She could feel it in the air between them, as though the atmosphere had been bound into a tight knot forcing them in different directions.

'Do it, Leah, or …'

'Or what?'

His jaw tensed. He grabbed her by the shoulders and shoved her back into the kitchen, clearing the doorway and his escape route. She didn't bother to follow him or try to stop him this time. Moments later, she heard the front door slam as he left.

She went into the dining room, sat at the table and sobbed silently, wondering where everything had begun to go so wrong.

CHAPTER TWENTY-TWO

At the station, Tom Stoddard was waiting in one of the cells. He had turned down everything from the presence of a duty solicitor to a drink of water and refused to speak other than to repeatedly insist that he'd had nothing to do with the death of Keira North.

In the main office, Alex and Chloe referred back to the description Jade had given of the man who had provided Amy Barker with the drugs: *Late teens/early twenties, quite tall – about 5'11" – with dark messy hair. He was wearing a black jacket, skinny joggers and bright blue trainers with a yellow tick on the side.*

'She said they were quite distinctive, didn't she? The trainers.'

Alex gave Chloe a sceptical look. 'I don't know now. It seemed to make sense when we saw them at the house, but I've never identified a suspect from a description of a pair of trainers before. First time for everything, I suppose.'

The trainers were definitely distinctive: Alex had noticed them the first time Tom Stoddard had been brought in for interview, and now she thought about it, she remembered seeing them again when she had gone into his bedroom on the day she'd taken Keira's parents to the house. Yet she hadn't made the connection when Jade had given her description. Her mind had been unfocused and she couldn't afford for it to stay like that. She glanced at Chloe, grateful that she had compensated for her error.

'This particular brand of trainers is pretty popular, isn't it? There are probably countless other young people in South Wales wearing similar pairs.'

Chloe nodded, unable to keep the disappointment from her face. She tried to suppress a yawn, but Alex didn't miss it.

'You sure you're not burning the candle at both ends?' she asked, knowing she sounded like her mother.

'I'm just a bit tired. It's not affecting my work.'

Alex raised an eyebrow. 'I hadn't suggested it was.'

Chloe had waited a long time to find happiness, and Alex didn't begrudge her that. If anything, there was a part of her that envied it. If she thought hard enough, she could remember what it had felt like to be young and in love. But only just. The memory of it was already so distant that it wouldn't be much longer before it evaporated altogether.

'The rest of the description is a match,' Chloe said, keen to return the focus to Tom Stoddard. 'How about we do a virtual ID?'

Alex tapped the desk for a moment, lost in thought. 'Where's Dan?'

'Out with uniform, I think.'

She nodded. 'It shouldn't take long to find a few matches with Tom, should it?' she said, thinking aloud. 'If you could get that set up and sent over to him, I can start interviewing Tom about Keira and those texts. Ask Dan to get straight over to Jade Richards' house if he can.'

In the interview room, Tom Stoddard wore the same lazy expression he had carried with him the first time he'd been there. He kept his gaze fixed to the wall somewhere behind Alex, as though by avoiding her eyes he might be able to conceal his guilt. It wasn't enough to fool her into believing that this young man considered himself without a care in the world. He was a liar; that much they were already sure of. All she needed to do was apply sufficient pressure for the cracks to begin to show.

'I've got a train to catch,' he said, still refusing to make eye contact.

'I imagine you've missed that one by now,' Alex said. 'There'll be another.'

Tom sighed and shrank further into his seat, his long legs stretched out to the side of the table. Either this was an elaborate pretence at nonchalance or he really was completely arrogant, Alex thought. Whichever, she was ready to put an end to it.

'I'd like to talk about our previous conversation about Keira.'

'OK. I don't know what there is to talk about, though. I've told you everything.'

'Really.' Alex reached for the file on the desk and removed the transcript of the text message dialogue between Keira's number and Tom's. 'You told me your relationship with Keira had been friendship, nothing more. You still sure about that?'

Tom said nothing. To illuminate her point, Alex began to read the text messages Chloe had relayed to her in the car.

'Doesn't sound like just friends to me, Tom.'

Tom sighed, threw his head back and looked up at the ceiling. 'I slept with her once. About six weeks ago. That was it.'

'So why not tell us that when you were here last time?'

'Because I know how it makes me look.'

'How does it make you look?'

He lowered his head to meet Alex's gaze, but didn't reply.

'If you had no involvement in Keira's death, you've got nothing to hide. Have you?'

The boy eyed her defiantly, his jaw strong, his grey eyes fixed on her intently. He might have liked to think himself tough, but Alex suspected the opposite to be true. In the face of solid evidence, Tom Stoddard's resolve was likely to crumble. They needed that evidence soon.

'Where were you on Monday evening?'

Tom looked away. Guilty, thought Alex.

'Why?'

She shrugged. 'Just curious. Monday must have been a difficult day for the three of you, your housemate having just died like that.'

'I was in the house.'

Alex nodded. 'What were you doing?'

'I don't know … watching TV.'

'What did you watch?'

Tom's eyes narrowed. 'I don't remember.'

Alex paused and exhaled. 'And Leah or Jamie will be able to corroborate this?'

There was a knock at the door, and Tom was saved from having to answer the question. Chloe's head appeared around the doorway, gesturing for Alex to join her in the corridor.

'Has Dan seen Jade?' Alex asked, closing the door behind her.

Chloe nodded. 'She gave a positive identification straight away, apparently.'

'Cocky little shit,' Alex said, looking at the door to the interview room. Tom's unexplained text message to Keira played on her mind: *Promise you won't tell anyone.* Was it a reference to his drug dealing? Had Keira found out what he was doing, and had someone pushed her off the ledge to keep her quiet?

Tom looked up suspiciously as the two women entered the room, his composure clearly shaken. 'What's going on?'

'Watching TV on Monday,' said Alex. 'You sure about that?'

'Yes.'

'So you didn't leave the house at all? Didn't pop out anywhere?'

'No … I told you. What the hell's going on? I thought this was about Keira?'

'A young girl's in hospital, Tom. Sixteen years old. She took a pill on Monday night and ended up in a coma. You've probably seen it on the news, with all the TV-watching you do.'

'What has this got to do with me?' Tom's voice was different now; panicked. He looked from one woman to the other, seeming to search for some sort of reassurance. He wasn't going to find any.

'Fusion nightclub. You been there before?'

Tom shrugged. 'Probably. Last year, maybe.'

'You weren't there on Monday night?'

'No.'

'OK. The thing is, someone matching your description was seen offering to supply Amy Barker with the drugs that landed her in hospital.'

Tom's stance eased suddenly, his shoulders visibly relaxing, his tensed jaw slackening. 'Right,' he said, dragging the word into a drawl. 'And how many other blokes my age fit my description?'

'Good point,' Alex said, rewarding his self-assurance with a nod. 'Or it would be, if we hadn't already had a positive ID.'

Tom opened his mouth to say something, but nothing came out. He looked again from Alex to Chloe, seeming to accept that his attempts at getting out of the situation were likely to prove futile.

He leaned back in his chair. 'I want to see a solicitor now.'

'All in good time. Tom Stoddard, I'm arresting you for the possession and supply of a class A substance. You do not have to …'

'What?'

'… say anything, but it may harm your defence …'

'No, this is ridiculous.'

'… if you do not mention when questioned something you may later rely on in court. Anything you do say may be given in evidence.'

'I was there, all right. I was there on Monday night. But I didn't give anyone any drugs.'

'So you're admitting you were at an under-eighteens' night?' Chloe said. 'You're in your twenties, Tom. Why would you be hanging around with teenage girls?' She raised her eyebrows and turned to Alex. 'Gets better, doesn't it?'

The panic on Tom's face was quickly spreading, the insinuation leaving him smarting. He refused to make eye contact with either woman and silently followed Chloe down the corridor and into the holding area, where she showed him to a cell.

'We'll let you know when the solicitor arrives,' she told him, closing the door and locking it behind her.

It seemed at that moment a minor victory; she imagined Alex felt the same. But she knew Tom Stoddard was a small fish in a huge pond; charging him with the supply of drugs was unlikely to mean getting any closer to the real perpetrators, the main suppliers who were bringing the stuff into South Wales and distributing it to the dealers.

And then there was Keira North. They might have Stoddard in custody, but none of them had wanted it to be for this reason. Unless they found something to link him to Keira's death, he was going to walk away from at least one of his crimes.

CHAPTER TWENTY-THREE

Hywel Moss, the duty solicitor, sat beside Tom Stoddard in the interview room. The boy had obviously been briefed in the detectives' absence, and for the time being at least he looked pretty self-assured once again. A shadow of a smirk sat upon his lips, and Alex found herself wanting to lean across the desk to slap it loose.

'Tell us a bit more about Keira,' she said. 'You say you slept with her just the once, about six weeks ago.'

Tom nodded.

'For the recording, please.'

'Yes. It was just the once.'

'So there's no chance you could have been the father of her baby?'

Tom folded his arms across her chest. 'It was six weeks ago,' he said. 'She was five months pregnant, wasn't she? You do the maths.'

Alex's lip curled.

'Can I ask what Keira North's death has to do with the allegation of drug dealing made against Mr Stoddard?' Hywel Moss asked.

'We need to ask these questions to get the answer to that,' Alex told him, finding it difficult to suppress her frustration. 'Were there drugs present at the party at your house on Sunday night, Tom?'

Tom rolled his eyes. 'It's a student house,' he said. 'Yes, there were drugs. But it's not me you want to be asking about that.'

Chloe raised her eyebrows. 'Meaning?'

'Meaning you should speak to Leah.'

Chloe glanced at Alex. 'Why would we want to do that?'

Tom sighed heavily and uncrossed his arms, letting them fall to his sides, dangling lazily. 'Anyone who was taking drugs that night either brought them with them or got them from Leah,' he declared. 'It was nothing to do with me.'

'So you admit to dealing drugs occasionally?' Alex said. 'Just not at the house party last weekend?'

Tom looked to the solicitor for guidance. Moss gave a slight shake of his head.

'No comment,' Tom said.

Alex shot Hywel Moss a glare. He was a regular at the station and infamous for finding loopholes, even when a suspect's guilt was evident to all. What frustrated Alex the most about him was that he always looked so smug about it.

'This seems a rather desperate attempt to get yourself off the hook, Tom,' she said. 'You've been positively identified as the person who supplied Amy Barker with the drugs, plus you've already admitted to being at the club that night. It would save us all a lot of time and energy if you started telling the truth.'

Tom once again looked to the solicitor for support. 'I said I was there. I never said I sold her those drugs, because I didn't. Whoever it was, it wasn't me.'

Alex produced a photograph of Amy Barker and placed it on the table in front of him. 'You'll have seen this photograph on TV, I expect. Do you deny seeing Amy Barker on Monday evening?'

'No,' Tom said hesitantly. 'I saw her outside the club, in the queue. We chatted briefly, that was it.'

'Why? Did you know her? Why would you stop to talk to her?'

'She was with another girl. She said something to me, we just got chatting. It was less than a minute or so and then I left.'

'Where did you go then?' Chloe asked.

'To a friend's house.'

'You didn't go inside the club at all that night?'

'No.'

'Referring back to the record of text messages sent between your phone and Keira's,' Alex said, 'you said to her, *Promise you won't tell anyone*. That was sent just a few days before she died. What were you talking about, Tom? What didn't you want her to tell anyone?'

There was a visible change in his expression. 'I don't know, I can't remember.'

'The text reads as though you were pretty concerned about something. I'm finding it hard to believe you can't recall it.'

The boy said nothing. He glanced at the clock as though lamenting the fact that his trip home to Leeds was now definitely postponed.

'Had Keira found out about your drug dealing?' Alex asked. 'Is that what you wanted her to keep quiet about? But she didn't reply to the message, did she? She didn't give you what you'd asked for – a promise not to tell anyone. Seems convenient that she fell to her death just a few days later.'

Tom looked up to meet her eye. 'I didn't touch her. I wasn't in that room when she fell.'

Alex brought the interview to an end. She and Chloe went out into the corridor, leaving Tom with the solicitor.

'I can't stand that man. What a weasel.'

'Do you believe him?' Chloe asked. 'Tom. About Leah?'

'I don't know,' Alex said, glancing at the clock. 'Let's speak with her again tomorrow, see what she's got to say. It could just be him trying to deflect us.'

'You going to keep him overnight?' Chloe asked.

'No. We haven't got enough on him – it's Jade's word against his, and she's admitted she didn't actually see him sell Amy those drugs; she just assumed it was him. Trust me,' Alex said, noting the disappointment on Chloe's face, 'there's nothing I'd like more than to charge that arrogant little sod. Anyway … off you go. You've got better places to be than stuck here any longer.'

Chloe gave her a smile. 'I won't be back late.'

'Please stop doing that,' Alex said, raising an eyebrow. 'You don't need to tell me what time you'll be home. You're making me feel ancient.'

She watched Chloe head away down the corridor, the spring in her step unmissable. She wondered whether happiness was something that would ever return to her own door. For the time being, she doubted it.

CHAPTER TWENTY-FOUR

Leah had started drinking at home. There was plenty of alcohol left over from the weekend's party, so by the time she left the house, she had already drunk almost a bottle of wine and a couple of canned cocktails she'd found at the back of the fridge. She didn't really know where she was going; she didn't really care. She wanted to forget for just a few hours at least: about Keira, about Leighton, about everything. After the first pub – a place usually packed with students, but strangely quiet now the summer had started – she ventured further towards Pontypridd, alcohol fuelling her pace as she hurried past groups of teenagers lurking around shops and couples holding hands as they waited for late-night buses.

The evening air made the effects of the alcohol all the more potent, and by the time she got to the next pub, she found herself ordering a pint of water with her glass of wine, trying to rehydrate slightly before beginning the next round. She didn't want to sober up. She wanted to get obliterated; the kind of obliterated that would wipe away everything else, if only for the next few hours. She sat at the bar and downed the water at record speed, then realised she needed to use the toilet. She asked the man behind the bar to keep an eye on her drink for her.

In the ladies', she leaned on the sink and studied her reflection in the mirror. She knew she was nothing special. She had never been the smartest or the prettiest or the sportiest. There had never been any superlative that could have been accurately used to describe her. But there were ways to make herself prettier and smarter, and as she'd got older, she'd worked out how to make those methods increasingly effective.

She knew how to get what she wanted.

She wiped beneath her left eye, where her mascara had smudged, then returned to the bar. She felt a pair of eyes watching her as she walked to her seat, and turned to look at the man whose gaze had followed her there. He was sitting with a group of men who all looked to be around his age; the attention of the others was distracted by football highlights being replayed on the TV screen near their table. He was good-looking, in a subtle, unobvious sort of way. Older than Leah by quite a bit, but that had never been an issue for her before. She wasn't interested in boys her own age.

She threw him a smile and it was instantly returned. Moments later, he left his friends and joined her at the bar.

'You on your own?'

'No,' she said, aware that the slur in her voice was evident with just one word. 'My friends are all invisible.'

The man smirked, apparently finding her sarcasm amusing.

'Can I join you?'

'Free country.'

He pulled up a bar stool and placed his drink next to hers, watching her with eyes that seemed impossibly blue. 'Bad day?'

'No.'

Her sulkiness apparently wasn't deterring him. If anything, he seemed to regard it as a challenge; something with which to break up the monotony that must have shaped the rest of his evening.

'My name's Eddie,' he said, waiting for Leah to return similar information. When she didn't, he finished the remains of his pint and asked the barman for another. 'Want one?' he asked, gesturing to her wine glass. It was still half full.

She shook her head.

'Not very talkative, are you?'

'What should we talk about?' she said. 'The weather? The football results?'

He turned further towards her, leaning in close. 'Your anger is very sexy.'

She smiled. 'Do you want sex?'

For a moment it was as though Eddie's confidence had been pulled from beneath him. He hadn't been expecting her response and now seemed unsure of how he was supposed to react. He was probably wondering whether she was winding him up, Leah thought; whether this was building up to some embarrassing moment in which she would attempt to humiliate him in front of his friends.

'Is that a trick question?'

Leah shrugged. 'Depends how you like it, I suppose.'

Eddie grinned, now responsive to her flirtation. 'You want to come back to mine and I'll show you how I like it?'

'No,' Leah scoffed. 'I don't want to go to yours – I don't even know you. What about through there?'

She nodded in the direction of the toilets. Eddie looked at her in disbelief, still not quite believing his luck. It wasn't even going to cost him the price of a drink, let alone a taxi fare home.

She stood from her bar stool, wobbly on her feet. 'Give me a couple of minutes. I'll be in the ladies'.'

In the toilets, she sat in a cubicle and held her head in her hands. A swell of headache was surging at her temples and blurring her vision like the onset of a migraine. She pulled the skirt of her dress up past her thighs, checking the smoothness of the skin beneath. She wanted to feel something, but she wasn't sure what.

A minute or two later, she heard the door to the ladies' open. She was the only person in there, and when he pushed open the door of the cubicle, she stood, sidestepping to let him into the narrow space. He grabbed her at the waist and tried to kiss her, but Leah turned away from him, her back to him, and pressed a forearm against the wall. She used the other hand to lift her dress.

'Jesus,' Eddie said. She heard him unzip his trousers. 'You are filthy.'

'Do me a favour,' she said. 'Stop talking.'

Her instructions only served to heighten his urgency. Within seconds he was pressed against her, his erection thrusting hard inside her. Leah felt her mind shut off. Thoughts of Leighton left her. Thoughts of Keira evaporated. She stopped feeling. For those moments, she could have been anyone; anywhere. The more forceful he became, the more she responded, pressing herself back against him, losing herself in the rhythm of his drunken enthusiasm.

'You on the pill?' he grunted against her neck.

'No.'

'Fuck.' He pulled out of her sharply and came in his hand, then fell against her, his weight holding her against the wall. She could feel his hot breath on the back of her bare neck, where her hair had fallen over her shoulder, leaving her skin exposed. His heavy breathing was warm in her ear. He was immediately repulsive now that the act was over. They all were.

She stood straight, pushing her elbows back to shove him off.

'What do we do now?' he asked pointlessly, leaning against the cubicle wall as he tried to catch his breath.

Leah adjusted her underwear and pulled down her dress. 'You can go back to your friends,' she suggested.

She stepped back, inviting him to leave first. He looked at her suspiciously for a moment, still wondering whether this was some kind of trick to catch him out; whether she was about to reveal the hidden camera that was going to broadcast the incident to the internet. When she raised her eyebrows as though to question why he was still there, he straightened his clothes and left, leaving Leah alone with the white noise of all the thoughts that had returned to her now it was over.

CHAPTER TWENTY-FIVE

Tom Stoddard stepped out of the police station and hurried across the main road towards the town centre. His time in custody had made something more than clear to him: he couldn't go to prison. If that girl was to wake up from her coma and tell police he'd sold her the drugs, no one was going to believe otherwise. Everything had gone to shit. The university would throw him off the course; his parents were going to go mental. He would end up with a criminal record and he'd never be able to get a decent job.

He checked his wallet. He had just enough change to buy himself a couple of pints, which would at least give him some time to think things through in peace. He cut through the town centre, past the betting shops and the off-licences, and crossed the main road to the Wetherspoon's. At the bar, he abandoned the idea of a pint and opted for something stronger, finding he had just enough cash to buy a double whisky. The alcohol burned as it travelled down his throat and left a churning, empty sensation as it hit his stomach. He realised he hadn't eaten anything since the previous morning.

He glanced at his mobile phone. He bet the police had gone through it, checking his messages and internet search history. He tried to think back, wondering what they might have seen. He supposed it didn't matter any more. Someone had apparently identified him as the person who'd sold the drugs to Amy Barker. He'd been there: he wondered if that would be enough. Amy was in hospital, still in a coma, so she couldn't have given the police the ID. It must have been that rough little cow she'd been with, he thought. Bitch. Why had she told them it was him?

Tom called Leah's number, the thought of one bitch leading him straight to another. It went to answerphone. He hung up midway through the pre-recorded message before calling back.

'Where are you?' he said. 'I need to speak to you. Fucking call me.'

He jabbed the end call button, locked the phone and shoved it back into his pocket. He could feel himself bubbling with anger; as he stood at the bar and sank the remainder of his whisky, he considered all the things he'd love to do to Leah once he got his hands on her. She'd played him like such an idiot, and he'd fallen for it. He wasn't sure who he was angrier at: her or himself.

She was going to pay for it.

When he'd finished his drink, he left the pub and set out on the walk home to Treforest, the world passing him by without his noticing it. Twenty minutes after leaving Pontypridd town centre, he was back on Railway Terrace, his stomach aching with the need for food. He was tired and felt dirty, but there was no way he was getting in the shower until he'd spoken with that devious cow.

There was a noise on the street behind him. Tom turned, his eyes adjusting to the darkness. Leah was staggering along the pavement towards him, her movements steered by alcohol. He felt anger race through him. He'd spent most of the day at the police station, being questioned about something he hadn't done, while she'd been out enjoying herself as though the past few days had never happened. As though everything was normal.

'Where the fuck have you been?' He grabbed her by the arm and shook her.

She fell against him, unable to hold her own weight. 'Not now, Tom. I feel so sick.'

Leah could feel her headache increasing, the dull surge that had started at the pub now an insistent throbbing that was making her nauseous. The lights in her head were getting brighter, pulsing against her brain and flashing behind her eyes like neon strobes. The street ahead was spinning; the pavement seemed to stretch, then narrow, contorting right before her eyes. She stopped for a moment, moved away from Tom and leaned against a lamp post, trying to force her vision to adjust.

He was speaking again, but she couldn't distinguish the words.

She staggered onwards, trying to shake Tom off as the night air and the alcohol joined forces to slow her progress. He had moved away as the lights became brighter, blinding now. She could see the house just five buildings or so ahead, but she knew she wasn't going to make it. The lights got sharper, heading straight for her. The street turned white, and then she stopped seeing.

CHAPTER TWENTY-SIX

It was gone 8.30 by the time Alex arrived at the nursing home. The building was so still at this time of the evening, almost other-worldly quiet; a completely different place to the one that was alive during the day, with its noises and its smells and incessant reminders of decrepitude. At night, there was a silence that to the inexperienced visitor might have suggested peace. But Alex knew otherwise. She had been coming to this place for a year now, since her mother had been assessed as having full-time nursing needs. Until then, they had somehow been coping at home, with Alex balancing her mother's care around work and employing paid help to assist her when she wasn't there.

Now they were at the stage of adult nappies and pureed dinners, thickened drinks and brief, incoherent exchanges.

Alex pressed the code into the keypad at the front door and waited for the electrical buzz that acknowledged her admittance to the building. The corridors were quiet and empty. She made her way to her mother's room and gently pushed the door open, knowing she would be asleep and not wanting to disturb her. The room smelled stale – the kind of smell she could only associate with this place – and she went to the window, eased it open quietly and allowed the night air to circulate in a warm blast around her. Her mother was lying on her back, her thin grey hair fanned out on the pillow around her head, so fine it was like feathers. She had a hand resting above the duvet. Her skin was so pale now, almost transparent; so delicate that Alex feared she would break it if she was to touch her.

'Hello, love.' Gillian's eyes opened and rested on her daughter. 'I didn't think I'd be seeing you today.'

It had been weeks since her mother had spoken this coherently, and Alex found herself not quite knowing how to respond. She sat in the chair by the bedside and took her mother's hand in hers. 'Hi, Mum.'

Gillian's eyes narrowed, her expression changing. Her thin face became even more pinched as she studied Alex. 'Are you my sister?'

Alex felt her stomach flip, as it always did when this happened. She had been a sister, brother, mother, husband. In recent weeks, she hadn't once been recognised as daughter.

'No, Mum,' she said, knowing that her disagreement would be pointless. 'It's me … Alex.'

Her mother's hand slid from hers and moved across the duvet, drawing away from her. 'I don't know you.' Her eyes closed and she turned her head towards the wall.

The words stung, though Alex realised she should have been used to this feeling by now. Her mother was confused, though there were the occasional days when Alex wondered whether Gillian knew exactly who she was and used her confusion as an excuse not to acknowledge her.

She tried to distract herself with thoughts of work. Charging Tom Stoddard would be a victory, though comparatively small and ineffectual. One dealer might have been identified, but how many more were there? South Wales's drugs issues were the same as those in every area of Britain: far too widespread for the police to keep under any sort of control. Stoddard was small fry. Alex could see the fear that had developed as his interview had progressed; he was little more than an idiot boy who had got himself involved with something way out of his league. Despite that, if it turned out he had sold those drugs to Amy Barker, then he'd known exactly what he was doing. He might be an idiot, but no idiot was stupid enough to not realise the harm that drugs could cause. How many more Amy Barkers would there be before people began to learn? But where drugs were concerned, Alex suspected the worst. People wouldn't learn.

The door to her mother's room opened and one of the carers appeared. She was young, little more than twenty; one of the regular carers Alex was familiar with.

'You're here late,' she said.

'Long day at work.'

The girl gave her a smile. 'Do you want a cup of tea or anything?'

'That'd be lovely, thanks. I'll come with you, save you bringing it back.'

They headed together down the corridor to the kitchen.

'She's in safe hands, you know,' the girl said, as though reading Alex's concerns.

In truth, Alex knew that safe hands weren't going to make any difference. The disease had spread so quickly – had taken such a firm and intense grip on her mother – that nothing and no one could prevent what it was now set to do.

'I know.'

She waited in the corridor as the carer went into the kitchen to make tea. She wondered if her mother would actually want her there if she was aware of what was happening. She knew she had been a disappointment to her; from school to her career choice, and then again when it had come to her failure to create a family. Her mother had always felt that Alex delayed things for too long, procrastinating until eventually choices were taken away from her.

Perhaps she hadn't been so far from the truth, Alex thought.

The carer reappeared from the kitchen and handed her a cup of tea.

'Thanks.'

'Do you mind if I make a suggestion?' the girl said.

'No.'

'Have the tea and then go home to bed. Everything will look better in the morning.'

Alex smiled at her youthful optimism. By the time she got to Alex's age, the girl would realise things rarely looked better in the morning.

She stayed a while longer in her mother's bedroom, listening to the steady purr of her breathing. She watched her chest rise and fall, the regular motion almost hypnotic. When she felt her eyes begin to grow heavy, she admitted defeat and left.

Her own home wasn't too far away, just a ten-minute drive when the traffic was quiet. When she got back, the place was in darkness and she suspected Chloe was still out with Scott. Perhaps she had finally decided to spend a night at his.

She showered and changed and went to the living room. She lay on the sofa and flipped through television channels, not really taking in what she was staring at. Her mind was lost to other things, to the day that fell behind her and the one that lay stretched out ahead. Her thoughts were lost to her mother, and the situation they had found themselves in.

She didn't want to go upstairs to bed. What had once been her marital bed – and had later become the bed to which she had returned with her by then ex-husband – now seemed a strange and alien place, as though the loneliness of it was rejecting her and casting her aside. Eventually she fell asleep on the sofa, the TV still on and the blanket she had pulled across twisted around her.

She was woken by the phone. Her mobile was on the carpet beside the sofa, still turned to silent since her visit to the nursing home. She was such a light sleeper, its vibrations alone were sufficient to wake her.

'Hello?'

'Boss … sorry to call you so early.'

She pulled the phone away from her ear and glanced at the time. It was twenty to five in the morning.

'What is it?' she asked.

'Leah Cross,' the officer told her. 'Looks like someone's tried to kill her.'

CHAPTER TWENTY-SEVEN

'Neither of you saw Leah earlier this evening?'

The uniformed policeman standing in the living room was studying them both with impatience, his left eyebrow raised in a question mark. His colleague was waiting by the doorway, as though expecting one of them to attempt an escape. Jamie wondered why they were being treated with such suspicion, although as soon as the thought crossed his mind, he realised how naïve that was. Of course they looked suspicious. First Keira, now Leah.

He sat forward on the sofa and rested his head in his hands. A part of him felt like crying, but the last thing he wanted was Tom seeing that. 'No, I didn't see her. I came home from work, had some dinner, watched TV for a bit and went to bed.'

'And you?' The policeman turned his attention to Tom, who had been uncharacteristically quiet since the police arrived.

'I was at the police station all day.'

'About?'

'Keira, of course.'

'What time did you leave the station?' the policeman asked.

'About nine thirty.'

'And you came straight back here?'

Tom shook his head. 'I went to the pub for a bit. Then I came home.'

'So what time was that?'

'About eleven.'

The policeman walked to the front window and pushed back the closed curtains. 'You didn't see Leah at all when you got back here?'

'No.'

'Is she OK?' Jamie asked. 'Is she going to be all right?'

'We've not heard anything from the hospital,' the policeman standing in the doorway told him. 'By all accounts she was in a bad state going in, though.'

Jamie sat back on the sofa and pressed his fingers against his temples, one eye on Tom. Tom was lying – he was always lying – but Jamie didn't know what about. He couldn't understand why he might lie, not now. He felt a swell of sickness pass through him. Tom had argued with Keira just before she died. The atmosphere between Leah and Tom had been fraught for days, and Jamie didn't think it was just because of what had happened on Sunday. Thinking back on things now, he realised they'd been weird around each other for weeks.

'Do you know who was driving the car that hit her?' he asked. He stood up, tiredness and anxiety making the room sway around him. He glanced down at Tom, not wanting to look at him for too long.

'Not yet, no.'

'Is there anything we can do?'

'Not for now,' the first policeman said, moving away from the window. 'If you think of anything, though, make sure you let us know. You can call the hospital in the morning – they'll tell you how she's doing.'

Jamie saw the two officers to the front door, then returned to the living room. 'Did you see Leah tonight? Why did you lie to them?'

Tom stood from the sofa and crossed the room. He squared up to Jamie, so close that Jamie was able to smell the alcohol on his breath. 'I've been at the station all day.'

'And why's that?' Jamie challenged, fuelled by an unexpected moment of bravado. 'What did you do to Keira? Did you push her from that ledge?'

Tom gripped him by the shoulders before shoving him aside. 'You're fucking pathetic. Still pining over her … She wasn't interested, you know that?'

'What would you know?' Jamie mumbled.

Tom turned back and shoved him for a second time. He wrapped a hand around Jamie's throat and pressed him against the wall, and in that moment Jamie's short-lived bravery fell away from him. 'She didn't seem too bothered about you while she was riding my cock six weeks ago.'

He raised a fist and pulled it back, and Jamie flinched, closing his eyes instinctively as he braced himself for the punch. It never came. Instead, Tom drove his fist into the wall, inches from the side of his head.

Jamie watched, breathless, as Tom left the room, slamming the living room door shut behind him. Like so many other moments in his life, he wished he'd been braver. He wished he'd fought back.

He had never hated anyone the way he hated Tom. His words rang in Jamie's ears, taunting him. Would Keira have slept with Tom? Jamie couldn't be sure. Tom seemed to have a way of getting what he wanted; in the same way that Jamie's life had a habit of serving up constant disappointment. Whatever had happened between them, Jamie now felt sure of one thing. Tom had killed Keira. He couldn't work out how, but he was probably responsible for what had happened to Leah too.

He sank on to the sofa as another thought enveloped him. Did that make him next?

CHAPTER TWENTY-EIGHT

Images of Keira North and Leah Cross were pinned side by side on the evidence board in the station's main incident room. They were surrounded by a gallery of faces: Tom Stoddard, Jamie Bateman, and a whole host of people who had attended the house party on Sunday night. The team had been called to meet first thing that morning for an update on both the Keira North case and that of Amy Barker, who was still in a critical condition in hospital.

Alex and Chloe had arrived early at the station. They sat alone in the room, both women focusing on the faces that stared out at them from the evidence board.

'You look exhausted.'

'Thanks.' Alex pulled her dark hair back and tied it into a stumpy ponytail.

'Do you think you might need a break? Take some time to spend with your mum?'

'In the middle of a murder investigation? I wouldn't have thought so.'

Chloe bit her lip, feeling her face flush. Alex rarely spoke to her like this – she rarely spoke to anyone like this – and her doing so was evidence that something was very wrong.

Alex sat with her arms folded across her chest and her eyes fixed on the faces on the wall, refusing to look at Chloe, though she presumably must have felt the other woman's gaze on her. Dark shadows circled her eyes and the whites were bloodshot. It looked as though she had at some point been crying.

Though Alex had been informed of the incident involving Leah Cross during the early hours of that morning, Chloe felt certain Alex's sleep had been disturbed before that. 'One housemate dead,' Alex said now, 'one dealing drugs, one a hit-and-run victim. I imagine Harry will be trying to tell me this was an accident as well.'

Over the next ten minutes, the team trailed into the incident room. Finally, the superintendent appeared in the doorway, and Alex began the briefing, addressing the team members sitting nearest her.

'Some of you will already be aware that Leah Cross was taken to hospital in the early hours of this morning. She was hit by a car just outside the house in which she lives in Treforest – the same property, as we know, at which Keira North died on Sunday. She's in a stable but serious condition, still unconscious. I'll be heading to the hospital after this. We need to find out what's been going on in that house. Yesterday Tom Stoddard was arrested for supplying the drugs that landed Amy Barker in hospital. He was released without charge, though Jade Richards, Amy's friend, has given a positive ID.'

As expected, there was an outbreak of whispered reaction to this news. A lot of the team had finished for the day by the time Tom Stoddard's interview had been held, so many of them didn't know he'd been released without charge. He was now a link between the two cases, although Alex couldn't yet see exactly where the connections could be made.

'Why wasn't he charged?' DC Jake Sullivan asked.

'At the moment, it's Jade's word against Tom's. She says she saw him at the club, but she admits she didn't actually see him selling Amy the drugs. Tom alleges that Leah is involved in dealing. Obviously this is something we'll want to talk to her about when she recovers.'

'If she recovers.'

Alex pursed her lips. 'Thank you, Jake.'

'Could he just be trying to save his own neck?' Dan suggested.

'Could be. We've got him unsettled now, so there's a chance we might be able to get more out of him. As you're all aware, Cardiff drugs squad is working on a full-scale ongoing investigation into the recent increase in drugs-related incidents in the city. We know they're currently focusing on two properties in the Canton area as having possible links. The official name for the drugs we know as "party smarties" is MDP. They've not been widely available in South Wales until the past few months. We're still waiting to hear back on whether the drug Amy Barker took was in fact one of these. Her reaction to it certainly seems to suggest so. There may not be a link to what's been happening in Cardiff, but if there is, we could be on to something huge. There are some brains behind this – it's a well-organised and thorough distribution set-up. Clearly I'm not referring to Tom bloody Stoddard, but he might have got himself mixed up with more than he bargained for.'

'He might be too scared to give names,' Chloe said.

'Maybe. But there's also a chance he's got no idea what he's involved in.'

'So where do the girls come into it all?' Dan asked.

'This is what we need to find out. Did the person who pushed Keira North from that roof have any connection with what happened last night to Leah? Is Leah involved in the drug dealing, and if so, was the person driving that car last night linked to Cardiff's inquiry? Cardiff's sent over a list of people currently under investigation. We're not expecting to find any of these faces directly linked to Amy Barker, but we might be able to find one of their dealers. Was Keira involved in the drug dealing? I know,' Alex added, responding to Dan's facial reaction to the suggestion. 'Seems unlikely, but at the moment we shouldn't be ruling anything out. We have a lot of unanswered questions. As always, time is against us.

'Dan, I'd like you and Chloe to go back to the house in Treforest with a search warrant. The rest of you I'd like here for now. We have a witness statement from the hit-and-run last night, but it needs corroborating – by all accounts, the man who saw the car driving away was so drunk it's a wonder he could see anything. There's CCTV footage from the off-licence on Railway Terrace, just up from the house – it might have picked something up, so it needs checking. OK. Any updates, I want to be informed straight away, please.'

Alex gave a nod, bringing the meeting to a close. She could feel the superintendent's eyes upon her; she had felt them for the past five minutes, scrutinising her. She was getting tired of having to justify each and every decision she made. If he was about to launch another attack on her judgement, she felt ready for retaliation.

CHAPTER TWENTY-NINE

Alex stood in the corridor outside the room in which Leah Cross lay hooked up to machinery. Just a few blocks away, in the intensive care unit, Amy Barker was still battling for her life. If there was any truth in Tom Stoddard's claim that Leah was involved in the drug dealing, Alex would have to fight the urge to drag the girl down the corridor and make her face up to the suffering her actions had caused another person. And not just Amy, Alex thought. Maybe she should leave Leah Cross with the girl's mother, let Ms Barker decide what to do with her.

But perhaps she was jumping to misguided conclusions. All she had was Tom Stoddard's word, and that had already proven unreliable. For now – and until there was evidence of anything to the contrary – Leah was a victim. Just like Keira. It seemed entirely plausible that Tom would attempt to incriminate his housemate in an effort to divert attention from himself. The two were supposed to be friends, but Alex doubted friendship meant very much to Tom.

'Has she woken at all yet?' she asked one of the nurses, an overweight, stern-looking woman whose bleary eyes and abrupt manner suggested her shift had started the night before and she was long overdue home. She breathed heavily and noisily, her uniform straining across her heavy bust and her chest rattling with every inhalation. She was hardly a poster girl for healthcare, Alex thought.

'Not yet.'

'How is she otherwise?'

'Bruising to the torso consistent with cracked or broken ribs,' the nurse told her. 'Head trauma, although the doctor says it's unclear to what extent at the moment. Do you know who hit her?'

Alex looked to the door of Leah's room and ignored the woman's question. 'Has her family been informed?'

The nurse shook her head. 'She doesn't seem to have any contacts for them. The officers who were here last night couldn't find anyone in her phone – no one listed as "Home" or "Mum" or anything like that.'

Alex nodded. 'I'll chase it up.'

'I'll be along the corridor if you need anything.'

The nurse left her alone outside Leah's room. Alex pushed the door open and sat on the hard armchair at the side of the bed. The girl just appeared to be sleeping, her eyelids heavy and her breathing steady. Her left eye was shadowed in bruising that looked too old to have been inflicted the previous evening. It looked more like the result of a fight than a hit-and-run. Her right arm was resting above the hospital blanket, and on her shoulder Alex could see more bruising, soft and green-tinged, peppered across the pale skin. Fingertip bruising.

She leaned closer, checking the pattern of the marks. What had happened to this girl before the car had hit her last night? she wondered.

Her thoughts roamed back to Tom Stoddard. Did she think him capable of drug dealing? Yes. Did she think him capable of violence? Without a doubt. Had he been driving that car the previous night? He didn't own a car, but he had a licence and might have had access to someone else's. He hadn't left the station until late the previous evening, but there had been a couple of hours between then and the time Leah was hit. But why would he do it? And was it connected to the death of Keira North?

They would need to find out where Leah Cross had been the previous evening, who she had been with before she arrived back on Railway Terrace. The eyewitness who had left the shop up the road shortly before the incident had claimed Leah had been walking towards the house, which suggested she was making her way home rather than heading out anywhere.

As she looked at the sleeping girl, Alex found herself consumed with a curious mix of pity and frustration. She remembered how Leah had cried for Keira during her interview at the station on Monday. She had seemed vulnerable in so many ways, yet there was something about the people in that house Alex just didn't trust. Tom and Leah had been arguing at the house the previous day, shortly before Alex and Chloe had taken Tom to the station. Had it been about drugs? And if she'd known something about his dealing, did she also know the truth about Keira North's death?

The two girls had been friends, or at least Keira had apparently thought as much. The photo collage pinned to the wall above Keira's bed had featured an array of images of the two girls together, arms circled around one another, faces smiling for the camera. Surely if she knew something about the death of her friend, Leah wouldn't be keeping it from the police?

Alex stood from the chair. If Leah had been lying to them, she was determined to find out why.

She left Leah's room and made her way out of the hospital and back to the car park. The university was just a couple of miles from the station – she would pass it on her way back to Pontypridd. It seemed an appropriate next stop. Perhaps the admin department there would be able to throw some light on Leah's background. Someone had to have a home address and contact number for her.

South Wales was still bathed in an uncharacteristic wash of blazing sunlight, and as Alex headed away from the hospital in Llantrisant and back towards Pontypridd, she felt herself almost calmed by the warmth that fell over the car. It had a deceptive quality, offering the false impression that everything was right with the world. She glanced at the Bluetooth screen on the dashboard. The clock read 11.10. She wondered whether her mother was awake, or even if she would wake at all that day.

Perhaps she should call, she thought. But she didn't.

She joined the stretch of A470 that would take her to the university campus just outside Pontypridd. It had undergone a recent revamp, the former University of Glamorgan having merged with the University of Wales in Cardiff to create a new University of South Wales with campuses in Cardiff, Newport and Treforest. The Treforest complex was a sprawl of buildings that could be seen from the main bypass; a mix of old and new, characterised by a series of huge white blocks like giant Lego pieces adorning the hillside. Alex veered left off the dual carriageway to meet the roundabout at Upper Boat and headed left towards the new road that would take her to the campus.

A secretary at the main reception pointed her in the direction of the English department, which was located in one of the university's older buildings. The campus was eerily quiet at this time of year, the majority of students having already left for the summer. There was a small reception area within the department building's foyer; here, Alex pressed the bell and waited for someone to come from the office. She introduced herself and showed her ID, explaining that she was looking for the home and family contact details of a student who'd been involved in a hit-and-run incident.

'Is she OK?' the woman asked.

'Too soon to tell at the moment.'

'I hope she'll be all right. Do you want to come through?' The woman moved from the desk and tapped a code that would allow Alex access to the office. She took the chair the woman offered her and waited as she logged on to the department's database.

'The system's so slow,' the woman said, talking more to the computer than to Alex. She tutted as she waited for the page to upload. 'OK. Leah Cross, you say?'

Alex nodded, and the woman typed the girl's name into the search bar.

'Here we go.' She turned the screen so that Alex could get a better view. There on the screen was a photograph of Leah, an image presumably taken on the department's registration day at the beginning of the previous academic year.

'I'll print this off for you, shall I?'

'Please.'

Alex glanced at the address on the screen as the woman set about her task. Newton Abbot, Devon. She had detected a hint of an accent in the girl's voice, though it wasn't strong.

The woman stretched awkwardly across the desk to retrieve the sheet from the printer.

'Thanks,' said Alex, standing. 'I think this should be all, but if there's anything else, I'll be in touch.'

'Of course. I hope she'll be all right.'

Alex left the building and reached for her mobile phone from her pocket. She keyed in the phone number provided on the printout as she walked back to the car park, waiting until she was inside the car before making the call. It was a landline and it rang for a while before someone answered. A woman's voice greeted her.

'Hello,' Alex said, 'this is Detective Inspector Alex King, South Wales Police. I'd like to speak with Mr or Mrs Cross if they're available.' There was a pause at the end of the line, and for a moment Alex thought the connection had been lost. 'Hello?'

'Hello,' the woman said. 'Sorry … there's no one here of that name.'

Alex glanced at the printout in her hand. 'I'm calling with regard to a Leah Cross.'

'Sorry,' the woman said again. 'I don't know that name. I'm afraid you've got the wrong number.'

Alex apologised and ended the call. She checked the number she had typed into her phone alongside the number that was printed on the page. She hadn't made a mistake: they were a definite match.

Why had Leah Cross provided the university with false contact details?

CHAPTER THIRTY

The traffic heading out of Pontypridd town centre was moving at a snail's pace. Dan and Chloe were stuck behind a bus packed with teenagers in school uniform. The two detectives were in one of the squad cars, making them anything but inconspicuous and drawing the unwanted attention of the schoolchildren, all of whom appeared to be kneeling on the back seat in order to jeer and pull faces at the officers behind them.

'Can't we just stick the siren on and dodge this lot?' Dan asked, pushing his head against the back of the passenger seat. Chloe shot him a glance; she could see he was fighting the urge to make a V sign at the boys on the bus.

'Not really supposed to,' she reminded him.

Dan sighed. Chloe was in agreement with the sentiment; surely rules were there to be broken every now and again. What was the point of being part of the police if you couldn't utilise the resources for a little personal advantage?

'Your kids behave like that?' she asked, gesturing to a boy who was now licking the back window, his tongue pressed grotesquely against the glass as he was jeered on by his classmates.

Dan shot her a look, offended by the suggestion. 'Do they hell,' he said.

Chloe smiled. She drummed her fingers on the steering wheel and sighed as the boy who'd been licking the window now grabbed one of his female classmates and proceeded to lick the side of her face instead. The girl squirmed in mock protest, the delight evident on her face.

'Sod this.'

Chloe flipped on the siren and lights and pulled out from the traffic jam, vehicles parting on either side to allow them to pass. 'I feel so powerful,' she said, shooting Dan a sarcastic smile. 'Like Moses.'

He laughed. 'It suits you.' He raised a hand to the window and not-so-surreptitiously flicked a V at the school bus. 'Reckon anyone will be there?'

Chloe shrugged and veered into the right-hand lane. 'If no one's home, we can pop around the corner, get the keys off Jamie Bateman. He works for an insurance company on Broadway.'

The traffic had thinned, so Chloe switched off the siren. She was grateful for the respite: she had always hated the sound. No good ever followed it. 'That eyewitness statement Alex mentioned this morning … Who was it?'

'Local drunk,' Dan told her. 'He'd not long left the off-licence at the other end of the street – went in there to restock on Special Brew.'

Chloe rolled her eyes. 'Reliable, then.'

'Maybe not as bad as we'd think. Turns out he had the sense to try to note down the number plate. Didn't get the last two numbers, though.'

Chloe waited for the traffic lights to change to green and then turned right. The primary school set back just from the main road was obviously on its break time; an array of short-sleeved arms and legs in grey shorts flailed across the yard, and the tinny sound of excited shrieks pierced the afternoon air.

'Black 4x4,' Chloe said, repeating the description she had heard that morning. 'With a missing last two numbers. That'll narrow it down then … I wonder how many vehicles in South Wales will fit that description?'

'We can but hope,' Dan said. Chloe admired his optimism. He seemed to have endless patience when it came to research and analysis, never complaining about the countless hours of CCTV footage he had to sit through or the seemingly endless email and phone trails he was asked to review. Being especially good at this particular aspect of the job meant that senior officers often landed this kind of work on his desk, but Dan seemed to relish it. Apparently the frustrations of whole days of monotonous scrutiny could be wiped out by the revelation of just one small detail someone else might have overlooked.

'Everything OK with DI King?' Dan asked.

Chloe swung a left onto Railway Terrace, deliberating over a response to the question. She clearly wasn't the only one to have noticed how fraught and tired Alex had seemed recently, although that didn't mean she felt comfortable discussing it with anyone else.

'Yeah, as far as I know.'

She could feel Dan's eyes on the side of her face; it was obvious he didn't believe her. 'She seems a bit stressed out.'

Chloe pulled up outside the house and cut the engine. Jamie Bateman's blue Fiat Punto was parked just up the street; unless he'd decided to walk to work that day, they were in luck. 'I think she feels she's got a lot to prove on this one,' she said, undoing her seat belt. 'With Blake leaving soon … I don't know, maybe I'm wrong. I mean, she's thorough in everything she does.'

Dan undid his own seat belt. 'You think she'll work her way up?'

'To superintendent? Alex? Christ, no. I mean, I think the further up you get, the more paper-pushing goes on. That's not Alex. She wants to be out here, in amongst things. It's what she does best.'

Realising she was beginning to sound as though she was defending her friend against some unspoken accusation, Chloe stepped quickly from the car and shoved the door shut behind her, hoping Dan's curiosity would subside there. Distractions from the job at hand were something they could all do without. She looked at the house in which Keira North had died; at the stretch of concrete just ahead of them on which Leah Cross had been hit by a car.

Whatever else was happening with Alex, she thought, she had been right about this. There was more going on behind the closed door of that house than any of them yet knew about. They needed to find out what, before someone else was hurt.

CHAPTER THIRTY-ONE

Alex made a call to the station, getting straight through to the investigating team's main incident room. Detective Constable Jake Sullivan answered the call.

'Boss. Any updates?'

'Not yet. Could you do me a favour?' she asked, wondering how he managed to sound so excitable even when answering the phone. 'Check Niche for Leah Cross.'

The Niche database held records of every arrest made over the past few years, as well as the details of every person who'd made contact with police. It had occurred to Alex as she'd been leaving the English department's building that Leah might have crossed paths with the police before, and if so, it would make things a lot easier for the investigating team. It wasn't the first time she had begun to find herself suspicious of someone who was supposedly a victim.

She waited a moment while Jake typed in the girl's details and waited for a result.

'No. Sorry … nothing.'

'OK.' It was annoying, but not unexpected. Leah hadn't struck her as the type of girl to get herself into trouble with the police, although time and experience had taught her there was never a type.

'Anything else come in?'

'Yep … we've heard back from the DVLA.'

'How many?'

'Six hundred and three.'

Six hundred and three vehicles listed in the South Wales area of the same colour and similar description, with plates that matched the first five numbers provided by the eyewitness who had seen the hit-and-run take place. It seemed a daunting task to find the right match, although Alex realised the numbers could have been worse. She'd worked on cases in which the odds against reaching results had been far greater, but they had managed in each case to get there one way or another. They would manage again.

'Try to find a link,' she said. 'This was no accident.'

Whoever had been driving that car last night had known Leah, of that much Alex felt certain. Had the incident been a warning? And was it linked to Tom Stoddard's drug dealing? Was Tom telling the truth when he said Leah was involved? Leah had been the victim of a hit-and-run. The focus should be upon finding out who had been behind the wheel of the car, and although doing so remained paramount, the mystery surrounding Leah Cross was beginning to take precedence in Alex's mind.

With nothing to work on from the database, she referred back to the printout she had been given by the secretary of the English department. She retrieved her iPad from the glove box, typed in the passcode and accessed the internet, then typed the address she had been given into the search engine. Finding little more than average street values and recent house sale prices, she moved the search to the local council and looked up their contact phone number. She was redirected to Teignbridge District Council's electoral services department and gave them the address she had been given by the university.

'Just a minute,' the man at the other end of the line said.

Alex was put on hold and found herself listening to the kind of background music that had once been played in the discount supermarkets she had visited with her mother; tinny keyboard versions of popular songs that made them so bad they became almost unrecognisable. The memory of those places was instant, the music taking her back, just as the smell of grilled bacon always reminded her of Saturday mornings, of her dad making sandwiches and singing along to the radio as he buttered thick slices of hand-cut bread. It would never be cut straight and the layer of butter he'd slather on would have sent a heart specialist into a panic, but those bacon sandwiches and sugary cups of tea first thing on a Saturday morning always tasted so good.

For a moment, Alex felt a cloud of sadness envelop her.

'Hello?'

She was brought back to the present by the abrupt halt of the music and the council worker's voice back at the other end of the line. 'OK, I have the names here for you.'

Alex retrieved a pen from the pocket of the car door and jotted down the names the man provided. Jonathan and Carol Brooks, both aged forty-five; living at the property for the previous thirteen years.

'Is their employment status recorded with you?' she asked.

'Yes,' the man replied. He was silent for a moment, gaining access to the information she had requested. 'Jonathan Brooks is a GP. Carol Brooks is registered as a self-employed childminder.'

'No one else living at the property? No children?'

'No, just the couple.'

'OK. Thank you – you've been a huge help.'

Alex cut the call and started the car. She stared at the address on the printout, wondering again why Leah Cross had provided the university with false details. She wondered if that was even the case. Had it been Carol Brooks she'd spoken with earlier, and could the woman have been lying when she'd claimed not to know Leah? There was so much the girl was hiding, Alex felt convinced of that now. Getting hold of the truth was likely to be complicated if they were to rely on Leah to start telling it.

She pulled out of the car park and back onto the main road headed north towards Pontypridd town centre. Almost immediately, her mobile began ringing; the name of her mother's nursing home flashed up on the Bluetooth screen on the dashboard.

'Hello?'

'Alex, it's Romy from Park View.'

Though she had known who was calling, the sound of the nurse's voice at the end of the line filled Alex with a sense of dread. They never rang her unless something was wrong; she realised in that moment that she had been waiting for this call, knowing it would come in the not-too-distant future.

'We've called the doctor out. Your mother has taken a bit of a turn during the night.'

Taken a turn, Alex thought. She wondered what that meant exactly, although the implications could be nothing but negative.

'Alex?'

'Yes, I'm here … sorry. Is the doctor still there?'

'At the moment, yes.'

'OK,' Alex said, turning right at the next set of traffic lights in order to redirect her route. 'I'm on my way.'

CHAPTER THIRTY-TWO

Jamie Bateman was still wearing pyjamas: grey flannel shorts and a long-sleeved superhero comic-strip top. His hair was cut too short to ever get dishevelled, but if his face could have been described as such, Chloe thought it would have been appropriate. His skin looked almost grey, and if it hadn't been for the stubble that peppered his chin, he would have looked about fourteen years old.

'How's Leah?'

'Too early to tell,' Chloe said, following him into the house. 'You didn't see her last night?'

Jamie shook his head and ran the palm of his hand over his face as though trying to rub the tiredness away. 'I was in my room all last night,' he said. 'Didn't see anyone. Police came round here early hours of the morning. Do you know who it was?'

Chloe shook her head. She could sense Dan beside her, his attention distracted by the living room.

'You stayed down here then?' he asked Jamie. 'After the police left.'

Chloe went into the living room, followed by the two men. There was a duvet on the sofa and an empty glass knocked over by its side.

Jamie nodded. 'Couldn't get back to sleep. They told us not to go to the hospital, not just yet. What's going on? First Keira and now Leah.'

Keira's name had got stuck in his throat, Chloe noticed, the sound of it half strangled as it left his mouth. He looked away from her to the floor, embarrassed by an imminent display of emotion.

'We don't know,' Chloe said. 'Yet. But this might help.' She reached into her jacket pocket and produced a search warrant. 'We need another look around.'

There was a knock at the front door and Dan went out into the hallway to let in the officers who'd be helping with the search of the property. Jamie eyed Chloe awkwardly as a uniformed officer joined them in the living room, evidently there to keep an eye on him while the rest of them went about their business.

'No objections?' Chloe asked.

Jamie shook his head.

Dan stepped from view of the open doorway and made a drinking gesture. He was right, thought Chloe as she followed him into the hallway: Jamie reeked of alcohol. She could smell it when he opened the door to them, as though the night before was following him in a toxic cloud. And perhaps it wasn't just the night before.

'Start upstairs and work our way down?' Dan suggested.

Chloe nodded. 'The girls are at the top, I'll start there. Boys are first floor. I'll meet you somewhere in the middle. If you two could make a start downstairs,' she said to the two remaining officers.

Dan followed her up the stairs. 'What do you make of him?' he asked once they were out of earshot of the living room.

Chloe shrugged. 'Harmless, I reckon.'

'Think he's got himself mixed up in something without realising?'

'Don't know,' Chloe admitted. 'He's obviously upset. I don't think that's faked, do you? If he's hiding anything, he's doing it well. Let's wait and see what we find.'

She headed upstairs to the second floor and stopped at the back room; what had once been Keira's bedroom. The furniture was still there: the bed now bare, the wardrobe emptied, the dresser that had housed her make-up and toiletries devoid of any evidence that the young woman had ever been there. She picked up a star-shaped pendant from the top of the drawers, wondering which of the girls it belonged to. There was already a smell to the room, she thought; that stale, disused, unloved smell that afflicted abandoned places.

It was so soon, though; perhaps she was imagining it.

She eased the door closed behind her, passed the girls' bathroom and went to Leah's bedroom at the front of the house. She hadn't been in this room before. It was neutrally decorated, with cream walls and pale grey curtains; a shadow of beige on the walls in the far corner that marked a spreading area of damp. The place was tidy, although that could have been down to the spring-clean the housemates had decided to have prior to Keira's parents' visit. The clutter was minimal: a few items of make-up on the windowsill, a pair of shoes left by the door. Other than that, the room seemed relatively sparse.

Chloe pulled a pair of latex gloves from her pocket and put them on. She went to the set of bedside drawers, a standard flat-pack piece of furniture that looked – along with everything else – to have already been there when the students started renting the house. She pulled open the bottom drawer to find it filled with stationery, pens and sticky labels; drawing pins and paper clips still in their boxes, unopened and unused. In the middle drawer she found paperwork: mostly receipts for clothing and a couple of bank statements. She pulled out a pile and put it on the bed beside her. The top drawer contained make-up, a hairbrush and cheap perfume.

The larger set of drawers, on the other side of the room, held nothing but clothes, so Chloe moved her attention to the wardrobe. There were dresses and coats hanging from the metal rail inside, but it was what was beneath them that interested her. Leah's laptop sat beside her shoes, its power lead wrapped in a swirl on top of it. Chloe took it and placed it on the bed before returning her attention to the bottom of the wardrobe. She moved Leah's collection of shoes to one side, searching for anything else among them.

It was then that she heard the hollow sound the base of the wardrobe made. She tapped twice on the thin plywood. There was a space beneath it.

She knelt on the carpet and began to take the shoes out of the wardrobe.

'Chloe.'

She leaned back. Dan was in the doorway of the bedroom, a small bag of white powder dangling from his gloved fingertips. 'Only enough for personal use, sadly.'

'Shit. We could have done with a bit more than that. Can you give me a hand with this?'

Dan put the bag in his pocket and crouched down to see what she was doing. She ran her hands around the side of the base, trying to find a gap. 'There's something beneath this,' she told him.

Dan reached under the narrow gap beneath the wardrobe as Chloe continued to search inside. 'Here,' she said, finding a space in the far corner. 'Wait a sec.' She slipped a finger into the gap and pulled back, but the piece of wood merely buckled slightly in the middle with the pressure. She yanked again; this time it lifted out, nearly taking the tip of her finger with it.

'Shit.' She stuck her finger in her mouth and sucked the nail, trying to numb the start of what would likely end up a decent bruise. Dan pulled the piece of wood from the wardrobe, exposing the gap beneath it. It was empty. If anything had once been kept there, someone had made sure to move it.

'Ever seen something like this in a wardrobe before?' Chloe asked, standing.

'Nope. Looks home-made, too.'

'Exactly.' Chloe sighed and sat back on the bed, returning her focus to the pile of paperwork she had pulled from the bedside drawer. She flicked through a selection of receipts: a £12.99 top from New Look, a pair of £25 jeans from Top Shop; a return slip for a dress Leah had taken back to the shop having changed her mind about it. Nothing out of the ordinary for a girl of her age. She scanned the bank statement. There were the standard direct debits and supermarket purchases; again, nothing unusual.

Until her attention was drawn to the top of the statement. She held it out to Dan, inviting him to take a closer look. 'Seem normal to you?' she asked.

CHAPTER THIRTY-THREE

It was too hot in the nurse's office despite the window having been opened. The air was stagnant, not helped by the number of people now crammed into the small room. An agency member of staff was sitting at a desk in the corner, riffling through a resident's file and pretending not to listen in on the conversation taking place behind her. Her feigned disinterest bordered on disrespect, and Alex found herself fighting back an urge to suggest the woman went and did something more useful than sit around listening to the unfolding of other people's misery.

Alex herself was standing, having refused the offer of a seat. With her were Romy, the duty nurse, and Dr Carter, a man she had met countless times in the year since her mother's admission to the home.

'We've spoken about this before,' the doctor was saying. 'It really was just a matter of time.'

The words seemed to wash over Alex, lost in a bubble that made them soft and hollow, barely audible. She knew she was supposed to react in a particular way – in an expected way – yet she still wasn't sure exactly what that was. For a moment she found herself unable to offer any kind of reaction at all.

'Any infection is likely to take its toll, and the antibiotics we've given your mother are just no longer taking effect. We've tried to—'

'How long?' Alex asked, cutting the doctor short.

Romy looked at the floor, as though the question made her uncomfortable. Alex didn't know why it should. People died there every day; it was what they went there to do. The home could try to dress up its 'quality of life' mantra in any way they wanted, but the underlying fact remained: no one who went in was leaving in anything other than an ambulance or with a funeral director. Why the nurse should find this simple truth uncomfortable after everything she had likely seen during her twenty-year career, Alex couldn't fathom.

'We're probably looking at days now.'

She appreciated the doctor's candour. The carers and nurses had made frequent attempts to fill her with false optimism, with tales of residents who'd been told they had a short time to live only to survive another two years and defy all the medical professionals' expectations. She didn't need to be bombarded with anecdotes and well-intended platitudes. What she needed was honesty, and finally she was getting it. She wondered why he was the only one prepared to offer it.

The thought that maybe this was the right time caught her off guard and left her reeling with guilt. She didn't want her mother to die. Yet at the same time, she couldn't bear to think of her continuing this existence, bed-bound and more often than not incoherent, plagued by the invisible intruders this ruthless disease had brought with it. It seemed inhumane. If a pet had been kept alive in these same conditions, people would have thought it cruel.

She nodded. 'OK. Was there anything else? I'll go and see her if not.'

The doctor shook his head and Alex left the office, Romy following her.

'I'm so sorry.'

Alex turned to her. 'What for?' She hadn't intended to make the nurse feel any more uncomfortable than she clearly already was, but apparently her few words had achieved just that. Romy glanced past her for a moment, reluctant to make eye contact.

'I know how difficult this must be for you,' she said. 'If you need anything, you know where we are.'

Alex doubted that was true. No one could know how difficult this was, not unless they had lived through the same thing. No one could possibly understand what it meant to watch a person alter so drastically in front of them, to see them change and deteriorate until eventually there was just a hollow shell that no longer remotely resembled the person who had once been in its place.

She had already been in mourning for the past eighteen months. Well intended as the nurse's words might have been, Alex doubted very much that she could understand that.

She mumbled her thanks and headed down the corridor to her mother's room.

CHAPTER THIRTY-FOUR

Back at the station, Dan and Chloe returned to the main office and were greeted by Jake with the news that the DVLA had come back with a list of the owners of the vehicles matching the description of the one that had hit Leah Cross the previous night.

'Has anyone seen Alex?' Chloe asked. 'I've tried her phone, but it's gone straight to voicemail.'

'I spoke to her earlier,' Jake told her. 'I thought she was on her way back here, but that was a while ago now.'

Chloe wanted to tell Alex about the bank statement she had found in Leah's bedroom. Neither she nor Dan could think of a legitimate reason why a second-year university student would have over thirty thousand pounds to her name, not unless she came from a wealthy and generous family. Even then, the money was unlikely to have been left sitting in a current account. As yet, Leah's family was still to be identified. Tom Stoddard's accusation against her was beginning to look increasingly plausible.

Dan glanced at the list of possible vehicles on his desk, scanning the information the DVLA had provided. 'Safe bet that what happened last night wasn't an accident,' he said to Chloe. 'So we're looking for a link with Leah Cross, yeah?'

Chloe nodded. 'Do you want me to take this? Your time might be better spent here.' She put Leah's laptop on the desk in front of him, offering him an apologetic smile. 'Go on … you know you love it.'

Dan rolled his eyes and gathered up the DVLA fax sheets from the desktop, handing them to Chloe. 'You can get me a coffee as a means of apology,' he suggested. 'Two sugars, please.'

'Deal.' Chloe passed by her desk and put the notes next to the computer before leaving the office and heading out into the corridor. At the coffee machine, she selected a white Americano and waited as the machine clicked and whirred into life. She took her mobile from her pocket and checked for a missed call or text message from Alex, despite already knowing one hadn't been received. She felt herself beginning to worry. Alex never had her phone off, not even on weekend evenings. Chloe wondered what had happened.

She moved the paper cup of Americano from the machine and pressed the button for a black coffee. Taking them back to the office, she returned to Dan's desk.

'Thanks,' he said, looking up from Leah's opened laptop. 'So what are we looking for?'

'Start with her desktop and emails?'

Dan nodded. 'Let me know if anything comes up in that list from the DVLA,' he said. 'Will do.' Chloe gestured to the laptop. 'Same for you.'

She made her way back to her desk, stopping at Jake's on the way. 'Did Alex say anything when you spoke to her earlier?'

He looked up at her with a pair of sharp blue eyes. 'About what?'

'Anything really. How was she?'

Jake shrugged. 'Seemed fine. I told her about the list of cars from the DVLA and she said she'd see me back here. That was it.'

Chloe nodded. She went back to her desk with a growing feeling of concern. Alex hadn't been herself those past few days and something was clearly wrong. But her reluctance to talk left Chloe guessing at the details.

She felt a mounting pressure to find something concrete to prove this case wasn't the runaround Superintendent Blake still seemed to think it was. For now, she had to believe that the money in Leah Cross's bank account would be the vital lead they needed. She didn't know yet where it might take them, but a link with the drugs ring the Cardiff branch was focused upon would prove a massive outcome, one that none of them could have foreseen a few days earlier.

She needed to do this for Alex. After everything Alex had done for her during those past six months, supporting her friend through this – whatever this might turn out to be – was the least she could do in return.

She turned her focus to the notes on her desk. First and foremost, there was Keira North. She was at the heart of this case. Chloe believed that identifying Keira's killer would mean finding the missing piece this case so desperately needed. She knew Alex believed the same.

She began to work her way through the list of vehicles, wishing she could share Dan's enthusiasm for such tasks. She felt as though she had a point to prove. Given how tedious the next few hours of her day were likely to be, she would need all her determination to get through them. When she finally caught up with Alex, she wanted to do it with something substantial.

CHAPTER THIRTY-FIVE

Tom stood in the yard at the back of the house and took a long drag of the joint he'd just rolled. The drug filled his lungs, relaxing him for a moment. It was the only thing that could. Feet in front of him lay the spot on which Keira had died. He stared at the ground, trying to erase the echoes of that scream from his mind. When he closed his eyes at night, he could still see her so clearly. Every word that had passed during that argument up in her bedroom came back to haunt him, replaying over and over, getting louder and louder.

Now all he could see was Leah being hit by that car. The flash of headlights that had seemed to come from nowhere blinded him, reappearing behind his eyes and sending a throb of headache searing through his brain. The angry screech of tyres, the thud of metal as the car made contact, the cracking of bones that he was sure he hadn't just imagined.

He had fallen back into the shadows of the hedges that lined the front of the houses just along the road from theirs, skulking backwards, trying to disappear. He had watched as the car reversed, turned and drove away, leaving Leah for dead on the roadside. Then he had done the same. He had checked the street, doubled back on himself and entered the house via the lane at the rear of the building.

He hadn't wanted whoever was driving that car to see him. First Keira, then Leah … Leah had got herself involved in something way beyond her control, and she was dragging him there with her. He wondered if her suppliers knew about him. Did they already know his name? And if they didn't, and Leah woke up, would she give it to them?

He leaned against the wall of the house and inhaled another lungful. He pictured Leah as he imagined she was now: lying flat in a hospital bed, hooked up to machines that beeped and whirred. He imagined himself in her room, standing next to her, just inches away from the buttons and switches that were keeping her alive.

Stubbing his joint out against the wall of the house, he realised what he had to do. He didn't have any choice. He took his mobile from his pocket and checked the screen. There was still plenty of time left until the end of visiting hours. No one was going to question a concerned friend going to visit a young woman in a coma.

He went back into the house and shut the kitchen door behind him, turning the key in the lock. As a sharp pain tore into his lower back, he fell against the glass panel. He opened his mouth, but nothing but a muted, strangled sob escaped him. He reached a hand to the edge of the kitchen worktop, trying to steady himself. He managed to turn his body around to face his attacker and opened his mouth again, but the pain had rendered him speechless. When the knife entered his body for a second time, this time in his chest, he slumped against the back door, feeling the life drain from him with the blood that seeped through his T-shirt. It was withdrawn and struck a third time; finally left embedded in his chest.

CHAPTER THIRTY-SIX

Chloe glanced at the clock. It was 4.40, and most of the team had now headed home, but there was no chance of her leaving the station while she still had so much to do. Lunch had consisted of a shared bag of chips and a carton of curry sauce. She and Dan had tried to lessen the guilt of the indulgence by sharing, although the rumble of Chloe's stomach was now making her wish she'd eaten a bag to herself.

She had worked through the list methodically, checking each name against records on both South Wales Police's Niche database and the Police National Computer, and running parallel internet searches in case any of them threw up anything of interest. She had so far searched for 212 of the 603 names provided by the DVLA, and though she realised that working through the entire list that evening would be an impossible task that would leave her useless for anything the following day, she didn't feel done just yet.

So far, a few of the names had come up on the PNC and she had listed them separately, along with the nature of their offences. She'd check later with Dan to see whether Leah's laptop showed any communication with any of them. She sipped her coffee, trying not to think about how many she had already consumed that day. She considered the possibility that her eagerness to continue in her task might have been fuelled as much by a caffeine rush as by anything else.

She typed the next name into the Niche database. It threw up an immediate match. She leaned forward, studying the details on the screen, then clicked back to the opened internet page and typed the name into the bar of the search engine. The results showed information on employment status: where the man worked. As she scrolled down, it became apparent that he had more than one job.

She put her coffee on the desk and clicked on one of the links: *University lecturer questioned over allegations of sexual harassment.*

It was a brief news article on the website of a local Rhondda newspaper, dated about twenty months earlier. Chloe scrolled through, absorbing the details of its contents.

> A student from Pontypridd has accused a member of the University of South Wales' English department of sexual harassment. The student, whose name cannot be given here due to legal reasons, claims that lecturer Leighton Matthews, 43, made sexual advances towards her, touched her inappropriately and offered her grades in return for sexual favours. Matthews, who has taught at the university since its opening, was arrested earlier this week but released without charge. He denies the allegations made against him. Police continue to investigate the claims.

She clicked back to return to the search list, then accessed Leighton Matthews' profile on the university's website. There was a photograph of him, stern-faced, younger-looking; she presumed the image had been taken when he had first joined the department. His profile gave his credentials: BA in English Studies from Leicester University; MA from the University of Cardiff. He had started working at the university there after the completion of his master's degree – having previously worked as a teacher in a sixth-form college – before moving to the University of South Wales. According to the profile, he was also a published author. Two book covers were shown beneath his photograph, each bearing his name.

Chloe opened another internet page and accessed Amazon UK's website. She typed *Leighton Matthews* into the books search bar and found the two novels. His debut had received 316 reviews, with an average rating of 3.5 stars; his second book had just 81 reviews, with an average rating of 3.

She minimised the web page and sipped her coffee, wincing at its bitterness. Dan had already left; he'd mentioned something about taking one of his kids to a gymnastics class, although much of what he'd said on his way out had managed to go straight past Chloe. She had been so engrossed in her task that he could have admitted to having been behind the wheel of the car that had hit Leah Cross and she would have missed it.

Returning to the university's website profile of Leighton Matthews, she sat back and stared at his photograph once again. Then she glanced at the clock and realised little more could realistically be done that evening. She needed to speak with Alex. Leah Cross was studying English at the University of South Wales, and a car belonging to one of the members of that department had been flagged up as matching the description and partial plate number provided by the eyewitness who'd seen the hit-and-run. In addition, this lecturer had previously been interviewed by police over an allegation of sexual harassment made by a former student at the university …

Perhaps there was no need to look into any of the other driver details, for the time being at least.

CHAPTER THIRTY-SEVEN

Chloe finally managed to get hold of Alex at gone 6.30 that evening. She'd left the station an hour earlier and had not long been back at their shared house in Caerphilly, having got stuck in traffic on the A470. She made herself a cheese sandwich and ate it in the garden, on one of Alex's rusting patio chairs. She wanted to take in some of the sunshine she'd so far managed to miss most of, and it was nice to be away for five minutes from the noise and activity that usually surrounded her.

Alex's garden had a lot of potential, though it would be a labour of love to tackle the overgrown bushes and tangles of weeds that now dominated what might have once been flower beds. Chloe knew that her friend had limited gardening skills – and even less enthusiasm – so she assumed it must have once been Alex's ex-husband who had dealt with maintenance beyond the walls of the house. Either that or her mother.

Alex had only ever spoken to Chloe in any sort of detail about her mother on one occasion, six months earlier, when they'd gone on a night out just before Christmas. By the time Alex had reached her third glass of wine, her truths were spilling across the table in free fall. The following day, her regret had been tangible. Chloe had learned that Alex's mother had gone to live with her shortly before her dementia diagnosis, when her increasingly unpredictable behaviour meant it had no longer been safe for her to live alone. By then, Alex and Rob had already been separated, but Alex had given the impression that her mother's move to the house had cemented the separation into permanence. There had been an entirely uncharacteristic but unmistakable bitterness in her voice.

Chloe hadn't judged. She didn't know enough to.

Finishing the sandwich, she tried Alex's number again, expecting the mobile to still be switched off. Alex answered on the third ring.

'Everything OK? I've been trying to get hold of you all afternoon.'

'Yeah, fine.'

The tone of her voice told Chloe everything was far from fine. Where had she been all afternoon? Chloe had an inkling that something might have happened to her mother, but if Alex didn't want to talk to her about it yet, then she wasn't going to force the subject. Trying to do so previously hadn't been met with the warmest of receptions.

'You can talk to me if you need to,' she offered.

'Everything's fine.' Alex's tone was curt, abrupt. Chloe took the hint and left the subject there. 'You're not still at the station?'

'Got back to the house about twenty minutes ago. We've got a few updates.'

'Can they wait until I see you? I'm on my way back now. What are your plans for this evening?'

'Shower, TV, bed.'

'You're not seeing Scott?'

'He's probably had enough of me for one week.'

'Leah Cross has apparently come round. The hospital say she's disorientated – it'll take a little while before they're able to assess the extent of any brain injury. I'm going to go back there to see her. You've had a long day, so don't worry if—'

'Oh no.' Chloe cut her short. 'I'll come with you. I'll explain when you get here.'

'OK. Pick you up in about fifteen minutes.'

Chloe stayed in the garden another five minutes, basking in what remained of her time outdoors. She sometimes felt like an incarcerated animal, particularly on days that kept her trapped within the confines of the station. She looked at her bare arms. Her pale skin could do with a bit of sunshine, she thought. Perhaps at some point in the hopefully not-too-distant future, she and Scott might be able to book a holiday. She wouldn't care where: anywhere warm.

She picked up her plate from the ground and went back into the house. Five minutes later, Alex was outside waiting for her.

'These updates then,' she prompted as Chloe fastened her seat belt.

'First thing,' Chloe told her. 'Leah Cross has more than thirty thousand pounds in her bank account.'

Alex shoved the car into first gear and pulled away from the pavement. 'Nice savings for a student.'

'Exactly. We've taken her laptop – Dan's been looking over it this afternoon. We should have more details on the bank account first thing tomorrow. The other thing is the vehicle check. I've only gone through about a third so far, but—'

'Already?'

Chloe shrugged. 'Time's against us, right?'

'Always. Sorry … I interrupted you.'

They were headed down Caerphilly Road now, past the GE Aviation buildings that lay sprawled in giant concrete blocks. The familiar stretch of A470 waited ahead, stretched out beneath a late-evening heat that held everything in a sticky grip.

'One of the vehicles on that list belongs to a lecturer at the university. A lecturer from the English department.'

Alex shot her a look. 'Could be a coincidence. We only have the first five numbers of the plate, remember.'

Chloe felt a wave of disappointment wash over her. Alex's reaction wasn't what she'd been expecting. She'd hoped the DI might see this development as something that would move the investigation on, and do so quickly, yet she seemed to be dismissing it outright.

'It's worth looking into, though?'

'Yeah.'

Alex took a right at the roundabout, silence falling between them, the atmosphere in the car cooling despite the warmth of the evening. Her attitude might have offended Chloe, but she knew her well enough to realise that something else lay behind her behaviour; something she had yet to share, and obviously wouldn't volunteer to do so without some persuasion. Alex reached for the radio and turned it on, obliterating the silence with a song that had been overplayed by every mainstream station during the past couple of weeks. There was nothing that could have stated more clearly that she didn't want to talk.

They were near the hospital by the time Chloe decided to break the uncomfortable mood. 'Any updates with you today?'

'Leah Cross has provided the university with false information,' Alex told her.

'False information regarding what?'

'Her home contact details, it seems. I went to the hospital earlier, but she was still unconscious. I tried the uni thinking I'd be able to contact her parents through them, but the phone number they gave me belonged to a woman who said she'd never heard of Leah.'

Chloe pushed her hair from her face and pulled it back into a stumpy ponytail. It had been too short for one until recently, but over the past few weeks it had grown long enough to tie back.

'Why would Leah do that?'

'No idea. Either she's lying, or the woman I spoke to on the phone lied to me about knowing her.'

Chloe sighed. 'Seems to keep a lot of secrets, doesn't she?' she said, throwing Alex a sideways glance.

Alex pulled off the main road and turned into the hospital's entrance. If she had picked up on Chloe's insinuation, she wasn't about to acknowledge it. It was the final attempt Chloe was going to make to get her to talk about her mother, and once again it failed.

'What do you make of the bank account then?' Chloe asked Alex as they headed down the corridor towards Leah Cross's hospital room. 'Makes Tom's accusations suddenly more plausible, doesn't it?'

'Maybe. I don't know. She might have been given the money – let's not jump to conclusions. I'm trying to keep an open mind until we speak to her, but she's certainly making that difficult.'

'What … the speaking-to-her bit or the keeping-an-open-mind bit?'

'Both.'

She needed to talk to someone from the university again, Alex thought. Unless it transpired that Leah's parents had moved house in the eighteen months since their daughter had started uni, something wasn't adding up. The university would have sent correspondence to Leah's home address prior to her starting there. If the address they'd always had for her was the address they had given her that morning, then that was where her letters would have been sent.

She pushed open the door to Leah's room. The bed was empty, the sheets gone. The leather sandals that had been beneath the window earlier that day when Alex had stopped by at the hospital were also gone.

'Can I help you?'

A nurse Alex hadn't seen before was standing in the doorway.

'Detective Inspector King,' Alex said, showing her ID. 'We're looking for Leah Cross.'

'She's gone,' the woman said.

'When?'

The nurse glanced at the clock on the wall. 'Last hour or so.'

'But surely she was in no condition just to walk out of here?'

'I'm sorry,' the woman said defensively. 'My shift has only just started – you'd have to speak with someone who'd seen her.'

Alex glanced at Chloe apologetically. Any hope either of them might have had of an early night was gone.

CHAPTER THIRTY-EIGHT

The house was quiet when Leah got back. A duvet was piled on one of the sofas in the living room and the TV still on; wherever the boys were, she doubted it'd be long before they were back. She didn't have much time. She went straight up to her bedroom, trying not to look at Keira's room as she passed. Pulling her gym bag out from under her bed, she packed some clothes and underwear. She peeled off the bloodstained dress she had been wearing the night before, replacing it with a pair of leggings and a T-shirt, then shoved the dress into her bag, resolving to dispose of it as soon as possible.

Sitting on the edge of the bed, she winced at the ache that pulled throughout her body. Her chest felt as though it had taken a beating, but she knew things could have been a lot worse. She reached for the bottom drawer of her bedside table and hunted about for a packet of paracetamol, taking two from their blister strip. Swallowing them down without bothering to get any water to help them along, she squeezed her eyes shut at the pain that continued to pulse through her head. She had known plenty of hangovers in her time, but this particular one was relentless.

She had heard them discussing her while she'd been lying in the hospital bed. The truth was there were a lot of things she couldn't remember: there was nothing between the bright lights that had headed straight for her and waking to hear voices at the end of the bed, and much of what had gone before remained a blur too. She had been careful not to open her eyes. She didn't want the doctors and nurses to know she was awake. She hadn't wanted that detective to know she'd woken up. As soon as they knew she was conscious, the questions would have started.

Trying to ignore the pain that consumed her body, Leah went to the wardrobe and opened its doors. She knew straight away something was wrong. Her shoes were arranged differently to when she'd seen them last, with her trainers now at the front of the wardrobe and not in the corner where they'd been shoved after she'd last used them. She felt a surge of panic. Where was her laptop?

She flung the shoes from the wardrobe and reached for the small gap at the back of the wardrobe's base. It had been tampered with. Someone had been in there.

Tom. It had to be Tom, she thought. But why would he have taken her laptop?

And then another thought occurred to her. The police had been here.

She stood, panicked, leaving everything as it was: shoes spilled onto the carpet and the wooden inner base of the wardrobe propped against the opened door. She grabbed her bag and went downstairs, heading for the kitchen. She was grateful she'd moved Leighton's money from the wardrobe. It would tide her over for the time being, at least.

She pushed open the kitchen door and stopped dead. Tom was slumped against the back door, the handle of a kitchen knife sticking out of his chest; the blade sunk deep enough to make it invisible. Leah steadied herself in the doorway as a surge of sickness swept through her. She could smell the blood that pooled beneath Tom's still body, metallic and rotten, like old rust. Pushing a hand to her mouth, she stepped back, unable to pull her focus from him. Tom's eyes were wide open, staring sightlessly across the kitchen. His last expression – one of fear and confusion – was fixed upon his face, immovable.

Seeing him brought something back, something Leah knew she wouldn't be able to forget. The previous evening, he had been there. He had been on the street when that car had hit her, yet one of the nurses she'd overheard that morning had told another that Leah had been brought in alone. Tom had left her for dead.

Swallowing back bile, she hurried back down the hallway and left the house, closing the front door quietly behind her. She went to the end of the row of terraces and into the narrow lane at the back, gaining access to the yard through the back gate. Her heart pounding, she grappled briefly with the metal padlock on the garden shed, twisting in the numbers of the four-digit code needed to release it. For a while she had faked an interest in gardening, as though anything could be done to improve the crappy narrow concrete space even the most convincing of estate agents would have struggled to describe as a garden. She had bought pot plants and some basic equipment: a small trowel, a fork, some gloves. It had given her an excuse to claim the shed as her own.

Inside was a small shelving unit that housed her tools and a stack of paint pots left by the house's previous tenants. On the bottom shelf, inside a black bin bag, was a box. Like the shed, it had a padlock that needed a code to gain access. Leah keyed in the number and opened the box. Retrieving the collection of rolled bank notes stashed there – as well as the pay-as-you-go mobile phone – she shoved them into the bottom of her sports bag, beneath her clothes, leaving the empty box open on the shelf.

She closed the shed door, but left it unlocked, then slipped back through the gate into the lane. She couldn't push the thought of Tom from her mind, already haunted by the sight of that knife; the smell of that blood. She had no idea where she would go; a B & B, she presumed, or a hotel chain; one of the big ones in Cardiff that would suck her in and allow her to go unnoticed until she'd worked out what the hell she was going to do.

She left the path and cut on to the main road, heading towards the train station. Her arm continued to throb and the paracetamol had so far done nothing to ease the pounding in her head. Her quick breaths reminded her of the bruising to her ribs, and as she hurried along she tried not to focus on all the things she was going to have to leave behind.

Well, she thought, the one thing she was going to have to leave behind. The one and only thing that mattered now.

She wondered not for the first time that day if he'd been behind the wheel of that car. She had thought so earlier, but what had happened to Tom changed everything. Now she wasn't so sure. What had she done? She wanted to see him, and nothing was going to change that.

She needed to speak to him before the police did.

CHAPTER THIRTY-NINE

That night, Alex couldn't sleep. She found herself repeatedly checking her phone, looking at it every two minutes though it was resting on the arm of the sofa right behind her with the sound on and the volume turned up. Things always seemed worst at night, her fears gathered in the darkness around her as though mocking her with their presence. That night was even worse. Her mother's pale inertia in her nursing-home bed – the paper-thin skin of her hands and the grey pallor of her face – seemed to be there with her now, embodied by the things she'd tried to avoid but had always known would catch up with her eventually.

Her laptop sat beside her on the sofa, a brief article on the allegations made against Leighton Matthews open on the internet. He had no criminal record: there had been insufficient evidence to support the student's claims. Alex would need to find out who had dealt with the allegations and what had happened during the investigation. Not being charged didn't necessarily mean not guilty.

Had Leighton Matthews been involved in a relationship with Leah Cross, and had it been his car that had hit her the previous night? Why? Perhaps she had threatened to expose the relationship, or had threatened to tell his wife. Had Keira found out something she wasn't supposed to? Her death remained at the heart of this case, of that Alex felt certain. Without a suspect, though, she felt herself getting further away from ever discovering what had happened on that rooftop. She needed something soon, or Harry would be given justification to bring the case to a close.

She was woken from her thoughts by a piercing scream that cut through the silence of the house. She recognised it, its sound now familiar to her. Chloe had been having nightmares for the previous five months, since she had first come to stay with Alex. They were not as regular now as they'd been back then, but their effect was always the same.

Alex shoved the laptop aside and headed up the stairs. A second shout followed, incoherent words muffled by a fitful struggle in which Chloe fought off the man who continued to haunt her sleep. She had been dealing so well with what had happened to her months earlier; during waking hours, at least. Her insistence on putting on a brave face meant her fears were saved for the witching hours, when her subconscious would recreate things she'd stored away during the day and present them in their rawest form, alive and real; inescapable. Her refusal to talk about what had happened meant these things continued to eat away at her, from the inside out, a parasite.

Pushing open the door to Chloe's room, Alex realised the irony of her thoughts. Wasn't she doing exactly the same?

'Chloe,' she said firmly, placing a hand on the younger woman's shoulder. 'Chloe, wake up.'

She had learned over the previous few months that this was the best way to deal with the nightmares. At first she had been tentative, unsure how to manage the transition between sleep and reality. Experience had taught her she should snap Chloe from the nightmare as quickly as possible.

Chloe's eyes opened, trance-like. As they adjusted to the darkness, Alex could see her realising where she was. That she was safe. Her breathing slowed and she pushed herself up in the bed.

'Shit, I'm so sorry. Did I wake you?'

'No. I was awake.'

Chloe reached for her phone, flipped open the case and pressed a button so that the screen lit up and she could see the clock. It was 1.20 in the morning. 'Why were you still awake?'

Alex shrugged. 'Couldn't sleep. Same dream?'

Chloe nodded. She took the glass of water that was on the bedside table and drained it. 'Sorry,' she said again.

'Stop apologising. Look ... I think you should talk to someone. You can always talk to me, you know that, but I think you need someone professional, someone who knows what to do to help you through this.'

Chloe pressed a hand to her eyes, wiping away sleep. 'I'm OK. They're just dreams. They don't mean anything.'

Alex didn't think that was true. She didn't believe Chloe really thought it was true either. There was a reason why sleep was evading Alex, and unwanted dreams were in part responsible. She didn't want to go to all the places her sleep took her. Dreams weren't always meaningless. Sometimes they were an indication that something was very wrong.

'Consider it properly, at least.'

Chloe nodded. 'And when are you going to talk to someone about what's going on with you?'

Alex folded her arms in an automatic gesture of defence. 'I'll let you get back to sleep. Early start tomorrow.'

'It's your mum, isn't it?' Chloe said, ignoring Alex's attempts to evade the subject. 'What's happened?'

Alex looked at the carpet, embarrassed by Chloe's concern. 'It's nothing that wasn't expected.'

'Is she OK?'

Alex shook her head. 'She's dying. I mean, she's been dying for a long time, but the doctor thinks it's not long now.'

Chloe pushed back the duvet and stood from the bed. She was wearing a pair of patterned pyjamas that made her look even younger than her twenty-six years, little more than a teenager. 'Why haven't you told anyone? You should tell Blake, take some time off.'

'Now? Not really a great time, is it?'

'Alex,' Chloe said, stooping down to retrieve a pair of socks from the floor. 'Nothing is more important than this.' She sat down on the edge of the bed and pulled on the socks. 'You should be with your mum.'

Alex sighed. 'We don't even like each other, not really. Our relationship's been terrible for years.'

'All the more reason to put things right now then, don't you think? If only for your own sake. Come on,' Chloe said, standing again. 'I'm putting the kettle on.'

CHAPTER FORTY

Later that morning, Alex and Chloe pulled up outside the semi-detached house in Llandaff that belonged to Leighton Matthews and his wife. This was an affluent area of Cardiff, characterised by large houses and sprawling gardens. The wide driveway housed a Mini convertible, but the first thing both women noticed was the absence of a 4x4.

'Nice,' Chloe said, gesturing to the house. 'Didn't think lecturers were paid that well.'

'Wife does all right for herself, by the looks of things. Owns three salons.'

'Maybe I could get my roots done while we're here.' Chloe stepped from the car. She was tired after the previous evening's restless night, but the make-up she'd applied carefully that morning was doing a good job of concealing the telltale signs of her need for sleep. It had been worth staying awake to get Alex to finally talk.

They walked up the driveway and rang the bell. Moments later, Leighton Matthews answered. He was tall and athletic in frame, quite different from the suggestions offered by the photographs Chloe and Alex had seen of him online. He was wearing fashionable clothes that seemed to Chloe slightly out of place on a man of his age, although even as the thought occurred to her she wondered what he was supposed to be wearing now he was in his forties, as if hitting a certain decade meant a life committed to sensible shoes and corduroy trousers. 'Detective Inspector Alex King.' Alex introduced herself. 'This is Detective Constable Chloe Lane. Do you have a few minutes?'

Leighton Matthews didn't move from the doorway, seemingly reluctant to let them into the house. 'Now? I mean … I'm a bit busy at the moment.'

'With what?' Alex asked. 'Term's over, isn't it?'

Matthews looked unsettled by the comment, disconcerted by the fact that they knew enough about him to know what his job was. 'What's this about?'

'We're investigating a hit-and-run that took place the night before last. We're just talking to people to eliminate them from enquiries.' Alex glanced to the fence that divided Leighton's driveway from the one next door. The neighbour was at his recycling bin, the lid held half open as he stood listening to the conversation taking place on the other side of the fence. She nodded an acknowledgement before turning back to Matthews. 'We can continue out here if you like, or perhaps you'd prefer a bit of privacy.'

Matthews stepped back reluctantly to allow them to enter the house. Inside, the property was something taken straight from the pages of an interior design magazine. Everything was in neutral colours, from the white walls to the pale grey furniture. The decor was sparse, and light poured into the hallway from a huge window at the top of the wide staircase. The place looked barely lived in – a show home – and the air smelled of plug-in fragrances, so strong it caught Chloe in the back of the throat.

They followed Leighton Matthews through to the kitchen, where a teenage girl wearing a tiny pair of pyjama shorts and a vest top was standing waiting for the kettle to boil. She threw the two detectives a glance, her eyes lingering on Chloe's outfit for a moment, before turning her attention back to tea-making.

'My daughter,' Matthews said, though the girl hadn't acknowledged him. 'Younger.'

The girl left the room, eyeing the two women with suspicion before heading upstairs with her cup of tea. Matthews returned to where he'd obviously been working at the table. His laptop was open beside a pile of paperwork.

'Next book?' Chloe asked.

He looked at her in surprise. 'Yes. I mean … it's just notes at the moment, but hopefully.'

Once again, he seemed disconcerted at the fact that they already seemed to know so much about him.

'What do you write?'

'Literary fiction.'

Chloe raised her eyebrows, but said nothing. She wondered whether a proficiency for writing fiction made someone a good liar.

'Look,' he said, folding his arms across his chest. 'I don't really know why you're here. I don't know anything about a hit-and-run.'

'Do you know Leah Cross?' Alex asked.

His reaction made the answer clear. At the mention of the girl's name, he flinched. 'She's a student at the university. Why?'

'She was hit by a car on Wednesday night.'

He was silent for a moment, avoiding eye contact with either woman. 'Oh. Well … I'm sorry to hear that.' He pointlessly pushed a pile of paperwork to one side. 'Is she OK?' he asked, his face turned from them.

'She'll live,' Alex told him. 'Could you tell us where you were on Wednesday night, Mr Matthews? Between the hours of eleven p.m. and one a.m.'

'I was here,' Matthews said without hesitation. 'In bed.'

'Was your wife home?'

'Yes.'

Alex nodded, taking in the details of the expensive kitchen: huge American-style fridge, chrome fittings, bi-folding doors that looked out on to an expanse of neatly tended back garden. 'The thing is, Mr Matthews,' she said, taking a seat at the table, 'a car of the same make and colour as yours was seen leaving the scene of the incident on Wednesday night.'

'There are hundreds of cars like mine on the roads. Thousands, probably.'

'We have an eyewitness. The number plate is a close match with yours.'

'A close match. So not exact, then?'

'Where is your car, Mr Matthews?' Chloe asked.

Matthews hesitated. 'It's in the garage.'

'Your garage here at the house, or do you mean another garage?'

He looked from Chloe to Alex. 'It's cut out on me a few times over the past couple of weeks. I took it in to have it checked over.'

'When did you take it in?' Alex asked.

'Yesterday.'

'Right,' she said. She shot Chloe a look. Leighton Matthews had taken his car to a garage the morning after the hit-and-run. They needed to get their hands on it before further evidence was lost, if it wasn't already too late for that. 'And the name of the garage?'

'Lockley's down on Western Avenue. Look …' Matthews glanced at the huge clock that hung on the wall above the sink. 'Is there anything else? I really am very busy.'

Alex sat back, making it clear she was in no hurry to leave. 'You don't seem too concerned about the welfare of your student, Mr Matthews.'

He leaned on the back of the chair that faced her. 'You said she's OK.'

'How well do you know Leah Cross?'

Matthews exhaled. 'As well as I know any of the students. She comes to my lectures, she writes me essays, I mark them and hand them back. I don't know any of them particularly well.'

'What about Siobhan O'Leary?' Chloe asked. 'Did you know her well?'

His face fell for a moment. It wasn't long before the look of surprise morphed into an expression of anger. His fists gripped the back of the chair in front of him. 'I said everything there was to say about that at the time. There were no charges brought against me and the reason for that was because she was lying. There was something wrong with that girl, everyone knew it.'

'Something wrong with her?'

'Delusional. Obsessive. There was no truth in any of her claims. Now … are we done here?'

Alex stood. 'That'll depend on your car, won't it?' She was interrupted by the sound of her mobile phone. 'DI King,' she said, heading out into the hallway as she took the call. There was a lengthy pause. 'OK … we're on our way.' She came back into the kitchen. 'We'll be in touch, Mr Matthews,' she said, nodding Chloe from the room.

'Everything OK?' Chloe asked as the door to the Matthews house was closed behind them.

'Tom Stoddard. He's been murdered.'

CHAPTER FORTY-ONE

Leah turned off the television. She had put it on in the hope that it would be a distraction from her thoughts and from the pain that continued its assault on her body, and had turned up the volume when the people staying in the room next door had decided to pop back to the hotel for a noisy bout of midday sex. Once they'd finished and were gone again, she realised the television wasn't helping to ward off anything. She couldn't keep herself away from her thoughts. What was she going to do now? Where was she going to go?

She stood at the window for a while and watched the city outside. Endless streams of traffic filtered along the main road and past the hotel, and commuters and shoppers dodged cyclists as they went about their daily business. The world moved below Leah in a flood of colour and life. Everyone had a purpose. Everyone had somewhere to go; something to head towards. Everyone had someone.

The inert expressions of the stone animals that lined the wall of the castle opposite Leah's window seemed to taunt her. Their cold faces were a mixture of fear and sadness: the hyena with its snarling teeth but terrified eyes; the lion that should have looked majestic but seemed instead oddly vulnerable, frozen there on the curve of the wall as though in punishment.

She thought she knew how it might feel.

Things weren't supposed to have been this way. She'd had a plan – a solid one, one that had taken so much preparation – and none of it had involved any of the things that had happened during the past week. She wasn't a bad person, but who would believe that now?

She went to the bed and winced as she sat on the duvet. She had listened to the nurses listing her injuries, yet none of the bruises and fractures hurt nearly as much as the pain of what she feared might still await her. She unzipped her bag, searching among her belongings for her mobile phone. She wanted to check the internet for news on Amy Barker. She'd thought about going to visit her when she'd been at the hospital, but it would have been difficult to explain who she was and what she was doing there. She tapped the girl's name into Google and scanned through the results.

Girl still in coma after overdose.

She closed the internet page and opened the photographs stored in her phone, searching for the last few taken of her and Keira. Smiling selfies at Keira's birthday party months earlier, documenting the night as it had happened, hour by hour. If she flicked through the images quickly enough, she could make them come alive, like those flip books that kids in school had drawn of footballers scoring goals and stick men falling off cliff edges, meeting their fate in a splodge of red ink on the final page.

If she did it fast enough, she could bring Keira back to life.

She looked away from the photographs. Tears had filled her eyes, bringing with them an unsettling nausea that hung leaden in her stomach. Keira had been her friend, no matter what anyone now said.

Realising she couldn't stay at the hotel for more than a couple of nights – maybe three, at a push – Leah searched through her contacts list. She hadn't wanted to do this, but circumstances had left her with little other option. If she grovelled enough – if she swallowed her pride and begged forgiveness, though she thought it might kill her to do so – perhaps they would take her back.

Perhaps.

She pressed call. Within a few rings, Carol answered.

'Hello?'

'It's me. It's Leah. Please don't hang up.'

There was silence.

'I know you're still mad at me and I don't blame you,' Leah said, the words spilling from her thick and fast. 'I'm sorry for what I did, you know I am.'

'Sorry you got caught out, you mean,' Carol said.

Leah clutched the mobile to her ear and drew her legs beneath her. When she spoke, her words made her sound like a child again. 'I want to come home.'

Silence. If she listened closely enough, she could hear the sound of Carol's breathing. She remembered that last afternoon. She had never seen Carol like it before: calm, kind Carol reduced to a screaming red-faced witch. And Leah had been responsible for it.

'This isn't your home.'

Even as Carol spoke the words, Leah could hear the doubt behind them. She might have thought she meant them, but Leah realised it wasn't in Carol's nature to be mean for the sake of meanness or cruel even when she thought it might have been deserved. She tended to see the good in everyone, something Leah had never quite been able to understand or emulate. Still, the words burned, and she felt tears prick her eyes as she continued her plea.

'Please,' she said, hearing her own voice cracking. 'I've got nowhere else to go.'

'You should have thought of that before,' Carol said, steadying her words in an attempt to make them sound more convincing. 'The police rang here looking for you, by the way. I suppose that's what this is really all about.'

Leah pulled the duvet over her, suddenly feeling cold. Why had the police called Carol? How had they known where she lived?

'You don't bring trouble to this house any more,' Carol told her, the words more a statement than a warning.

Leah opened her mouth to speak, but it was too late: Carol had already gone. She thought about ringing back, but knew the attempt was likely to be met with an engaged tone. She turned her mobile off. She couldn't stay here, not now. Turning over in the duvet and cradling her injuries, she cocooned herself in its comfort and cried until she fell asleep.

CHAPTER FORTY-TWO

The cordon that ran across the front of the house at Railway Terrace was surrounded by rubberneckers, and when Alex and Chloe arrived, uniformed officers were in the process of trying to disperse the crowd. One held up the police tape so that the two detectives could duck beneath it. In the living room, an officer was sitting with Jamie Bateman. The young man's face looked deathly pale, tear-stained, and he had never appeared more childlike. He looked at but seemed to barely see the two women as they entered the room.

'What happened, Jamie?'

Alex sat beside him on the sofa, nodding to the officer that she was free to leave to help the others outside. When the boy spoke, his words were barely coherent. 'He's still … he's in there … there's …'

'Jamie, take a deep breath and start at the beginning. Tom's in the kitchen, is that right?'

The young man nodded, fighting back tears. He was evidently still in shock. Alex and Chloe had yet to see the body, but the phone call Alex had received had made it clear how unpleasant the scene was.

'You found him?' Alex asked. 'When was that?'

'This mor—' Jamie stopped, unable to speak. He inhaled sharply, in short bursts, as he tried to catch his breath. 'This morning.'

'You didn't sleep here last night?'

Jamie shook his head. 'I wanted to get away. Everything with Keira, and then Leah … I didn't want to be here.'

Alex shot Chloe a glance. What the hell had gone on in this house? Two housemates were dead, a third was now missing. The boy sitting beside her looked pathetic, vulnerable, but Alex knew she couldn't allow herself to be fooled by appearances.

'Where did you stay?' Chloe asked.

'With someone from work. He knows what's been going on – he said I could have his sofa for the night if I needed a break.' He put his head in his hands and leaned forward, hiding his face from the two women. 'Oh God, there was so much blood,' he said, his voice breaking on the words.

Alex gave Chloe a nod and the two women went out into the hallway. 'Stay with him for five, give him a chance to calm down a bit,' Alex said. 'I'll go and see the pathologist.'

She headed down to the dining room and stopped at the doorway, where a SOCO was dusting for prints. The man lowered the mask he was wearing and passed her a set of protective shoe covers.

'Pathologist here yet?' she asked as she pulled them on.

The man nodded. 'In the kitchen.'

Alex passed through the dining room, bracing herself for the scene that would greet her. In her seventeen years with the police she had seen some truly horrific things, yet she had always prepared herself with the thought that there was something worse she could encounter. Whatever nightmarish visions she could conjure in her mind, someone somewhere was macabre enough to make those imaginings a reality.

Tom Stoddard was slumped against the glass panel of the back door. His skin looked faded to a pale grey, almost blending with the T-shirt he was wearing. The front of the T-shirt was stained in blood that had spilled from his chest to the floor. No matter the amount of blood, the thing Alex already knew would remain with her was the young man's eyes, alert yet visionless, still staring at the last sight he was likely to have seen: his killer.

'There are at least three stab wounds, but I'll be able to tell more once he's in the lab.'

Alex's attention was drawn from Tom's body as Helen Collier, a pathologist from the University of Wales Hospital, appeared like a ghost at her side, clad from head to foot in white protective clothing. Alex had been oblivious to all three people in the room: Helen, and the two SOCOs who were busy retrieving potential evidence.

'Where's the third?' she asked. The two stab wounds to Tom's chest were evident from the patterns of blood that stained his T-shirt. The knife was still embedded in his chest, but a second wound was obvious from the stream of blood that had coursed down the left-hand side of his body on to the kitchen's laminate flooring.

'Look.' Helen Collier crouched beside the body and gestured to where the boy sat against the end of the kitchen unit. 'This pool of blood here – it's come from his back.'

'How long do you think he's been dead?'

'Initial estimate, between twelve and eighteen hours. Like I said, I'll be able to tell more once we get him to the lab.'

Alex left the kitchen and went back to the living room. Chloe was standing at the doorway, trying not to focus for too long on Jamie, who was still sitting on the sofa, his head hidden in his hands.

'You'll need to come to the station to make a statement, Jamie. Are you OK to do that?'

The boy looked up and nodded. 'And then what? I can't come back here.'

'Where do your parents live?'

'Carmarthen. I'm not going there, not so they can say they told me so. They never wanted me to move away in the first place.'

'What about the friend you stayed with last night?' Chloe asked. 'Could you go there for a while longer?'

Jamie shrugged. 'What the hell's going on here?' he asked, the words filled with fear. 'I feel like I'm living in some sort of nightmare.'

'Have you heard from Leah?' Alex asked.

'Leah? No. I thought she was at the hospital. Has she woken up?'

'Come on,' Alex said, gesturing him through to the hallway and ignoring his questions. 'We'll take you to the station.'

CHAPTER FORTY-THREE

After taking Jamie to the station and leaving him with Dan to make a statement, Alex and Chloe headed to the University of South Wales. Tom Stoddard's death had thrown yet another complication into the case, and Leighton Matthews remained the only link they currently had to any of the students.

Anna Stapleton's office was a shambles. Alex wondered how anyone could achieve anything amid the mess and chaos that littered the room: towering stacks of paperwork so high they looked as though a single misdirected sneeze would topple the lot; books and magazines scattered on the floor; half-eaten food and forgotten cups of coffee that had grown fur coats left on any and every available surface.

She shot Chloe a glance. The younger woman's face had paled at the sight of a half-eaten ham sandwich that looked as though something might have started living in its dehydrated depths.

'Ignore the mess,' Anna said, waving a hand dismissively.

She too looked generally dishevelled, her auburn hair piled high in a messy mass of metal slides and her skirt, too long, twisted at the waist so that the zip had caught at her side, snagging on her loose blouse. Anna Stapleton looked like a woman who'd had a long and busy summer term and should probably be spending the next couple of months in recovery rather than still here at the university doing whatever it was she was doing.

'We'd like to talk to you about a student called Leah Cross,' Alex said.

Anna cleared two chairs, which involved a swift swipe of an arm across a pile of clutter. She gestured to Alex and Chloe to take a seat, which Chloe did tentatively.

'Leah. Yes. She was on my fiction-writing module.'

'Good student?'

Anna tilted her head. 'Are any of them good any more?' she asked, more to herself than to either of the women sitting opposite her. 'Chasing other people's deadlines has become part of my job description, apparently. I've got a couple of decent workers, but I think most of them are here for a three-year party and that's about it.'

'Leah Cross included?' Chloe asked.

'I don't know Leah too well,' Anna admitted. 'She doesn't really engage much during sessions – she tends to keep herself to herself.'

'What are her grades like?'

'Well,' Anna said, crossing one leg over the other and smoothing out the creases in her skirt. 'Good. Surprisingly good for someone who doesn't seem to do much work.'

Alex caught Chloe's eye. They were already on the same page, thinking the same thing. Something about Leighton Matthews and Leah Cross wasn't adding up, particularly in light of what they'd found out from the garage earlier that morning. Despite Matthews' claims that the car had been cutting out, it turned out it had not only been cleaned inside and out, but had also had a dent to the front bumper repaired.

Why would Leighton Matthews want to harm Leah Cross? If they could get to the bottom of what was going on between the pair, perhaps it might lead to a link to Keira. And where did Tom come into any of this? Alex was starting to wonder whether their initial assumption had been the right one all along. Had Tom pushed Keira from that roof, and if so, had Leah discharged herself from the hospital in order to take her revenge?

She tried to rein in her theories. Tom had been seen by too many people downstairs at the time Keira had fallen, and besides, none of this explained why Leah had been hit by a car on Wednesday night. She still wasn't ready to rule out Jamie Bateman, although the thought of his involvement seemed unlikely. They'd have to wait until the post-mortem results on Tom came back, as well as the results on the evidence lifted by the SOCOs.

'Leighton Matthews,' Alex said. 'A couple of years ago he was accused of harassment by a female student who attended the university.'

'Falsely accused,' Anna said quickly. 'He was investigated but there was no evidence found.'

'Doesn't necessarily make him innocent,' Chloe quipped.

'What happened to innocent until proven guilty?'

In an ideal world, Alex thought. But they were working in a far from ideal world. In the superintendent's perfect scenario, the death of Keira North would be marked down as an accident and they could all move swiftly on from it. She was sure he had been hoping the post-mortem would find a high level of alcohol in the girl's system, so he could chalk it up as a drunken mishap. Alex knew she was being cynical, and it wasn't like her to think so poorly of Harry, but his attitude towards this young woman's death was something she couldn't condone. It bordered on indifference.

Anna Stapleton's face had flushed. She looked offended by the insinuation of Leighton's impropriety, as though Alex and Chloe had suggested something about her rather than about her colleague. 'Leighton is a creative mind. He's an artist, in the true sense of the word.' She stood and went to one of the bookcases that lined the far wall of her office. She reached for a paperback and passed it to Alex. 'Have you read it?'

Alex studied the book. It was black, with a single white feather embossed on its front cover. *Resurrection*, the title read. 'Can't say I've had the pleasure.'

'Take it, please,' Anna said, Alex's sarcasm lost on her. 'I have a couple of copies. It really is a beautiful piece of work. Raw. Relevant.'

'We're investigating a suspicious death,' Alex said. Clearly the woman needed some reminding. As thrilling as an afternoon might be spent discussing the literary abilities of a man who was seemingly angry at the world and everyone in it, Alex didn't have the time to listen to this woman's sycophantic praise of her colleague. Nor did she have time to listen to Anna Stapleton skirt around information she was clearly loath to provide.

Anna's expression changed as she sat back down, her defiance collapsing slightly. 'That poor girl. She was pregnant, wasn't she?'

Alex ignored the question. It was public knowledge that Keira North had been five months pregnant when she died; now that the details of her death had been broadcast, the girl's secret was no longer her own.

'I understand that you may feel a sense of loyalty to your colleague, Ms Stapleton, but the time for withholding information from us isn't now. You seem to be a woman who champions honesty. The truth. That's all we're asking for.'

Anna shifted uncomfortably in her seat. 'I've questioned some of Leah's grades,' she confessed. 'I …'

Alex raised an eyebrow. 'Go on,' she prompted.

'I've spoken to Leighton about it already, but the marks have been submitted now.'

'Spoken to Leighton about what?' Alex pressed, her growing impatience now obvious.

'She got a first for one of her essays.' Anna Stapleton hesitated, avoiding Alex's eye. Why was the woman so obviously reluctant to speak about her colleague?

'And?' Alex pressed.

'I just don't think her work merits that.'

'And Leighton awarded the grade?' Chloe asked.

'Well, yes, but—'

'I'd like a copy of that essay, please, Ms Stapleton,' Alex interrupted.

Again Anna look flustered. 'What … now?'

'Yes, now.'

Anna stood and began rummaging in one of the filing cabinets at the back of the office. With the woman's back to them, Alex raised the book in her hand and gave Chloe a roll of her eyes. Her colleague smiled.

'If there was no truth in Siobhan O'Leary's allegations against Leighton,' Alex asked, 'why do you think she made them? Why lie about something like that … if it was a lie?'

Anna turned from the filing cabinet. 'I have no idea.'

Alex didn't believe the woman. Anna was on the defensive, and again she wondered why. What was it about Leighton Matthews that seemed to draw women towards him, regardless of how poorly he might treat them? She had met plenty of people during her life who seemed to possess an innate ability to avoid the consequences of their actions, but from recent accounts of his character, Leighton Matthews seemed to have made the habit a life skill.

'Are you sure?' she asked. 'Only it seems to me you might have a pretty good idea.'

Anna's face flushed again. She moved away from the filing cabinet and sat back down. 'Look,' she said, 'you'll find out soon enough, I suppose. A few years ago, Leighton had a relationship with a student.'

Alex sighed. Everything was starting to make sense, but the more truths they uncovered, the more she realised she was being lied to by the very people who could help them find out exactly what had happened on that rooftop.

'You surprise me. Go on.'

'There was nothing illegal in what he did.'

Chloe gave an involuntary snort. 'There are plenty of legal things that are morally questionable,' she said. 'She was his student. Isn't that an abuse of his position?'

'I know,' Anna said defensively, 'and I'm not suggesting I condone what he did.'

'Why do you think this relationship, as you put it, is relevant to Siobhan O'Leary's allegations of sexual harassment?'

'It made Leighton an easy target. She probably thought it made her lies more convincing. From what I saw of it, she loved the attention. Some girls can be very calculating. Siobhan saw an opportunity and she exploited it. Leighton was foolish for getting involved with the other girl, but that doesn't make him a bad man.'

Foolish, Alex thought. That was one word for it.

'Suspecting him of anything criminal is ridiculous,' Anna concluded.

Alex stood. 'We'll be the judges of that. Now if we could have that essay, please.'

CHAPTER FORTY-FOUR

Leighton Matthews was sitting in one of the station's interview rooms, looking as though he would rather have been anywhere else. It was an expression most people wore in this room, including the officers and the duty solicitors who attended. The only people Alex had ever seen show enthusiasm for the place were the ones who'd reoffended in the hope of making it back inside, usually before Christmas, where they'd be guaranteed heating and a two-course dinner. It was a sad truth, but such incidents were on the rise and the same faces were becoming increasingly familiar.

'We've spoken to the garage,' she told him. 'They've had to fix a bit of a dent to the front bumper, apparently.'

She studied the man, waiting for a response. Matthews kept his head lowered, eyes fixed to the table, trying to hide any reaction. He pressed his long fingers to his temples. Alex gave Chloe a sideways glance. Her colleague was usually quite perceptive when it came to body language, and she wondered what she might be reading into this.

'Did you ever have any contact with Keira North?'

Matthews looked up at the mention of the young woman's name. 'No.'

'OK.' Alex opened the file on the desk in front of her and removed copies of some of the messages Dan had retrieved from Keira's laptop and email account. 'This demonstrates that she had contact with you, at least. April the fourth,' she said, checking the date the message had been sent. 'Keira sent you an email about one of Leah's essays. Ring any bells yet?'

Matthews pushed a hand through his dark hair and shifted in his seat. 'No.'

'Did you reply to the email?'

'I don't know,' he said, his voice rising. 'Maybe. I get lots of emails, from lots of students. I can't be expected to remember them all.'

'*Dear Mr Matthews,*' Alex read. '*You teach my friend and house-mate, Leah Cross. She told me last night that she has missed the deadline on a piece of coursework and that the department won't accept a late submission. A draft of the work in question – an essay on post-modern American fiction – was delivered a week before the deadline: I know this because I dropped it into your office myself, as Leah was unwell. You weren't there at the time, so I left it on your desk. I saw one of the other members of staff – she said it was fine to leave it there. Please allow Leah to submit the essay – she is very upset about the impact this might have on her end-of-year result, and if it was anyone's fault the work didn't end up with you then it's mine. Thank you. Keira North.*'

She put the page on the desk in front of her and looked at Matthews expectantly. He looked back, his expression having morphed from concern to exasperation.

'I don't understand this,' he said. 'You've brought me in here to question me about an email?'

'No. We've brought you in here to question you about a murder. And possibly an attempted murder too. No one drives their car at someone without intending them harm.'

'You're suggesting I went to a student house party and pushed a girl off a roof?' he said. 'Everyone knows what happened to Keira, and it's tragic. But this is ridiculous. If I'd been at that party, plenty of people would have seen me. I'd have looked a bit out of place, don't you think? And what the hell would I have been doing there in the first place?'

Chloe raised an eyebrow. 'You tell us.'

The unspoken insinuation rested in the air between them, silencing the room for a moment.

'And Wednesday night?' Alex said. 'What about then? We have an ID of a vehicle that closely matches yours, along with the fact that you conveniently happened to take your car to a garage the following morning, and that visit just happened to involve a full clean and valet. There was no mention of any engine failure, by the way. They told us they fixed a dent on the bumper. What's your excuse for that?'

'I did that ages ago,' Matthews said, holding her gaze.

'Where?'

He hesitated. 'I don't remember – it was quite a while back.'

'Convenient.'

'It was a narrow lane,' he said, 'I remember now. I swerved to avoid a sheep.'

'Of course you did,' Chloe said. 'And were there flying pigs around this lane at the same time?'

'Do you have evidence of any of these accusations?' Matthews asked, ignoring Chloe and returning his focus to Alex.

They didn't, not yet, but Alex wasn't about to tell him that. What they needed was something concrete, something that would place Leighton Matthews at the scene of the hit-and-run. By having the car cleaned, the clever bastard had managed to erase any trace of Leah's blood or fibres from her clothing that they might have been able to retrieve from his vehicle.

Matthews looked from Alex to Chloe and back again. 'I'm not involved in any of this,' he said. 'I'd like to speak to my solicitor.'

Alex pushed her chair back and stood. 'Fine. Though if you're not involved, you shouldn't have anything to worry about, should you?'

CHAPTER FORTY-FIVE

While they waited for Leighton Matthews' solicitor to arrive, Alex and Chloe went to the incident room to speak with the rest of the team. The room was a buzz of activity, with much of the team now confined to their desks while CCTV footage was checked and communications between suspects reviewed. Superintendent Blake was present, watching over proceedings in his usual quiet manner.

'You're all aware of Tom Stoddard's death,' Alex told the team. 'I've asked for the PM to be considered a priority. Leah Cross, as you know, has gone AWOL from the hospital – let's make finding her a priority, please. We need to speak with as many people from Railway Terrace as we can, see if anyone saw her between five o'clock yesterday afternoon and ten this morning. Leighton Matthews has been brought in for questioning. We're waiting for his solicitor to arrive. In the meantime, there have been a few developments. Turns out he took his car to a garage yesterday morning for a full valet. There was also a dent to the front bumper that was repaired. Leighton claimed he'd taken the car in because the engine kept cutting out on him, but the garage said there was no evidence of that.'

There were murmurs among the team members.

'Enough to nail him?' DC Jake Sullivan asked.

'Unlikely,' Alex admitted. 'We're not going to get a confession any time soon, so we're going to have to broaden our review of the CCTV footage from the area – we're not looking wide enough. We need to put his car within a mile radius of Leah Cross's house on Wednesday night. We might have to think a bit sideways here with

regard to what route he might have taken to get to Treforest. He's
not stupid … this was likely to have been planned well in advance.'

'There's also the fact that the car seemed to have been waiting
there,' Chloe said. 'Matthews couldn't have known what time Leah
would be home, so he must have waited for her to come back.
How long did he wait? Perhaps we're not checking the footage
early enough.'

Alex addressed Jake, who was sitting in front of her. 'I'd like you
to go and speak with Melissa Matthews, Leighton's wife. He claims
he was with her all of Wednesday evening … let's see if she offers
the same account. We've got reason to suspect that Matthews may
have been involved with Leah Cross. His colleague at the university,
Anna Stapleton, claims he had a relationship with an ex-student
a few years ago, plus there's the allegation made against him by
another student that we already know about.'

'Has he admitted to being involved with Leah?' Dan asked.

Alex shook her head. 'He's not prepared to say much until his
solicitor arrives. He's been in a similar situation before; he knows
the drill.'

'So we're thinking Matthews hit Leah Cross with his car because
he was having a relationship with her and wanted to shut her up?'

The question came from Superintendent Blake, whose eyes Alex
had felt fixed upon her during the last few minutes. His scepticism
was tangible, even now.

'For the moment, yes. His car is with forensics; there might still
be something they're able to pick up.'

'And how does this link to Keira North's death?'

The room fell silent for a moment, the tension between the two
apparent to everyone present. Alex held the superintendent's stare.
This was her team; once he was gone, she was going to have to
continue working with them. She wasn't going to be undermined
in front of them, not by Blake or anyone else.

'That's what we need to find out,' she admitted. 'It might be the case that Keira found out about the relationship between Leah and Matthews. If so, he could have wanted her kept quiet too. Another affair exposed – how much more could his marriage be put through before it snapped? How much more could he get away with before his position at the university was compromised? There's also Tom Stoddard's drug dealing to consider. We don't yet know if his death is linked to that, or if it's linked to what happened to the two girls. Perhaps all three incidents are connected. In his interview, Tom accused Leah of orchestrating the drug dealing. Keira might have got herself unwittingly involved in something there. Wherever she comes into this, I believe Keira North was an innocent. She got herself mixed up somewhere she wasn't wanted and she paid the price with her life.'

Blake looked away for the first time. Alex didn't want their working relationship to end on a negative note, but at the moment he was making that possibility difficult to avoid.

'The party was the perfect place for someone to kill her. There were lots of people there, plenty of noise – plenty of alcohol, and apparent drug use too. Her death might have easily been written off as an accident.'

Alex knew Blake would realise her last words were intended for him.

'There was no sign of a break-in at the house on Railway Terrace this morning,' she continued. 'Jamie Bateman stayed with a colleague last night, which has been corroborated.'

'Surely the catalyst in all this is Leah?' Chloe said.

'Definitely. Leah Cross, who has now conveniently gone AWOL. She discharged herself from hospital yesterday. I know it's been a long day already, but let's try to get on to her bank statements. Dan, we need to know how that money was paid in. Was it cash or transfers? If it was transfers, who from? Let's get a trace on her phone. Let's try to find her today, please.'

'Think she might have gone home?' Jake asked. 'To her parents, I mean.'

Alex exhaled loudly. 'Brownie points to whoever is able to find out where "home" is. Leah Cross provided the university with a false home address. The woman who lives there claims not to know her, so one of them is lying. We need to know why. And whoever speaks to Leah first, just remember it's becoming increasingly probable we can't trust a word this girl says.'

She was interrupted by Stuart, one of the desk sergeants, entering the room. 'Boss,' he said, 'we've just had a call from the hospital. Amy Barker's woken up.'

CHAPTER FORTY-SIX

There is blood on my hands now. It is ugly and real and not the way things were supposed to be. When I close my eyes, I see him looking back at me. That expression of shock, of fear, returns to haunt me, and I know it will be a long time before it leaves. But he had to die. If I keep my cool, if I stay calm, then nothing will come back on me. There is still every chance that someone else will pay, and when they do, justice will be served at last.

The police are focused on the two people who deserve it most in the world. If she survives the hit-and-run, I will have to find another way to silence her. I wanted to kill her, but perhaps things will be better this way. How much damage have I done to her? How much suffering will she have to endure as a result of what I've done? Perhaps this punishment will be fairer than death.

She is dangerous: more dangerous than I anticipated. But I have learned how to be bad. It has developed in me, spreading like an illness; if I focus hard enough, I can feel it growing. I have watched corruption and learned by example.

When all this is over, I am going to leave South Wales. There is nothing here for me any more. I can start anew somewhere, live a different life. There will be nobody to ruin anything or make me feel the way I've felt for so long now. Maybe I can shed this anger, abandon this resentment. I can leave them here, with the old me.

I need to see her again, and I know the way to bring her to me.

The job isn't finished yet. Until it is, I won't be going anywhere.

CHAPTER FORTY-SEVEN

Leighton Matthews' solicitor was a heavy-set woman with a bottle-blonde bob and a manner that suggested she considered time spent at the station wasted time. Somehow, Matthews seemed easily able to fool the women in his life into believing he was an innocent man victimised by circumstance. Intelligent, educated women such as his colleague, Anna Stapleton, and his solicitor, Frankie Piper, seemed taken in by his 'poor me' act.

Alex watched him across the table; he was scowling at her while surreptitiously checking the clock on the far wall.

Perhaps it was his charm, she thought.

'I'd like to refer back to the email sent to you by Keira North.'

'I believe my client has already discussed that matter with you,' Frankie said, pushing a length of blonde hair from her face.

'Yes,' Alex said, 'but I'd like to go over it again. You say you never saw the essay Keira claimed to have left in your office.'

Leighton Matthews shook his head.

'Keira writes in her email that she left it on your desk. Do you often leave your office unlocked?'

He rolled his eyes. 'I work in a university, not a prison.'

'What about this?' Alex asked, reaching for the file on the table and removing the copy of Leah North's essay given to her by Anna Stapleton. 'Do you recognise it?'

Alex had read the piece. It was the opening of a novel, moody and angst-ridden; more the rantings of a disgruntled teen than the work of a literature student. She had also read half a chapter from Anna Stapleton's copy of *Resurrection*, Leighton Matthews' masterpiece. Apparently it was about one man's descent into madness, although the opening of the book had been enough to make her feel she was likely to lose parts of her mind too if she carried on reading any further.

She was no literary expert – whatever reading she got to do mostly involved suspect profiles and case histories – but she was pretty certain Leah Cross's efforts hadn't been worthy of a first.

Matthews took a look at the work. 'Yes, of course I recognise it. I marked it.'

'Got a good grade, did it?'

He said nothing. Frankie Piper was watching Alex questioningly. 'I'm not sure how any of this is relevant.'

'There's been a suggestion you may have awarded Leah Cross an undeserved mark.'

'This is ridiculous.' Leighton Matthews shoved back his chair and glared angrily across the table at Alex. 'You've dragged me in here to question my marking? Am I under arrest?'

'No.'

'So I'm free to go?'

'Your car is still with forensics,' Alex reminded him. She gave him a smile. 'Even the best valets sometimes miss a bit.'

Matthews had been ready to stand from his seat; now he eased back, sighing heavily.

'It's in your interests to cooperate with us on this, Mr Matthews. We're trying to find out the truth about what happened to Keira North as well as who was responsible for the hit-and-run that left Leah Cross in hospital. Cooperating may mean we're able to eliminate you from enquiries more quickly.'

Alex didn't believe for a second this was true. She suspected Leighton Matthews was hiding something; they just needed to find out what it was. She imagined he'd spent much of his adult life walking away from the chaos he'd created, never having to face the consequences of his choices. The line he'd given them about his car having cut out several times during recent weeks had been yet another of his lies; told so casually, as she imagined all his lies were.

'Did your wife know about your relationship with your student Natalie Sanderson?'

The question appeared to throw Matthews off balance. He'd known the police would have access to the details of Siobhan O'Leary's allegations against him, but had seemingly believed them ignorant of his affair with another former student.

He glanced awkwardly at Frankie. 'Can they ask about this?'

She shrugged. 'They can ask. You don't have to answer. But if you want to prove your innocence, I suggest you talk about it now.'

Obviously Frankie Piper already knew of his extramarital affair, although Alex doubted there had only been the one. She wondered how many times this solicitor had been called upon by Matthews for advice. One thing seemed certain: even Piper was now starting to doubt him.

'Yes, she knew about it,' Leighton answered reluctantly. 'I mean, not while it was going on, not at first. She found out later.'

'How did she find out?'

'She ... I still don't know why this is relevant. I never met Keira North and I know Leah Cross from my classes. That's all. We're just going around in circles here.'

There was a knock at the door and DC Daniel Mason popped his head into the room. 'Boss, sorry to interrupt ... have you got a minute?'

Alex went out into the corridor and closed the interview room door behind him. 'I'm not going to get anything out of him,' she said. 'It's like pulling bloody teeth.'

'You might not need to,' Dan said.

She followed him upstairs to the main incident room, where they went to Dan's computer. 'Traffic lights near the College Arms in Treforest,' he said. 'Six minutes past twelve – five minutes after Leah was apparently hit by the car.'

Alex looked at the image paused on the screen. It had been taken from CCTV at a set of pedestrian-crossing traffic lights near the pub and showed a black Ford Kuga driving south towards Cardiff. The number plate was perfectly visible; this time, all of it. It was a match with Leighton Matthews' car.

She gave Dan a grateful smile. 'Let's see how he tries to talk himself out of this one.'

CHAPTER FORTY-EIGHT

'Yes, I went there,' Leighton Matthews said, looking up from the CCTV image that sat on the desk in front of him. 'But I didn't hit her.'

He glanced at Frankie Piper as though to check the solicitor still believed him. Judging by the stern expression that had fixed itself on the woman's face, Alex doubted that was now likely.

Chloe had joined them for this second part of the interview. She sat by Alex's side, quietly taking in the panic that had set in on the man's face now they had produced a piece of physical evidence against him.

'This is your car, yes?'

'Yes.'

'So why did you go there? Why would you go to the home of one of your students? Unless, of course …'

Alex left the insinuation hanging in the air between them. An hour earlier, Frankie Piper would have jumped to her client's defence. Now it seemed she had given up on him. She too was looking to him, waiting for an explanation.

'I didn't hit her,' he repeated, ignoring Alex's question. 'I went there, but I changed my mind. I didn't go to her house, I didn't see her.'

'What time did you get to the house?'

'I don't know,' Matthews said, looking and sounding increasingly flustered. 'Elevenish.'

'So you drove to her house, stayed in the car, then turned round and drove back home.'

He hesitated. 'Pretty much, yeah.'

'Why did you go there?'

Once again, he refused to answer the question.

Alex pushed the photograph towards him. 'This camera picked up your car at a set of traffic lights near the College Arms in Treforest at 12.06. It's only a few minutes from Leah's house. If you went to Treforest at around eleven o'clock and didn't stay long, as you claim, the times don't really match up, do they?'

She sat back and waited for him to say something. His face had paled, the arrogance gone now, wiped away by the evidence that lay in front of him. He was staring at the photograph on the desk, knowing they had him cornered.

'What's the name of the street?' asked Alex.

'What?'

'The name of the street Leah lives on. What is it?'

He looked at each of the women in turn, confusion stamped across his face. 'I ... I ...' he bumbled. 'I don't remember.'

'Describe the street for me, please, Mr Matthews.'

He looked imploringly at his solicitor, his panic becoming evident. 'I went there at night. It was dark. It's just ... it's just a terraced street.'

Alex sat back and studied the man. 'Are you or have you ever been involved in a relationship with Leah Cross?'

'No.'

'We've now got evidence that places your car not far from where Leah was hit by a vehicle matching its description, yet you told us this morning that you and your wife were in bed at midnight on Wednesday. What possible reason could you have had to be in this area,' she tapped the photograph in front of her, 'if not to pay Leah a visit? What did she threaten you with, Leighton? Was she going to tell the university you'd been helping her pass the course? Or did you try to break it off with her? Was she upset that you'd ended the affair? Did she threaten to tell your wife everything? You've already admitted to us that your wife knew about your previous relationship

… surely this one would have been the final straw. Did you decide to shut Leah up before she could expose you?'

'No!' He slammed a fist on the desk. The noise was quickly replaced by an uncomfortable silence that fell over all four of them. Frankie Piper was no longer able to hide her disdain behind a mask of stoic professionalism. Her painted eyebrows were raised, but Matthews refused to meet her eye.

Alex wondered where Tom Stoddard came into all this. Had he been aware of a relationship between Leah and her lecturer? Had Matthews killed him to keep him quiet?

'We know you're lying about something, Leighton. If there was anything going on between you and Leah, don't you think she's bound to tell us now?'

There was no reason for him to know that Leah had gone AWOL, not unless she had been in touch with him. His phone would now be checked for that. Had she known it was Matthews who'd hit her with his car? Was she in love with him, Alex wondered, or at the very least, did she believe herself to be? Perhaps, through some misguided notion of loyalty towards him, she would attempt to protect him even though she knew he was guilty.

They needed to get hold of her, and the best and most likely way of achieving that now was through Leighton Matthews.

'You'd have lost everything, wouldn't you, Leighton? Wife, family, home, career. Easier just to shut her up.'

He was shaking his head now, his eyes lowered to his lap. He looked suddenly dejected, all the arrogance and certainty drained from him. 'You've got it all wrong.'

'Did you have a sexual relationship with Leah Cross?' Alex asked again.

'No, I didn't.' He looked up from his lap and met Alex's eyes, the aggression gone now. 'Leah is my daughter.'

CHAPTER FORTY-NINE

By the time Leighton had been released from the police station, it was gone ten o'clock in the evening. His house keys were returned to him, separated from the car keys that had been given to the forensics department. The spare change he'd had in his pocket was also returned. The police kept his phone. He racked his brains for what might have still been on there, or what they might be able to find when they looked into its history. The police had ways of retrieving deleted messages and information, but he had been careful: he'd never given Leah his personal number but had used a pay-as-you-go mobile on which she was able to contact him. There was nothing to be found on what they had.

Melissa was in the reception area waiting for him. She looked tired, but mostly she looked angry. Her eyes bore evidence of tears, though she had reapplied her make-up in an attempt to conceal their aftermath. Her strength had once been one of the things Leighton had admired about her. She didn't give in to anything. She wore a mask even on her toughest days and found a way around every obstacle thrown in her path. There had once been something attractive in her resilience.

Now he wondered. Was it a mask, or was she simply in denial? Had she stood by him because she was a strong woman, or because she was inherently weak? Either way, he knew he had long ago stopped deserving her forgiveness.

She refused to meet his eye as they left the building, and they walked to the car park in silence, both lost in their own thoughts. She unlocked her Mini convertible and got into the driver's side. Leighton got in beside her, resentful of the silence. He might almost have preferred her anger visible, he thought, as he'd seen it back in the days when she had screamed, fought, retaliated. This silence was the worst form of treatment; unbearable.

'Have you been charged?' she eventually asked, five minutes into their journey home.

'No. Not yet. I've been released on police bail.'

'Meaning what exactly?'

'Meaning I'm still under investigation.'

'They interviewed me.'

'What did you tell them?'

'The truth.'

Leighton nodded and turned his head to the window. 'They're going to ask again. When they do, tell them—'

'I get it,' she said, cutting his sentence short. 'You're going to do the right thing … for once in your sorry little life.'

That night, Leighton slept in the spare bedroom. Melissa had gone to bed as soon as they'd got back to the house, their conversation having ended abruptly in the car on their journey home. He hadn't tried to resurrect it. She knew what had happened. The rest of his truths would have to come out now, but for tonight they could wait. He wasn't yet sure how he was going to break it to her.

He had retrieved the pay-as-you-go phone from the cupboard in the office and taken it upstairs to bed with him. He passed his bedroom, where he could hear Melissa crying. The thought of going in and attempting to console her barely crossed his mind; he had tried that before and it had never been welcomed. More often than not it had resulted in a blazing row, one of which had only been ended when the neighbour came over to complain about the noise.

Their younger daughter, Olivia, was in bed; there was no sound from her room. He wondered how much she knew about what was going on. She was sixteen and they barely saw her these days – he barely saw either of his daughters; when she wasn't in her bedroom, she was at her boyfriend's house. Her AS level exams had finished a couple of weeks earlier, though she'd barely spoken about them to either of her parents. Perhaps he should have taken more interest, but like everything else, it was now too late.

He turned the phone on and pressed the sound off. There were five missed calls and four messages, all from Leah.

Where are you? I need to speak to you.

Call me when you get this.

Was it you?

I need to speak with you. Please call me.

He stared at the messages, wondering where his life had gone so wrong. Of course he knew the answer to that, but fooling himself that there was still someone else to blame was an attempt to shield himself from the effects of all the damage he'd done. It didn't work. This was his fault, all of it.

He remembered the night he had met her, all those years ago. She had been young and beautiful and exciting; all the things his life had been missing at the time. He'd had so much responsibility at such a young age, and he wasn't ready for any of it. He knew it was a pathetic excuse, but it was the only one he had. He'd seen something he wanted. He'd taken it.

It had become a habit he'd never quite been able to break.

The screen lit up, the name Sean flashing up at him in the darkness. It was her. He had stored her number under a different name – the name of one of his colleagues at the university – in case Melissa ever found the phone.

He ignored it. It didn't matter what she did now; she had caused enough damage. There was nothing more she could do.

The call ended, but the phone lit up again within moments. Then again. And again. A message came through. *I'm outside.*

Leighton sat up in bed. He didn't doubt for a moment she was telling the truth; the girl was crazy enough. He pushed open the door to the spare room and stepped out onto the landing. There was silence from his bedroom; Melissa would be asleep by now. He eased his way down the stairs, taking two at a time.

Another message came through. *If you don't come out now, I swear to God I'll scream the place down and tell her everything.*

He went into the living room and pushed the closed curtain to one side. His stomach flipped at the sight of her standing on the driveway looking up at the bedroom window. He dropped the curtain and tried to catch his breath. An involuntary image appeared in his mind: his hands closed around her neck, squeezing the life from her; making her finally go away, for good this time.

If he went out there, he was sure he would end up killing her.

He went to the kitchen and left the house through the back door, walking down the side of the building to meet her on the driveway.

'What the hell do you think you're playing at?' he hissed.

'We need to talk.'

There was little time in which to consider his options, and a mere moment was sufficient time to realise he didn't have any. Melissa was going to find out the truth soon enough anyway, but he didn't want it to be that night. Not like this. He grabbed Leah by the arm, his fingers pressing into her skin.

'You'd better let go of me,' she said, her warning slick and assured.

He dropped her arm, his eyes narrowing. 'I'll talk to you,' he said, 'but not here. Follow me.'

She followed him down the path that ran alongside the house and into the garden. Leighton crossed the lawn, heading for the summer house at the end. He opened it and ushered her inside, closing the door behind him.

'It's over,' he said, before she had a chance to speak. 'I've told the police who you are.'

CHAPTER FIFTY

Alex indicated and pulled the car on to the slip road. This stretch of the A470 – a concrete link between Cardiff and Brecon that got greyer the nearer it drew towards the city – often felt like a kind of second home. She had driven it so often that she was now able to navigate her route without paying attention to the road, her thoughts often snared by work. That evening, it wasn't the job that was keeping her mind preoccupied.

Chloe was sitting beside her in the passenger seat, her frustration still obvious. She was playing distractedly with an elastic band, stretching it between her fingers in a form of ineffectual stress therapy. 'We let him go,' she said, stating the fact as though still struggling to comprehend it. It wasn't the outcome any of them had expected, Alex included. Not a couple of hours earlier, at least.

She had her reasons.

'We've got bloody proof he was in the area that night,' Chloe said, winding the elastic band around her thumb until the circulation was cut off and the tip turned white. 'He had no other reason to be there. And we let him go.'

Alex pressed her foot further to the accelerator, speeding up the journey home. She was keen to get back to the house and have a shower, feeling as though she hadn't been home in days. She understood Chloe's frustrations, but for now all she wanted was to stand beneath a powerful stream of hot water, drink a cup of tea and fall into bed. Tomorrow she would explain everything to the team.

Chloe had started to say something else, undeterred by Alex's lack of response. She was interrupted by the ringing of Alex's mobile through the Bluetooth system, and though Alex was initially grateful for the distraction, her reaction altered when she saw the number. This was a conversation she would have preferred to keep from Chloe, but the speaker meant she would hear everything. She could have left it until they got to the house and called back then, but she didn't want to chance it.

'You might want to come up,' the nurse told her. 'I'm so sorry … it won't be long now.'

Alex felt her grip on the steering wheel tighten. She hadn't wanted it to end this way, in an alien room surrounded by institutional furniture and blank walls. She had wanted her mother to be at home, where she would have wanted to be. It seemed only right – the last decent thing she could do for her amid a host of forced decisions that she'd never wanted to have to take – yet she wasn't entirely sure where 'home' might be. To her mother, it would have meant the house in which she'd shared the majority of her adult life with Alex's father; not Alex's house, to which she had moved reluctantly, still refusing to accept it wasn't safe for her to continue to manage alone.

Chloe looked at Alex questioningly as she ended the call. She'd stopped playing with the elastic band and shoved it into her pocket.

'I'll drop you home and go straight up,' Alex said.

'I'll come with you,' Chloe told her.

'No, I—'

'You shouldn't be on your own, not now. I won't come in with you … I'll wait in the car. But you should have someone there with you.'

Alex headed off the roundabout at the first exit and drove up Nantgarw Hill towards Caerphilly. 'I appreciate it,' she said, keeping her eyes fixed to the road ahead, 'but I really just want to get there. On my own.'

She slowed for the speed camera, pressing her foot back to the accelerator once they'd passed it.

Chloe bit her lip and sat back. 'If you change your mind, you know where I am. My phone will be on. I'll stay up.'

'OK. Thanks. But honestly, there's no need.'

They made the rest of the journey in silence, passing the places that had once made Alex feel secure but in recent years had come to represent all the things that had kept her trapped. It was strange how a changing life could alter perceptions of things that had remained solid and dependable for years. The crossroads that had once signalled the closeness of home now appeared to be taunting her: Still here? it seemed to ask; an accusation, almost. The church on the corner that stood so tall and grand, once so beautiful, seemed now forbidding, as though it was sitting in judgement on her. The mountain that stood behind her home, once upon a time a kind of silent protector, was now a guard that kept her imprisoned in this town.

They hadn't changed, Alex realised. She had.

She pulled into her street and drove to the end, stopping outside the house.

'Stay in touch,' Chloe said.

Alex nodded. 'If you really want to help me out,' she told her, 'go and get a good night's rest. I need everyone on top form tomorrow. There's a reason I opted for police bail for Leighton Matthews. He wasn't driving that car. He's covering for someone.'

Chloe looked at her incredulously. 'What?'

'I just don't believe he did it. That's why I let him go. We could have charged him, but we'd have been charging the wrong person. Think about it – he didn't really seem to have a clue what time he was supposed to have been there. He couldn't describe the street, and when I asked him to, he reacted with panic. Who else might have taken that car?'

Chloe's eyes widened. 'Melissa.'

'Exactly. She assumed the same as us – that Leighton was having an affair with Leah. It's one affair too many, so she takes matters into her own hands. If we'd kept him in custody, he'd have had no contact with her. This way, we get to catch them out. They're going to try to cover for one another and they'll slip up somewhere.'

She glanced at the clock on the dashboard. 'Sorry, Chloe, I really have to go. We'll speak about this more tomorrow.'

CHAPTER FIFTY-ONE

'You've done what?'

Leah looked at him in shock. She had never expected him to come clean to anyone; she had never thought he would be prepared to risk everything he had for her. Then she realised this wasn't about her; he was protecting himself.

She sank onto one of the wicker seats in the corner of the summer house, her body heavy with the weight of her injuries. 'Was it you? Were you driving that car?'

'I had to tell them,' Leighton told her, not answering the question. 'The police thought we were sleeping together. They've got it into their heads that Keira found out about us and that's why she died. They asked if I'd ever slept with her. They probably thought I was the father of her child. What else was I supposed to do?'

'Keira?' Leah gripped the arm of the wicker chair as though stopping herself from falling.

'You shouldn't be here – I'm not supposed to have contact with you. Should you even be out of hospital yet?' Leighton asked. He obviously didn't really care what sort of state she was in; he just wanted to make sure that she wasn't going to keel over on his property.

'I'm fine,' she said, her bottom lip jutting in a pout.

'You can't see me any more. This … all of it … it's over.'

Leah looked at him. The smile that crept over her face seemingly had a life of its own. She couldn't believe that after everything, all he could think of was himself. It didn't matter that a girl was dead or that Leah was being kept in the shadows by his lies. All that mattered to Leighton was Leighton. She had been naïve to assume – naïve to hope – that this might ever change.

'Do you love me?'

The question seemed to set him off balance. He looked at her in horror, as though she'd just confessed to him that she'd already told his wife all his dirty secrets. The past life he'd kept hidden all these years. The daughter he had thought he would be able to write out of his life and simply forget about.

He had needed reminding. He had forgotten about her and he had needed to remember that she existed. That he had responsibilities – years of them – that he had chosen to ignore. Now she was here, she wasn't going anywhere.

He didn't answer her. He didn't even open his mouth and try to say something, even if that something might be a lie. Leah thought she might have preferred a lie; it might have softened the blow somehow. This – this silence – was almost more than she was able to bear. It was an insult. He didn't respect her enough to lie to her.

She stood. 'Do you love me?' she asked again, as though his silence hadn't already answered the question for her. 'Like Isobel. Like Olivia. You love them, don't you?'

Leighton pressed a hand to his head, closing his eyes and blocking out the sight of her. 'You need to leave, Leah. This has all gone too far. I should never have let it get to this point.'

'And if I won't?' She gripped him by the wrist, her face defiant. She wouldn't be fobbed off by him, not this time. It wasn't fair. None of this was fair.

Her body tensed as he moved towards her and shook his hand free.

'No,' he said suddenly. 'No, Leah, I don't love you. You're not my daughter, not like they are. You never will be. Look at what you do to people. You ruin lives. You are a hateful, devious, manipulative little cow. How could anyone love you?'

His words were a slap to the face. She could already feel tears, hot and sharp, burning at her eyes. It was just moments before their heat was coursing down her cheeks.

But there was no sympathy from him. If anything, her tears made him angrier. He moved forward, suddenly towering above her, and put a hand on either shoulder, his weight holding her steady. 'I could have told them plenty more,' he said, his voice soft and threatening. 'But I didn't. And you should be grateful for that.'

'Grateful?' Leah laughed bitterly. 'Oh. In that case, thank you. Thank you so much.'

His weight was pressing more heavily on her shoulders, his thumbs digging into her skin, returning to the place where he had already bruised her days earlier. In that moment, she was scared of him. Behind his eyes, she could see how much he hated her. It hurt, but it was almost a good kind of pain; the kind of pain that reminded her she could still feel something.

She studied the darkness in his eyes and wondered if the same hands that were pressing down on her were the ones responsible for ending Tom's life. But why? It didn't make any sense.

He moved his right hand away, and for the briefest moment Leah thought he was going to hit her. His face had reddened, crimson flooding his unnaturally pale skin.

'Why don't you take this as the warning it probably is,' he suggested, stepping back from her. 'You've been given enough already – how many more do you think you'll get?'

All Leah heard in his words was a challenge. She had never liked to be told what she could or couldn't do; even as a young child, she had preferred things on her own terms or not at all. The problem was, things rarely happened that way. She had become used to disappointment, programmed to it by the succession of miserable events that had shaped her childhood. She had been taught she should accept disappointment; she should accept coming second best, although no one had ever told her the reason why.

Why should she always come last?

Why should she always be the one to go without?

Forgetting the agony that flooded her body, she rushed towards Leighton and reached for the neck of his cotton T-shirt. His reactions were delayed – he had been expecting her to leave, an admission of eventual defeat – and he wasn't quick enough to resist her. He was taller than her, but on tiptoes she was able to reach him easily. Her mouth met his, and she tried to part his lips with her tongue, but he shoved her back, sending her falling against the wicker chair.

'What the fuck are you doing?'

He ran the back of his hand across his mouth, trying to wipe away the taste of her. He was shaking; no longer with anger, but with something else. Disgust. Leah put a hand to her shoulder, tentatively tracing her fingertips across the tender patch of skin he had bruised.

'There's something wrong with you,' he said accusingly, his eyes boring into hers and his body shaking with the shock of her attack. 'You are seriously fucked up, you realise that?'

A sob caught in the back of Leah's throat. She could feel anger rising in the pit of her stomach, bubbling inside her; boiling. She pushed the heel of her right hand against her eye, smudging her mascara in a black smear. When she looked back at him, she was expecting something different. Sympathy. Forgiveness, maybe.

Instead, she saw nothing but contempt.

She ran from the summer house, slamming the door shut behind her.

CHAPTER FIFTY-TWO

Alex sat by the bedside, holding her mother's hand loosely, letting it rest in hers. Holding hands seemed strange; alien. It wasn't something they'd ever done much, not even when Alex had been a small child. It wasn't that her mother had been a bad mother. She just hadn't been like a lot of others.

Chloe's words were preying on her mind. *All the more reason to put things right now.* For years, Alex's relationship with her mother had been fraught with complications and blighted by disappointments her mother had never quite been able to conceal. They had always been there – little comments about what Alex had chosen to wear to an end-of-year school party, facial reactions to her exam results. Then tensions that had created a divide when Alex was a teenager went on to become the things that would in later years carve an impassable crevasse between them.

She knew she should say something. She just didn't know what.

Do you remember that time you told me I'd never amount to much? she thought.

'Hi, Mum,' she said, still sceptical that Gillian would even hear the words. 'It's me. I've opened the window a bit – it was so warm in here. I know you don't like to be too warm. The weather's been lovely. Sandal weather, you used to call it … do you remember?'

God, she thought, I'm talking about the weather. She sat back in the chair, her mother's hand still resting in hers. Where had things gone so wrong that in these final moments all she could find to talk about was the weather?

There was a sound at the door and one of the carers popped her head into the room, offering Alex a sympathetic smile. 'Shall I get you a cup of tea?'

Alex nodded. 'Thanks.'

The girl left again, leaving them alone to the unsettling silence. It was punctuated every now and then by a rattle from her mother's chest, weak and distant, but there all the same.

'I'm sorry I disappointed you, Mum,' Alex said. 'I'm sorry I could never be the straight-A student you wanted … It was never really going to happen, though, was it?'

She could remember still – as clearly as though it had been the previous afternoon – the argument she had overheard between her mum and dad: her father telling his wife that Alex had tried her best and there was nothing more they could ask from her; her mother declaring that it wasn't good enough.

And Alex had continued to disappoint. She'd moved between bar jobs and shops for a while, unsure what she wanted to do with her life. That uncertainty had continued for years, right up until her father had died suddenly of a heart attack when she was twenty-seven. His death had been unexpected, ripping the ground from beneath her feet, changing everything. A week after his funeral, she heard a radio advertisement for police recruitment. The following week, she handed in her notice at the restaurant where she'd been working. But by then it was too late to change her mother's fixed opinion of her.

The sound of Gillian's breathing had faded into an almost inaudible hum. She looked peaceful, and for that Alex was grateful. There had been anger, confusion, bitterness, denial. All of it leading to this.

She would never forget that hospital; that diagnosis. The memory of the smell of the place – the disinfectant tinge that coated the air – and the stark whiteness that pervaded every room brought everything flooding back: that office in which she had sat barely hearing the doctor's words; the room in which her mother lay for a total of twelve days, with the window that wouldn't shut properly, allowing the whistling wind to filter in with a continual angry hiss; the stretch of corridor that linked the unit to the restaurant, and those endless walks for pointless cups of tea that went untouched.

Thoughts of the past were interrupted by the carer's arrival with Alex's tea, which she placed on the bedside table. Yet another cup that would be left to go cold.

'You OK?' she asked.

Alex nodded. She felt sorry for the girl. She probably felt obliged to say something, but there was nothing to say. How many times had she had to do this?

'Let us know if you need anything.'

'Thanks.'

The carer left the room, leaving Alex and her mother in silence. It was pitch dark outside now; she closed the window and drew the curtains, shutting out the night. She returned to the seat and took her mother's hand in hers again, tracing her pale, bony knuckles with her fingertips.

She wondered if this was normal. She couldn't cry. She wasn't sure what she felt, or if in that moment she even felt anything at all. Did it make her cold; inhuman somehow? Was there a set of rules for times such as this?

If their relationship been different, she might not have felt like this now. It was difficult to forget the things her mother had said to her, particularly as her illness had worsened. She knew that often it had been the dementia talking and not Gillian, yet the accusations and recriminations that had left her mouth had been based somewhere in truth, heightened versions of what had already gone before. Alex's failed relationships. Her childlessness. Her divorce. She respected the fact that her mother was entitled to an opinion, but that didn't mean she had to appreciate hearing it at every opportunity Gillian had deemed suitable to offer it up.

Though it was the dementia that had disinhibited her mother's brain, there was no doubt in Alex's mind that the hurtful things it was throwing out had been there all along, years before she had been afflicted by the awful disease that had cost her everything. Many of them had been said and heard before.

But despite everything, she had stood by her mother throughout her illness. She had moved her into the house shortly before her ex-husband had left, although by then their marriage had already been in its final stages. Her mother's condition had deteriorated more rapidly than either she or the doctors had foreseen; eventually Gillian had become unable to walk, and at that point Alex had been advised that the house was no longer a safe place for her. The guilt was something that was never going to go away, regardless of the misery her mother had sometimes caused her.

'I'm sorry it hasn't been what you wanted,' Alex told her now. 'If I could have made things different, I would have. It wasn't all bad, was it?'

She remembered the beach holidays they'd had when she was a child: the long afternoons spent searching rock pools for crabs and eating sandwiches that had turned to mush in the heat of the afternoon. But her father had been there then. It seemed to Alex now that this was where everything had changed. They had worked as three, in their own unique way, but they had never worked as two. Losing her father had been the moment when Alex's relationship with her mother had finally come to its end.

'Say hi to Dad for me,' she said.

She let her mother's hand slip from hers and rest on the duvet. Her face was relaxed, her chest still. And Alex realised she was already gone.

CHAPTER FIFTY-THREE

Chloe and Dan walked the length of the corridor that led to Amy Barker's hospital room. Chloe's tiredness was visible; even her carefully applied make-up couldn't manage to disguise it. She had waited up to hear from Alex – checking her phone every five minutes for news – but hadn't heard anything. At just gone one in the morning she had called her. Gillian had passed away a couple of hours earlier.

'Have you spoken to Alex yet?' Dan asked.

Chloe nodded. 'She's gone home to get some sleep. She was with her mother until after three this morning.'

'She's not going to turn up for work later, surely?'

Chloe gave him a look. 'What do you think?'

She had tried to argue the point with Alex when she'd seen her briefly that morning, but Alex wasn't having any of it. She needed time off now, but Chloe knew she would refuse to take it while they were in the middle of their two ongoing cases. She had contemplated speaking to Superintendent Blake about it, but it would undoubtedly have got back to Alex and she would likely see it as Chloe having interfered. The best thing Chloe could do was let Alex do what she wanted, and be there later to try to catch the falling pieces.

'She can't let Keira North go,' Chloe admitted. 'She feels a sense of duty to her, and to her parents.'

She contemplated mentioning to Dan what Alex had said about Leighton Matthews the previous evening, but decided against it. Alex would want to talk to the team about it herself, and without any more details it wasn't really for Chloe to discuss. Thinking back on the previous day's interview, she realised Alex might be on to something. Matthews couldn't give a reason for having been to Leah's house, unless his reluctance was explained by his embarrassment at having to admit that Leah was his daughter; a daughter his wife apparently knew nothing about. No wonder he'd been so unwilling to talk about her.

Yet he didn't strike Chloe as the type of man to be stricken by embarrassment. Certain questions had been deliberately evaded, obviously in the hope that his secret third daughter might be kept just that. He'd been put at ease by the fact that the police weren't going to be volunteering the information to his wife, though he'd realised he was now going to have to break the news himself.

The timeline he'd given hadn't matched the timing suggested by the CCTV footage. Was he lying about something else?

'She's awake,' Dan said.

They had reached Amy's room. Through the window they could see Janet Barker sitting by her daughter's bedside. She stood when she saw Chloe and Dan and came out into the hallway to greet them. She looked exhausted still, her face pale with the flood of relief that had come from Amy's having woken up.

'It's a miracle,' she said, fighting back tears. 'I think the doctors were starting to give up on her ever coming round.' She bit her bottom lip, trying to hold back her emotion.

'An arrest was made in connection with the drugs that were sold to Amy,' Chloe told her.

Janet nodded. 'The liaison officer told me. Do you still want to speak with Amy? I thought this would all be done with now.'

'We only have Jade's statement,' Chloe told her. 'We really need to speak to Amy herself to get her to confirm that it was in fact this person who sold her the drugs.'

Finding out whether Tom Stoddard had been involved in drug dealing, and on what scale, might give a clue as to who had killed him and why.

'OK. Can I stay with her?'

Chloe nodded and they followed Janet into the hospital room. Without make-up, Amy was still just a little girl. Her face filled with fear at the sight of them, panic setting in behind her glazed and sleep-filled eyes. Chloe wondered when she'd started to look like a police officer.

'How are you feeling, Amy?'

Janet gestured to the chair and Chloe sat beside Amy. Dan stood to the side, while Amy's mother waited at the foot of the bed, quietly standing guard over her daughter. Amy began to cry, silent tears that ran quickly down her face, looking to her mother for help.

'You're not in any trouble,' Chloe reassured her. 'That's not why we're here. I think you've already learned a painful enough lesson, don't you?'

Amy looked away; too proud to admit to having done something stupid. Chloe reached into her bag and took out the file she'd brought with her. She removed a photograph of Tom Stoddard. 'Your friend Jade has identified the person who sold you the drugs you took. It would be really helpful to us if you could also identify them for us.'

Amy turned back to her and glanced down at the photograph, which Chloe had placed on the bed. Then she looked back up. 'He didn't sell me the drugs,' she said. 'I bought them off a girl.'

Chloe shot Dan a look. She returned her focus to the file and produced a second photograph. 'Not this one, by any chance?'

CHAPTER FIFTY-FOUR

Chloe stood in the incident room studying the array of photographs pinned to the evidence board. What had started as a small collection had turned into a gallery of faces: Keira North, Leah Cross, Tom Stoddard, Jamie Bateman, Leighton Matthews, Amy Barker. Undoubtedly their current cases were interlinked in some way or another, yet the more faces that came to adorn this board, the further Chloe felt herself getting from the truth.

Then there were the other people who had attended the party that night at the house on Railway Terrace; the ones they knew about, at least. Countless other people were likely to have been in and out of the house that evening, and locating them all had proven an impossible task. Chloe wondered how many more names and faces would be added to the collection before they finally got to the truth of what had happened that night.

The lines and notes that had been drawn between images had expanded into a scrawling web of possibilities. Tom's name was connected to Amy Barker, with a tentative second line joining them both to Leah Cross added later.

They needed to find Leah urgently. The fact that she had fled the hospital and seemingly not let anyone know of her whereabouts suggested she was guilty of something. Did she know what had happened to Tom? Had she killed him?

Tracing Leah's mobile had only led them back to the house in Treforest, where it had been found by uniform in her room. That meant she had returned to the house sometime between leaving the hospital and Tom's body being found by Jamie the following morning. From whichever angle they looked at things, Leah looked increasingly like a suspect. Wherever she was now, she was either without a phone or she had access to another.

'Everything OK? You look a bit lost there.'

Chloe turned. Dan was standing behind her, a handful of papers clutched in his fist.

'Lost in thought,' she told him. 'What have you got there?'

'Leah Cross's bank account details.'

'Anything?'

Dan pulled a chair across and sat down. Chloe did the same. He spread the paperwork out on the desk in front of them. 'No recent transactions to give us a clue as to where she might be, but take a look at this.' He pointed to a figure on the statement. 'Two thousand pounds transferred to Leah's account from an account in Leighton Matthews' name. And that's not the only one. They go back as far as February last year … a total of twelve thousand pounds.'

Chloe sat back. She needed to get hold of Alex and let her know the latest. No wonder Leah hadn't wanted them to catch up with her. First the possible drug dealing, now this. No wonder the girl told so many lies. She had plenty she needed to try to conceal.

'So Leah enrols at the university knowing Leighton works there,' Chloe said, her thoughts spilling from her mouth as her brain went into overdrive, 'and knowing he's her father. She tells him who she is and … what? He gives her money to make up for all the time he's missed?'

Dan raised a sceptical eyebrow.

'OK. She blackmails him. He pays her to keep quiet, presumably to save his marriage.'

Dan nodded. 'Sounds more likely. Clever girl.'

'Devious girl.' Chloe leaned forward, rested her elbows on her knees and her chin in her hands and sighed. 'Alex said something last night about Leighton covering for someone else. That's why she let him leave here without charging him.'

'For Melissa?'

'She didn't really say any more about it, but yeah, Melissa.'

'Makes sense, I suppose. I wish she'd said something earlier, though – there's been no end of speculation knocking about this place today. I don't think the super was too happy about Leighton walking out of here, although he seems to have eased off a bit now he's heard the news about Alex's mother.'

'I trust Alex,' Chloe said. 'Whatever decisions she's made, she'll have done so for good reason.'

'So Melissa finds out about Leah,' Dan said, 'maybe through this?' He gestured to Leah's bank details. 'Perhaps she found evidence of these transactions and confronted him about it. Do you reckon she knows Leah's his daughter, though?'

Chloe shook her head. 'It'd be entirely plausible that she found out about the money and believed the same as we did – that Leighton was having an affair with Leah. Maybe she questioned him about it and he had no choice but to tell her he was being blackmailed. Better to say she was his lover rather than admit she's his daughter. Maybe he thought Melissa would forgive him yet another affair.'

'So Melissa finds out where Leah lives and goes to the house in Treforest to confront her?'

Chloe exhaled loudly, her thoughts colliding as she tried to make sense of every possible scenario. 'Perhaps,' she said. 'But I just don't see where Tom comes into any of this.'

Her attention was caught by the images on the evidence board: Leah Cross and Keira North pinned alongside one another.

'There's something else,' she said, getting up and gesturing to the two girls' faces. Something had been bothering her all day and she'd been unable to shake it off. The more she went over it, the more it made sense. She studied the images of the two girls for a moment before turning her attention back to Dan.

'Notice anything?'

CHAPTER FIFTY-FIVE

No one had thought they would be seeing Alex that day, so her arrival at the station later that morning was unexpected. News of her mother's death had quickly spread among the team, with speculation as to who would head up the current cases when she was on leave. Chloe didn't bother to correct them by suggesting that Alex was unlikely to take any time off work. She suspected her colleague wouldn't be going anywhere.

'You sure this is a good idea?' she asked Alex as the team began to filter into the incident room.

'Yes. I need updating on what I've missed.'

Chloe held her gaze for a moment. 'How are you?' she asked.

'Fine.'

'I'm so sorry, Alex.'

Alex glanced over Chloe's shoulder and asked the team to assemble as quickly as possible. A couple of people had already left for the day, so she now clearly felt a pressing sense of urgency to speak with those who were still present.

Chloe moved away and sat down. Perhaps Alex would speak to her about it later, without the prying eyes and ears of others.

Perhaps not.

'I know a lot of you will be wondering why Leighton Matthews was allowed to leave here yesterday without being charged,' Alex said, addressing the team, 'especially in light of the CCTV footage that places his car in a nearby location just minutes after Leah Cross was hit. You've probably all heard by now that Matthews gave us quite a revelation last night, although it wasn't the admission we'd all been expecting. He told us that Leah Cross is his daughter.'

There was an outbreak of chatter among the team at this point. Everyone had known about this, but the unlikelihood of the relationship meant it was still causing shock waves. Alex raised a hand and tried to bring some sense of order back to the meeting.

'We know the car was in the area,' she continued, 'but Leighton Matthews' little trip to the garage the morning after the hit-and-run means that any chance of retrieving physical evidence from the car has been removed. If anyone's car needs valeting any time in the near future, I'd suggest Lockley's on Western Avenue – they're bloody thorough.'

Chloe watched Alex intently, noting the tightening of her jaw and the increasing speed of her speech.

'Just because the car was there doesn't mean Leighton Matthews necessarily was. I don't think he was driving that car. I don't think he was even there that night. I think he's been lying to protect someone.'

'Who?' DC Jake Sullivan asked.

'His wife,' Chloe answered, meeting Alex's eye.

Alex gave her a nod. 'At the moment, they're each other's alibis. They both claim to have been in bed together, from ten thirty onwards on Wednesday night. My guess is this: Melissa Matthews assumed the same as the rest of us, that Leighton was having an affair with Leah Cross. Remember that this woman has already endured quite a bit in that marriage. Sexual harassment allegations against her husband, his affair with a former student … and they're just the things we're aware of. So let's assume she found out about Leah somehow. This is the final straw; it tips her over the edge. She takes his car, waits for Leah to come home and hits her with it. When she goes home, Leighton realises what she's done and takes the car first thing the following morning to be valeted. We turn up and he has a choice: let his wife shoulder responsibility for what she's done, or take the blame for her. He's already put her through enough; taking the blame might mean trying to compensate for some of the previous damage he's caused her.'

Chloe watched Alex with growing concern. Her words were falling from her mouth so quickly that each was tumbling into the next, as though her voice was desperately trying to keep up with the movement of her brain. She shouldn't have been there.

And yet everything she said made perfect sense.

'That's why I didn't want him charged,' Alex continued. 'We'd have been charging the wrong person. This way, he knows we're still suspicious. He'll know we don't believe his admission. If we keep applying the pressure, the cracks will start to show somewhere. Has anyone been to see Amy Barker yet?'

'Chloe and I went,' said Dan.

'How is she?'

'Physically OK, but she seemed very embarrassed at what's happened.'

'Did she ID Tom Stoddard?'

Dan shot Chloe a glance.

'No,' Chloe said. 'She recognised Tom – she said the same as Jade, that they'd spoken to him outside in the queue before going into the club – but Amy said he's not the one who sold her the drugs. Apparently, it was a female. Take one guess who she did positively ID, though.'

Alex's eyes widened, her mouth thinning into a tight line. 'Right,' she said, trying to process this new information. She ran a hand through her hair, getting it caught in a knotting tangle at the back of her head. 'You showed her a photo of Leah Cross?'

'Yep,' Dan said. 'Identified her straight away. No wonder she's gone AWOL. We've been trying to locate Leah this afternoon. Her phone was traced back to the house in Treforest – looks as though she left it there when she went back for her things. If she's involved in the dealing as Tom claimed, chances are she's got a second phone we know nothing about. I've checked with her bank to see if she's made any transactions in the past couple of days, in case we could trace her whereabouts that way.'

'And?'

'Her account's not been used for nearly a fortnight, other than for standing orders.'

Alex grimaced. 'Where does Tom fit into all this?' she wondered aloud. 'We've not had the post-mortem results back yet. I'll give the pathologist a call, see what's taking so long.'

'There was something else, though,' Dan told her. 'The unusually large amount of money in her bank account … a substantial amount of it has been transferred from accounts in Leighton Matthews' name.'

Alex's eyes widened once again. 'OK,' she said with a sigh. 'So what are we thinking? Blackmail?'

There were several nods in agreement.

'Leah turns up and announces she's Leighton's daughter,' Chloe said. 'She offers to stay quiet in return for money. Plus, if she's involved in the drug dealing – which we now have increasing reason to believe she is – she's been making extras that way.'

'Quite the little entrepreneur.' Alex glanced at the clock. 'It's Keira North's funeral this afternoon. I'll be going. I'd like the rest of you to keep looking for Leah Cross, please – we need to make this a priority. Let's go public with her image now – let the public know we're looking for her. Dan, Chloe, I'd like you both to speak with Melissa Matthews first thing. Let's see if we can get a confession from her.'

Chloe gave her a nod. 'How do you think Keira North fits into all this?'

'I still think she discovered something she wasn't supposed to. Before last night, it seemed likely she'd found out about an affair between Leah and Leighton and someone pushed her to keep her quiet. Perhaps it's still the case that she found out about the relationship between them, only not the relationship we'd originally assumed. Maybe not, though. Maybe she'd found out something to do with the drugs. Knowing what we now know about Leah, we know she can't be trusted. If she didn't have several witnesses to place her outside the building when Keira was pushed from the roof, I'd have her down as a main suspect.'

Chloe looked past Alex to the photographs of the two young women pinned side by side on the evidence board behind her. Keira. Leah.

'There's something else,' she said. She gestured to the board. Alex turned to study the gallery of faces. Chloe stood from her chair and joined her at the front of the group. 'Look,' she said, tracing a finger between the two girls. 'We asked Amy Barker to give a description of the woman who sold her the drugs at the club. The description she gave us fitted Leah Cross, but it could equally have described countless other girls her age.' She tapped her finger on the image of Keira North. 'It could have been a description of Keira.'

Alex met her eye.

'So what if Keira's death was an accident?' Chloe continued. 'Not in the sense that she fell, but in the sense that someone made a mistake? From behind, they wouldn't look dissimilar. I reckon someone pushed Keira from that roof thinking she was Leah.'

CHAPTER FIFTY-SIX

The church in Monmouthshire was small, set back from sight of the main road behind a gathering of tall oak trees. There was little parking available, so Alex found she had to head back the way she had come and leave the car in a lay-by where many of the other funeral attendees had obviously had the same idea. Men and women dressed in black and grey milled about at the roadside, offering one another meaningless condolences as they tried to conceal their discomfort on what was already a sweltering morning. Alex's thoughts couldn't help but stray to her mother's funeral. She would have to start making arrangements once the death certificate had been issued, but at the moment her brain seemed incapable of thinking that far ahead.

At least in her mother's case it had been the natural order of things, she thought. Losing a parent was difficult; when her father had died, she had thought she'd never get over it. The pain had been like a physical wound to her chest, one that she'd never fully recovered from but had learned to live with. Losing a child was something she was unable to imagine. No parent should ever have to endure burying a child. Alex imagined no one could ever fully come to terms with such a loss. In Louisa and David North's case, the true nature of their daughter's death had still not been revealed, which must only have added further suffering to their already monumental grief. It was impossible to comprehend the day that lay ahead of them.

Alex locked the car and made her way to the church. She had wanted to attend to pay her respects. She also hoped her presence there might reassure the Norths that the search for the person responsible for their daughter's death hadn't gone forgotten. Louisa North seemed to hold little faith in the police. Alex didn't blame her. Those first vital few hours of what should have been an investigation into the girl's death had been marred by procrastination, deliberation and short-sightedness. Valuable time had been lost, and they continued now to pay the price for those mistakes. The woman was also still angry about the post-mortem carried out on her daughter: one that had given them a possible motive but hadn't brought them any closer to finding out exactly what had happened.

Chloe's theory that someone might have pushed Keira believing her to be Leah held a lot of weight. Had it been Melissa Matthews? Had she gone looking for Leah to confront the girl about the affair Melissa believed she was having with her husband, only to expel her anger and jealousy upon the wrong person? Had she returned for Leah having realised her mistake?

It might have gone some way to explaining the relatively minor injuries Leah had sustained during the hit-and-run. Perhaps the guilt that had followed Keira's death meant Melissa Matthews had been unable to bring herself to kill for a second time, regardless of how deeply she might have felt she wanted to.

As Alex entered the church grounds and walked the path that led through the graveyard, she spotted Keira's parents near the church door, talking with the vicar. Louisa North was crying, dabbing at her eyes in an attempt to keep her make-up in place. Alex wasn't sure whether she found this strange or understandable. In the same situation, her appearance would be the last thing she would be concerned with. But perhaps the make-up was providing Louisa with a shield; something behind which she could hide until she got safely back behind the closed doors of her home.

David North turned and saw Alex approaching. They'd known she was coming: she had called to check they would be happy for her to do so, although happy was unlikely to be the right word to

describe the reaction the news had no doubt prompted from Louisa.
Whatever her husband had said to her following the telephone
conversation, it was obvious he had had a tough time persuading
her they should allow Alex to be there.

What Alex hadn't mentioned was that as well as wishing to
pay her respects, she wanted to keep an eye on the mourners. It
wasn't unheard of for a suspect to attend the funeral of a victim,
in much the same way guilty people often found ways to involve
themselves in the cases of missing people or murder investigations.
If anything suspicious or untoward were to happen, Alex wanted
to be there to witness it.

'Thank you for letting me be here today,' she said to David as
he approached. She reached out a hand and he took it, shaking
it briefly before letting go. His eyes were glazed, holding back an
onset of tears.

'Is there anything we should know? I'd rather find out now
than later.'

Alex shook her head. 'I promise you that when there is, you'll
be the first to hear.'

David nodded. 'I don't want to do this,' he said, his voice
breaking. 'I don't think I can.'

Alex put a hand on his arm. 'You'll find a way. If you need
anything at all, I'll be at the back of the room. I'll leave after the
service, but you've got my number.'

David nodded and looked away, not wanting her to see the tears
that had spiked at the corners of his eyes.

Mourners were beginning to filter into the church, and Alex
waited until the vicar and the Norths had entered before following
them in. She took a seat at the back of the room, near the doors.
She suspected that had Keira's family not requested that guests be
kept to a minimum of family and close friends, there might have
been many more there. Keira had by all accounts been popular, not

short of friends at school. Inevitably, funerals also attracted the usual rubberneckers and those who went to the burials or cremations of people they had barely known just to give them something to talk about. It had always seemed strange to Alex, who did everything she could to avoid having to attend them.

There was a large photograph of Keira propped on a stand at the front of the church. It looked as though it had been taken before a school prom; in the image, she was smiling boldly, her face so young and her excitement so visible and innocent that the sight of her was painful even to someone who hadn't known her. The numerous papers that had reported on Keira's death had all made note of her looks, as though the premature deaths of less attractive people were somehow less of a tragedy. Had she been plain or overweight, Alex reflected, the amount of page space devoted to her would probably have been less significant.

The room fell into silence as the vicar addressed his audience. 'Every death is tragic, but the death of someone of Keira's age, at the start of her young life and with so much ahead of her, is always all the more so. You all knew Keira, so you know the kind of young lady she was – caring, kind and ambitious. She was a bright student with a brilliant future ahead of her, but above all she was a loving daughter and a good friend to those she grew up with in the community.'

From the front of the room, Alex could hear the embittered sounds of Louisa North's tears. The woman's head was tilted forward, her chin resting on her chest as the vicar's words washed over her. The Norths' other daughter – a younger version of Keira – sat beside her, an arm around her mother's shoulders. There were more tears being shed elsewhere, in the rows of pews on the other side of the room. Alex looked over. An older woman was sitting with a handkerchief clutched to her mouth, her shoulders shifting heavily with the weight of her grief. Beside her, a teenage girl held her hand, clutching it tightly in the woman's lap.

Alex scanned the rest of the room as the vicar continued his speech. There were about thirty people present, none of whom she was familiar with.

'And now we're going to hear a poem read by one of Keira's close school friends.' The vicar looked to the second row and nodded to one of the young women sitting there. 'Bethan.' He offered her an encouraging smile. The woman stood. She had a shock of red hair pulled back into a ponytail, and when she turned to face the rows of people looking at her expectantly, Alex realised she had seen this girl before. She was one of the friends featured several times in the photo montage Keira had kept hanging above her bed.

The girl tried the first line, but her voice failed her, breaking as she spoke. She stopped and cleared her throat, refusing to make eye contact with anyone in an attempt to regain her composure.

'*I cannot say and I will not say that she is dead,*' she read. '*She is just away. With a cheery smile and a wave of the hand, she has wandered into an unknown land—*'

A sound at the back of the church interrupted the young woman's reading. Alex turned. Jamie Bateman was in the doorway, his eyes fixed to the photograph of Keira at the front. Louisa North had turned at the noise of the door and was gripping her husband's hand, urging him to do something. Her daughter's arm had slipped from her shoulders.

CHAPTER FIFTY-SEVEN

When Chloe and Dan arrived at the Matthews house that lunchtime, Leighton wasn't there. His wife had looked out from the bedroom window at the sound of the doorbell, and knowing she'd been spotted clearly realised she had little choice but to open the door and let them in.

'Why hasn't he been charged?' she demanded. Her face was a mask of expertly applied make-up, but the flush of colour at her cheeks was a telltale sign of the anger that lay beneath. She stood with her hands fixed to her hips, poised for confrontation.

Chloe found the question strange. Surely Melissa should be relieved at the fact that her husband had evaded a charge the previous evening, yet the tone of her voice suggested disappointment.

'There are still some facts we need to be clear about,' she told the woman. 'Where is your husband, Mrs Matthews?'

'He's gone for a walk,' Melissa said, leading them through to the kitchen. 'Said he needed to clear his head.'

'You don't know where he's gone?'

'No.'

Do you care? Chloe wondered. She studied Melissa Matthews for a moment. Despite the events of the previous few days and the allegations made against her husband, the woman was immaculately presented, from the carefully styled hair to the shop mannequin outfit of tailored trousers and layered shirt. Her smile was as stiff as the fabric. Every word she spoke seemed wooden, as though nothing that left her mouth was said with sincerity. She gave no purchase for anyone to connect to.

But none of this made her a liar, of course.

'Day off for you today?' Dan asked.

'Yes,' Melissa said, placing a hand on the kitchen worktop. 'Though actually, I was just about to head in. Paperwork.'

'We won't keep you long,' Chloe told her, wondering why she couldn't – or wouldn't – complete her paperwork at home. Perhaps it was just an excuse to avoid her husband for the day. 'We were just wondering if you could go back over what happened on Wednesday night – the night of the hit-and-run.'

Melissa seemed to fight back the urge to roll her eyes. They were a perfect match, Chloe thought: Leighton with his surly impatience and Melissa with her everything-is-too-much-for-me demeanour. Some people deserved each other.

Moving from the worktop to the table, Melissa Matthews pulled out a chair and sat down. She gestured to the chairs opposite, silently inviting Chloe and Dan to join her.

'I haven't been honest with you,' she said, her face betraying no regret at the fact.

Dan shot Chloe a glance. It was what they'd all hoped for, but neither of them had expected Melissa to be so forthcoming so quickly.

'I know who that girl is, and I know what's going on.'

It was Chloe's turn to look to Dan. Was Melissa referring to the fact that Leah Cross was Leighton's daughter, or was she, as they suspected, under the misapprehension that the girl had been having an affair with her husband?

'You'll have to elaborate, Mrs Matthews.'

'Leah Cross,' Melissa said, evidently unimpressed at being made to speak the girl's name aloud. 'I know she's been having an affair with my husband. Old habits die hard, apparently.'

The woman's face was set in a stern grimace. Her husband's history of infidelity was clearly a bitter pill she had yet to swallow.

Why was she still with him? Looking around the couple's luxury kitchen and through the bi-folding doors that opened out on to a wide expanse of back garden, Chloe thought she might have an idea. Perhaps the facade of a happily married life – the magazine-worthy home, the picture-perfect offspring – was sufficient compensation for her husband's myriad misdemeanours. Perhaps she was prepared to overlook his infidelities for the sake of maintaining appearances. Either that, or she loved him too much to let him go.

'Where were you on Wednesday night, Mrs Matthews?' Chloe asked.

Melissa met her eye. 'I was here. In bed, like I told you.'

'And your husband?'

Melissa looked from Chloe to Dan and back again. 'He was out,' she said. 'He was out all evening … he came in at around twelve thirty.'

'Why did you lie to us? You previously claimed he was in bed with you at that time.'

Melissa sighed. 'I thought I was protecting him. Then I wondered what for. I've been protecting him for years – listening to his excuses, putting up with his lies. I'm not doing it any more.'

Chloe studied the woman's face as she spoke. Her anger was visible, snagging at the sharp edges of her tensed jaw; flitting behind the intensity of her dark eyes. Was she telling the truth, or was Alex right? Was Melissa Matthews letting her husband take the blame for her revenge?

'When he got back, did Leighton tell you what he'd done?' Chloe asked.

Melissa shook her head. 'He never confesses to his sins. It takes someone to force them out of him. Now,' she said, standing. 'Are we done here?'

CHAPTER FIFTY-EIGHT

'When were you going to have a funeral for the baby?' Jamie asked, his words directed to the front of the church and his voice breaking through the uncomfortable silence that had settled over the mourners. 'Or has she just been forgotten about?'

There was a succession of gasps before a loud sob emanated from the row where Keira's parents were sitting. Alex stood hurriedly and sidled out from her pew. She grabbed Jamie by the arm and pulled him out of the church. 'You're not supposed to be here. Close friends and family only, you know that. What the hell do you think you're playing at, going in there and mentioning the baby like that?'

The young man looked for a moment as though he might push past her to go back into the church. 'I am close,' he told her. 'Closer than most of that lot in there.' He waved an arm in exasperation and turned away from Alex, folding his arms across his chest in a gesture of childish defiance. It didn't last long; moments later, the boy was in tears. 'I haven't had a chance to say goodbye.'

Alex wondered how Jamie Bateman had survived living with Tom Stoddard for the past nine months. The two young men were polar opposites: one brash and obnoxious, the other quiet and sensitive. From what she'd seen of him so far, Jamie seemed the type to be scared by his own shadow; this was the first time she had detected any fire in him. Perhaps he'd had enough of fading into the background. It was difficult for Alex to look at him without considering him a suspect, but she knew that until they found out the truth about what had gone on at that house, everyone remained guilty until proven innocent. Had he hated Tom enough to kill him?

'I know,' she said. 'But you need to find another way. It's nothing personal to you, Jamie, but any reminder of the house in Treforest is a reminder of what happened to Keira. You understand that, don't you?'

Jamie turned back to her. His eyes were red-rimmed with tears. 'They don't know her, not really. Not like I did.'

Alex watched as he ran a hand over his eyes, looking so much younger than his twenty years. There was something a bit pathetic about him, she thought; something vulnerable. He had the kind of face that looked as though it didn't know where it belonged. Lost.

'Have they even mentioned the baby?' he said, his voice rising. 'Has anyone even mentioned the baby?'

Keira's pregnancy was no longer a secret, but the Norths – Louisa in particular – had on several occasions made it clear they wanted nothing said about it in front of them. As far as Alex could see, they were in denial. If they refused to speak about the unborn child or hear a word spoken about the pregnancy, they might be able to convince themselves it hadn't been true after all.

Alex shook her head. 'Not today. Today's about Keira.'

'So when does the baby get a funeral?' Jamie snapped, moving closer to her. 'Or has no one even thought of that?'

Alex smelled alcohol on his breath. 'Have you been drinking, Jamie?'

He stepped back, apparently aware of his sudden aggression.

'Bloody hell,' she muttered. 'Jamie, don't you think there's already enough going on without creating more trouble for yourself?' She reached into her bag for her car keys. 'Come on.'

'Where are we going?'

'I'm taking you home,' she said.

She walked away, confident Jamie would follow her. His brief moment of bravado had been followed by obvious embarrassment, if the red flush of his neck and cheeks was anything to go by.

'What about my car?'

'You've got two choices,' Alex said, turning back to him. 'You can get back in that car and I'll arrest you for driving under the influence, or you can get a lift home with me and find a way back up here tomorrow to collect it. Which will it be?'

Admitting defeat, Jamie sighed and followed her through the graveyard towards the main road.

'Why didn't you tell us before?'

'Tell you what?' he asked, trailing alongside her like a reprimanded schoolboy being taken to face the head teacher.

Alex stopped for a moment. 'That you were the father of Keira's baby.'

Jamie's eyes dropped to the floor; Alex couldn't tell whether through embarrassment or as an attempt to hide imminent tears. He shifted from one foot to the other. 'I know how it would have made things look. You might have thought I'd killed her. I'd never have hurt her.'

Alex sighed and led him to the car. Once they were settled inside, she asked him about the extent of his relationship with Keira.

'It was only once,' he told her, 'but the dates matched up. When I found out … I don't know. A few things started to make sense, looking back. She went really awkward around me for a while after.'

'She didn't tell you about it?'

He shook his head. 'I only found out when …' He trailed off, unable to put her death into words. Alex understood. If you spoke something aloud, it made it real. Ignore it for long enough and it might go away. Only it never did. It festered and developed, usually evolving into something even more difficult to face.

'Did Keira have any enemies that you know of, Jamie? Anyone who might have wanted to cause her harm?'

He looked at her questioningly, his face creased with a look of hurt. He'd apparently taken the suggestion personally. 'No. No one. She was a kind girl. Everyone liked her. There was nothing not to like.'

'What about Leah and Tom?' Alex asked, realising that Jamie's opinion of Keira was clouded in a mist of bias. 'Know of any enemies either of them might have made?'

She couldn't get her mind off what Chloe had said during the previous evening's meeting. It made so much sense that someone might have pushed Keira thinking she was Leah, but if that did turn out to be the case, Alex was frustrated with herself for not having noticed the resemblance and the possibility sooner.

She was grateful that Chloe had, though. Someone needed to keep on top of things while her own focus was elsewhere.

'Tom makes enemies like other people make cups of tea,' Jamie told her. 'He's not ... he wasn't the nicest of people, didn't you notice?' He looked at Alex as though trying to read her reactions. 'You think I killed him, don't you? I didn't. I hated him, but I could never do that to anyone.' There was a moment's silence. 'Keira slept with Tom, didn't she?'

Alex didn't respond to the question, keeping her eyes fixed on the road ahead.

'It's OK,' Jamie said. 'I know she did. He only did it to get at me. He'd never shown any interest in her before ... It was only when he knew I liked her.'

Alex glanced at the boy sitting in the passenger seat beside her, his hands balled into fists in his lap. He had turned his face to the window, not wanting her to see him.

'I did really like her,' he said. 'I might have loved her ... I don't know. I don't really know what that's supposed to feel like. But I'd have done the right thing by her and the baby, I know that. Why didn't she tell me? If she'd told me, maybe none of this would have happened. Maybe she'd still be here and we'd be …'

His words fell short, silenced by a swell of stifled tears. He ran his sleeve across his face and kept his eyes fixed to the window, watching the landscape move past in a blur of green fields and blue sky.

Alex believed him. She believed that this young man – still little more than a boy himself – would have done the right thing by Keira and her daughter; or at the very least, he would have tried. It was a sad fact that in a world filled with Tom Stoddards and Leighton Matthewses, Jamie Batemans were few and far between.

Unless she'd got him wrong, she thought. And just how bad were the others really?

Increasingly it seemed to Alex that the true catalyst of harm in all this mess wasn't any of these men.

It was Leah Cross.

CHAPTER FIFTY-NINE

Alex sat at the computer in her office and studied the post-mortem report that Helen Collier had sent over that afternoon. As Helen had anticipated at the murder scene, Tom Stoddard had received three stab wounds: one to the right kidney, a second to the chest, a third that had pierced his left lung. According to Helen, the first was likely to have been deliberately placed and used to debilitate him. The attack would have been incredibly painful, to the extent that it might have rendered him unable to cry for help.

Helen had concluded in her report that Tom was likely to have died of his injuries within minutes of the final stab wound being inflicted. There had been no attempt made to remove the knife from his chest.

The door to the office opened, and Chloe came in carrying a cup of coffee. She placed it on the desk in front of Alex. 'How did this morning go?'

'Other than the impromptu arrival of Jamie Bateman? He's the father of Keira's baby.' She gestured to the coffee. 'Thanks.'

'But he didn't think to mention it earlier?'

Alex reached for the coffee and took a sip. 'He said he knew it would make him look suspicious.'

'Well he looks a whole load more suspicious now,' Chloe said, pulling up a chair and sitting beside Alex.

'Look,' Alex said, gesturing to the computer monitor. 'Post-mortem results on Tom Stoddard.' She sat back and gave Chloe a few minutes to read the key details.

'Fingerprints are going to prove useless,' Chloe said, sitting back once she was done.

'Exactly what I'd already thought. There were countless prints lifted from that kitchen. If things had been done properly that bloody Sunday …' She let her words drift. Being angry about the multitude of errors made on the night of Keira's death wasn't going to alter the situation they now found themselves in. 'There were no prints on the knife, so whoever did this, it was planned. The pattern of the stab wounds suggests the same.'

'Did he know his killer, do you think?'

Alex sighed. 'Not enough evidence to suggest either way. Tom was at the kitchen door when he was stabbed, his back to his killer. He was either about to go out into the yard, or he'd just come in and had his back turned to lock the door. He turned to whoever attacked him and then received the second stab wound. The third and final wound was at an angle that suggests he had already slumped to the floor by that point. Look,' she said, referring to one of the images attached along with the report. 'Sorry,' she added, noting Chloe's response to the close-up of Tom Stoddard's punctured chest. 'Never gets any easier, does it?' She minimised the image. 'He didn't seem to put up any sort of fight. Perhaps the stab wound to the kidney had rendered him unable to retaliate. Either that, or he saw his attacker and the initial shock delayed any fight he might have put up against her.'

'Her?' Chloe said, turning in her seat. 'Leah, you mean?'

Alex raised an eyebrow. 'We know she went back to that house. Her phone was there, when the previous day she'd had it at the hospital with her – we know that because officers had tried to find a next-of-kin contact number on it. Where is she now? If she didn't do this, why didn't she raise the alarm when she found Tom's body?' She took another sip of her coffee. 'Anything useful come in since we went public with her image?'

Chloe shook her head. 'We've had the usual might-have-beens, but other than that, nothing.' She returned her focus to the report on the computer screen. 'I thought Jamie told you on his way to the station that he didn't recognise that knife, though? He said it hadn't come from the house.'

'She could have bought it between leaving the hospital and returning to the house. She didn't even have to buy it – she may have stolen it. I tell you something,' Alex said, returning her coffee mug to the desk. 'I don't think anything you could tell me about Leah Cross would surprise me any more. We need to find out which shops stock this particular make of knife. If it was bought and we can find out from where, perhaps we can identify her that way.'

'What do you make of the bruising to the knuckles on Tom's right hand, then?'

'Obviously not self-defence – the pathologist reckons it's a few days old. It suggests a fight, but with who is anyone's guess.'

The two women fell silent, both lost in their own thoughts. Whether or not Leah Cross had physically inflicted those fatal stabs wounds, Alex was convinced that the girl was in some way or another responsible for Tom Stoddard's death. They just had to find a way to prove it.

CHAPTER SIXTY

Leighton Matthews was back in the interview room. He had pushed a paper cup aimlessly around the table for the previous ten minutes, allowing the untouched murky tea to go lukewarm. His solicitor sat beside him, her bottle-blonde hair pulled into a painfully tight ponytail that made her look like a middle-aged cheerleader in an eighties power suit.

Alex and Chloe were outside in the corridor.

'I can get someone else in with me to do this,' Chloe suggested.

Alex shook her head.

Chloe studied her tentatively. Alex's eyes were dark and edged with heavy, exhausted shadows. 'I'm not sure you should be here.'

'I'm not sure I asked for your opinion on the subject.' Alex pushed the interview room door open and gestured for Chloe to go in. Chloe felt her face colour at her superior's curtness.

Alex sat opposite Leighton Matthews, Chloe taking the seat beside her. She pressed a button on the tape recorder. 'Saturday 17th June. Interview with Leighton Matthews, commencing at 17.04. Mr Matthews, when you were last here, you told us that Leah Cross is your daughter. We'd like to ask you some more about the relationship between the two of you.'

Matthews looked at his solicitor. 'Is that necessary? I thought you were investigating the hit-and-run. I don't see why any of this is relevant.'

'That's for us to think about,' Alex told him. 'We're currently looking for Leah in connection with this incident, but also in relation to a separate case. You might be able to help us locate her.'

'I very much doubt that.'

'Again, we'll be the judges of that. When did you first find out who Leah was?'

Matthews slid his hands from the desk and balled them into fists in his lap. He sat back in his chair, pushed his head back and looked up at the ceiling. 'Do we have to do this?' When no one responded to the question, he sighed and wearily began his version of events.

'It was the November before last. We were a couple of months into the first term of that year. I hadn't really noticed Leah – she was sitting one of my modules, but it was lecture-based that term so I didn't really get to know any of the students. She came to my office one day with a piece of work and told me who she was.'

He stopped abruptly, as if this was sufficient explanation.

'So what happened?' Alex asked. 'She just walked in and said, "Hi, Daddy … surprise"?'

Matthews' jaw tensed. 'Not quite, obviously. She told me she knew someone who used to know me – I didn't really think anything of it at first. Then she asked me if I remembered a woman called Carol Chambers.'

'Which you did,' Chloe said, taking in the reaction that had etched itself on Matthews' face at the mere mention of the name.

'Yes, I did.' He glanced at his solicitor again, as though embarrassed to reveal any more in front of her. 'Leah told me Carol was her mother. It didn't take long to understand what she was implying.'

'Tell us about Carol.'

He pressed his fingertips against his eyelids. 'I'm not proud of what happened.'

'Which part?' Alex asked sharply.

Chloe shot her a look. Alex's anger was radiating in a static aura, keeping everyone around her at arm's length. She realised that the investigation into Keira's death was getting to her – it was starting to get to them all, but now, in the aftermath of Gillian's death, it was evident Alex wasn't coping. The case had already been marred by error and misjudgement. Chloe didn't want Alex to be responsible for any mistakes that might follow; she knew her colleague would never forgive herself.

'Tell us what happened,' she prompted.

'It was the summer of 1996. I was a few years out of uni and working as a teacher. Melissa and I had been married nearly a year. Our first child was on the way. She was having a rough time of it: morning sickness, tiredness … we weren't getting on very well. I mean, that wasn't the reason why, there were lots of things at the time, but we decided to have a break from one another, just for a couple of weeks, to get our heads straight. She went to stay with her mother and I went to Cornwall to stay at my cousin's. He was away that summer – he let me have his flat for a while so I could concentrate on finishing the book I was working on.'

His speech was flowing freely now. Despite his earlier reluctance to tell the truth, confession now seemed to come naturally to him.

'I met Carol on the second day I was there. She was working behind the bar at this place not far away and we got chatting. I never told her I was married. I didn't mean for things to happen the way they did, but she was young and fun and it was everything Melissa and I didn't have at the time. I felt … I don't know … trapped. It was like a two-week holiday from my life, I suppose.'

'What a heart-warming tale,' Alex said. 'So you shacked up with the barmaid for a fortnight, didn't get the book finished … and then what? Went home to your pregnant wife and never said a word?'

'DI King,' Frankie Piper interjected. 'Mr Matthews has told you what happened, as requested.'

Alex ignored the woman. 'You never said anything to your wife about this?' she asked again.

Matthews shook his head.

'So nineteen years later, a teenager turns up in your office and tells you she's your daughter?'

'Yes. Like I said, I'm not proud of what happened. But I'd never heard from Carol since that trip to Cornwall – I had no idea she'd got pregnant.'

'How did you react when you found out?' Chloe asked.

'Well … as you'd expect. Shocked. This was the first I'd known about it.'

'And how did you react to Leah? Were you kind to her? Or did you tell her she shouldn't have looked for you?'

'I admit I wasn't very nice, not the first time. I was in shock. I realise now that probably made things worse.'

'The blackmail, you mean?'

He nodded.

'We have copies of Leah's bank statements here,' Chloe said, gesturing to the paperwork on the desk. 'You've made considerable transfers to her account in recent months. How much have you given her in total?'

Matthews hesitated on the answer, as though reluctant to admit it even to himself. 'Fifteen thousand pounds.' He sighed loudly, as though the loss had physically pained him.

Chloe raised her eyebrows. 'Quite a steep price to pay to buy her silence.'

'Did you ever ask her for proof?' Alex asked. 'A DNA test, for example?'

'Of course I did,' Matthews said, exasperated by the question, 'but she told me she'd tell my wife everything – I wasn't going to risk that. My family, my career … everything I've worked for. She had enough proof anyway. She knew everything about that time in Cornwall and how I'd met her mother. She had photographs of them together – of her as a baby and then as a teenager. She came to South Wales with a plan. I don't think she ever wanted a relationship with me – it wasn't about that. That girl is devious … calculating.'

'Must be something in the genes,' Alex mused.

Chloe shot her another look.

'DI King,' Frankie Piper said in a warning tone, glaring at Alex across the table. The look was met with a mirrored expression.

'Do you know where Leah is now?' Chloe asked.

'No idea,' Matthews told her. 'Hopefully as far away from here as possible.'

'Your last interview,' Alex said, resting her elbows on the table. 'Who were you covering for?'

He appeared unsettled by the question. 'I don't know what you mean.'

'Oh, I think you do. You were trying to protect somebody – who was it? Your wife?'

Matthews shook his head. 'Look,' he said, 'I wasn't honest with you, OK? I wasn't protecting anyone. Well … only myself. I did it, OK? I hit Leah with my car. She was never going to go away and leave us alone … I didn't know what else to do.'

'OK,' Alex said, sitting back. She clearly still didn't believe a word of it, but perhaps the threat of a charge against him might force the truth. 'Leighton Matthews, I'm arresting you for the attempted murder of Leah Cross.'

CHAPTER SIXTY-ONE

'I think you should go home. Just for the rest of the day, OK?'

Alex was standing in the superintendent's office, summoned there following Leighton Matthews' arrest. Harry had been in the recording room watching on screen as the interview unfolded. Like Chloe – and like the solicitor, if her angry complaints had been anything to go by – she surmised that Harry didn't feel she had conducted the interview appropriately, although he hadn't said as much.

'We've got a confession and an arrest,' she said defensively. 'What more do you want? This is the way you like things, isn't it, sir? Nicely wrapped up and packed away.'

She was angry. She was convinced Matthews was lying, but the pressure to secure a charge was weighing over her. She could now only hope that proof of Melissa's guilt would make itself apparent before he went to court.

Superintendent Blake's eyes remained fixed on her. 'I'm going to let that one go,' he said steadily, 'considering what you've been through over the past couple of days. But the past couple of days are the exact reason you shouldn't be here. You need to go home, get some sleep. I'm not saying don't turn up for work tomorrow, not if that's what you feel you need to do. I'm just suggesting you call it a day now.'

'There are still things that need doing.'

'They'll wait until tomorrow.'

Alex rolled her eyes. 'Waiting until tomorrow is the reason we've got ourselves into this mess. If we'd done things properly the night Keira died, we might have found her killer by now.'

'I know why this case is getting to you so much, Alex.'

She held his eye, well aware of what he was referring to. 'It makes no difference.'

'Doesn't it? Keira's death has become personal. That's why you need to take a step back.'

'I think Leah Cross killed Tom Stoddard,' she said, changing the subject. 'She had the opportunity, and there's a likelihood his death is linked to Keira's. If we find out there's also a link to the drug dealing, we might end up with something bigger on our hands. We need to involve Cardiff – get them on board with us.'

Blake nodded. 'I think you might be right.'

'There's a first.'

He sighed. 'Not at all, Alex, and you know that's not true. There are people here who care about you, me included. We don't want to see you run yourself into the ground.'

'I know Keira's death wasn't an accident, sir. I've always known it. Chloe's theory about the similarities between the two girls holds a lot of weight.'

'I agree, and I'm sorry if you feel I was working against you. We work differently – we always have. We need proof, Alex – that doesn't change, you know that.'

She nodded. She hadn't realised the extent to which she had needed the super's support. Not needed, she thought; wanted. It would be a shame for their working relationship to end on a negative note. Nor, she realised now, did she want to lose his friendship.

'She's a smart kid,' Harry said, referring to Chloe. 'You've brought out the best in her.'

'I don't know about that.' In truth, Alex suspected that for the previous couple of months it might have worked the other way around. Would she have functioned effectively without Chloe to fall back on? It seemed to Alex that Chloe might have helped her hide a multitude of flaws from the outside world.

She turned to leave the office. 'Boss,' she said, looking back, 'I'm sorry. I've said some hurtful things. Let's try to end this on a positive, shall we?'

Harry gave a nod; it was all Alex needed. She left the office and went back into the corridor feeling differently towards the case, a fresh sense of energy powering her step. There were things she couldn't control. Her mother's illness, the relationship they'd shared; the awful death that had dragged on for years before its eventual arrival, draining them both of every reserve of energy. These were the things she had always struggled with: things she had no control over.

But she could control this. There were ways of finding the truth, and she had them at her disposal. She could also control the way she reacted to others, and she needed to apologise to Chloe for not having done so. The way she had spoken to her earlier that afternoon had been unnecessary and unfair.

She found her in the main investigation room, talking to Dan. 'Chloe ... have you got a minute?' They crossed the room to a quieter corner. 'I'm sorry for what I said to you before.'

'Don't worry, it's forgotten.'

'No,' Alex said, 'it was wrong ... I know you were only looking out for me.'

Chloe nodded. 'Honestly, you don't need to apologise.'

Alex managed a smile. 'Thank you. Harry was a bit less forgiving at first. He was watching the interview.'

'Don't worry about it. You did what you had to; we got a confession. Think Matthews is telling the truth?'

Alex shook her head.

'Me neither.'

'The woman he told us about,' Alex said. 'Carol Chambers.'

'What about her?'

'Well, the address in Devon – the one Leah gave the university as her home address – belongs to a couple called Jonathan and

Carol Brooks. Chambers might have been her maiden name. It shouldn't be too difficult to find out.'

Chloe looked confused. 'But when you called, the woman you spoke to said she'd never heard of Leah Cross.'

'Exactly. Why might a mother lie about knowing her own daughter?'

'I don't know. Unless she's managed to upset her as well. Seems Leah makes pissing people off a bit of a habit.'

Alex nodded in Dan's direction. 'How's he getting on with her social media accounts?'

DC Mason had been requested to access Leah Cross's Facebook account in the hope it might shed some light on her whereabouts. It was a long shot – Alex suspected Leah would be too clever to reveal anything incriminating on social media – but if they didn't check it, it would only be added to the list of things that had already been overlooked.

'He's into her account,' Chloe told her, 'but there's been nothing posted recently. She's not done an online check-in anywhere either. He's still working through it.'

Alex nodded. 'Keep going. I'm going to go and make another phone call to a certain Mrs Brooks.'

Chloe hesitated over her next words, choosing them carefully. 'You know if you want to talk about anything, I'm here. No one's trying to interfere. I just wonder if being at work is the right thing for you.'

'I'm fine. I can't change what's happened. At least here I can do something constructive.'

'There must be a lot to organise, for your mum.'

Alex shook her head, dismissing the thought of the already countless administrative tasks she would have to undertake as a result of her mother's death. Between them and this place, she was being kept busy. It was the very thing she needed. 'I'm fine,' she said again, trying to make the words sound more convincing this time.

Chloe gave a sad smile. 'We're going to work this out,' she told her.

Alex returned the smile. This was why she needed Chloe working by her side: that eternal youthful optimism. Hours earlier, she might have doubted Chloe's faith in their abilities.

Now, there seemed no reason why she shouldn't be right.

CHAPTER SIXTY-TWO

His car wasn't at the house, but Leah presumed the police were still holding it. Evidence. She wondered how much evidence they had against her, but surely if it had been sufficient they'd have found a way of getting hold of her by now. She'd have been arrested.

Or would she? Would they even believe him, with his track record?

She wasn't sure whether anything she'd done involving Leighton was illegal, but there were always the drugs to go on. She had been stupid to go out that Monday night. Keira's death had left her reeling; she hadn't been thinking straight. All she'd known at the time was that she needed to escape that house – escape her own life – and start again somewhere new, somewhere no one knew her. And the only way to access freedom was through money.

She tapped at the front door, expecting him to be waiting for her on the other side. When he didn't answer, she tried the handle. The door was unlocked. She pushed it open and paused a moment before calling his name. The place was empty and couldn't have looked more like a rental property if it'd had an announcement pinned to the door: magnolia walls, industrial-grade brown carpets that wore the telltale signs of age and neglect; peeling wallpaper at the edges of the ceiling, painted over in an attempt to conceal its existence.

'Leighton,' she called again.

She heard a noise along the corridor. She passed the living room, empty but for a sofa and a TV unit, but there was no one there. What was she going to say to him? She didn't know; she was just grateful that he wanted to see her again.

She had never said sorry for anything in her life; at least she'd never said it and really meant it. With him, she was beginning to think she would mean it. She had seen enough of his life to know she wanted to be a part of it. She missed not having a father figure, someone she could turn to when things weren't making sense. She wanted to be the photo on someone's desk at work. She had imagined what it might be like to go home to the house where his family lived. Didn't she deserve a piece of that, no matter how small?

There was so much she regretted now that she could see the damage she had done. She wished more than anything that she could go back to the start and do things again, differently this time.

She'd reached the kitchen. Pushing the door wide, she saw someone standing at the sink at the far side of the room, back turned. It wasn't Leighton. It was a woman. Long blonde hair that fell down her back in thick waves.

'Sit down,' the woman said, without turning to look at Leah. 'We need a chat.'

Leah stayed where she was. She thought about leaving, about running back down the hallway and out onto the street, but her conversation with Carol over the phone had reminded her that she had nowhere to go. She had spent so long running from things, got so far away, there was no turning back now.

The woman turned. When she saw her face, Leah realised she wasn't as old as she'd suspected. Much younger, in fact; about her own age. Pretty face. Familiar.

The girl had been crying. Her eyes were red-rimmed and her cheeks were flushed. There was smudged mascara on the bridge of her nose. 'Sit down,' she said again.

Leah sat, compliant. She could have turned and left, but things were already beginning to become clear: a series of awful, impossible events that she had until now judged entirely incorrectly. The past week played out in front of her, their missing pieces starting to fall into place.

She knew who this young woman was. She thought she knew what she'd done.

Isobel Matthews crossed the room and reached to one of the shelves. She pulled from it a kitchen knife and moved to stand near the door. In that moment, Leah realised her mistake. All her mistakes. She had thought the place empty, but Isobel had made provision. She had tried to hurt her before; this time, she was going to make sure she finished what she had started.

Leah wasn't sure she would go through with it, but then she thought of what the girl had already been capable of.

'How long?' Isobel asked. The knife in her hand was shaking.

'I don't know what you're talking about.'

'How long?' she said again. She held the knife out, her arm shaking unsteadily.

Did this girl think the same as the police? Did she think Leah had been sleeping with Leighton?

Leah stood, shoving the chair from beneath her. She wasn't being silenced by this family any longer. 'Get out of my way,' she said calmly.

Isobel stood her ground, refusing to move. She looked defiant, filled with anger, and in that moment everything that had gone before seemed so clear, spread out before Leah as though she were watching it in film projected on to the walls of the kitchen.

'It was you driving that car, wasn't it?'

Isobel looked her up and down, her mouth contorting into a sneer. 'He's always had shit taste,' she said, 'but my God, his standards have dropped.'

Leah was thirteen again, being taunted about the state of her clothes: the shabby coat she'd been wearing for the previous two years; the trainers from the discount shop that had a hole in the rubber sole. Her mother had insisted on repeatedly using glue to mend it, despite the fact that it never succeeded in holding anything in place; her shoe had come unstuck in the middle of a netball match against the school's main rivals and she had tripped over the flapping sole, falling over and losing the team the final points that went on to cost them the game.

Keeley Porter, captain of netball – spoilt little rich girl and notorious Year 9 bully – had sauntered past her, shoving her sideways while she was crouched at her broken shoe. 'Fucking gyppo.'

Leah heard those words again so clearly now, as clearly as though Isobel had spoken them. Isobel Matthews, who thought the world owed her an explanation and she could click her fingers and everything would fall into her lap. Keeley Porter, who'd made her life a living hell throughout the whole of secondary school and had never been held to account over anything. Nobody beautiful could ever possibly be bad.

'You fucking bitch.'

Leah forgot that Isobel was holding a knife. She forgot the pain she was still in from the hit-and-run. For a moment, everything else was wiped away and she was thirteen years old again, humiliated on a netball pitch with no one to fight her corner. Her arm flew towards the girl, her fist meeting the side of her face. Isobel recoiled, crying out in pain, and as she fell back against the kitchen door, Leah landed a second blow. The knife was dropped to the floor. Leah swung again and again, her anger with the world culminating in a torrent of violent rage. Isobel tried to fight back, but Leah's strength overpowered her and she found herself cornered, helpless to do anything other than accept the repeated blows landing upon her. She slid to the floor, desperately trying to cover her face with her arms as Leah continued like a madwoman; a girl possessed.

At last Leah stopped. The red mist faded, dropping to the floor like a fallen curtain. Then she saw what she'd done. She stopped, stood back; saw the bloodied mess she had made of Leighton's older daughter. She saw the violence she was capable of; all those years of suffering and endurance built up into one seething outburst of uncontrollable rage. She leaned down and took the knife from the floor. Isobel looked up at her, barely able to speak; desperate pleas leaving her mouth in an incoherent babble of pain and fear.

Leah stood back, the knife trembling in her hand, before she drew it back and plunged it into her stomach.

CHAPTER SIXTY-THREE

Alex wondered whether there was ever going to be an evening when she would make it home before receiving a call that sent her veering off course yet again. She and Chloe had just turned onto the mountain road when her mobile began to ring. They had stayed at the station far later than intended, both frustrated by the absence of answers out there. Repeated calls to Carol Brooks's home had gone unanswered, and though Alex found out fairly easily where the woman worked, the offices had closed at six and there was no one there to speak with.

'DI King,' the officer at the other end of the call said. 'There's been an incident at a house on Broadway – two young women involved in an altercation. One's been stabbed.'

Alex rolled her eyes, wondering whether the uncharacteristic heat of the summer was turning everyone mad.

'One of the officers who attended the call recognised one of the women. Looks like we've found Leah Cross.'

Alex stopped the car at the kerbside and glanced at Chloe. 'Where is she now?'

'University Hospital in Cardiff. Emergency unit.'

'Do we know who the other woman is?'

'Isobel Matthews.'

Alex pulled a face and sat back in the driving seat, trying for a moment to process the information. Isobel Matthews was Leighton Matthews' daughter. Had Leah gone to her, or had she sought out Leah?

Was this a reaction to her father's arrest?

'We're on our way,' she told the officer. 'Another thing … you said there's been a stabbing. Which of the girls has been stabbed?'

'Leah Cross.'

It wasn't the answer Alex was expecting. The girl seemed already responsible for so much harm that her immediate assumption was that Isobel had been the injured party. She ended the call and pulled away from the roadside, her mind racing with the possibilities of what they might find when they arrived at the hospital. Where Leah Cross was concerned, nothing seemed straightforward.

'She just flew at me. I couldn't do anything to stop her.'

Leah Cross was lying in a hospital bed, propped up on a mountain of pillows. Her make-up was smudged around her eyes in thick black smears, and when she moved, she winced, putting a hand to the dressing that covered the stab wound to her stomach. If they hadn't already known so much about her, the act might almost have been convincing.

'We've already been to see Isobel,' Alex told her. 'She's in quite a state.'

'I had to,' Leah said. 'She went crazy … she was out of control.'

'So you beat her up before or after she stabbed you?' Chloe asked.

'I didn't beat her up; it was self-defence.' The girl's eyes moved from one woman to the other. 'She attacked me, I fought back. If I hadn't, she would have kept going … she'd have killed me. She was driving the car, you know, the one that hit me. It was her. Ask her.'

Alex studied Leah in disbelief. Even now, lying in a hospital room with a stab wound, her priority was incriminating others. Perhaps Leighton Matthews' assessment of her character hadn't been entirely inaccurate.

'You managed to give her quite a beating considering the pain you must have been in,' Chloe mused.

Leah narrowed her eyes but said nothing.

'Where have you been for the past couple of days, Leah?'

The girl shrugged. 'Staying with mates. I couldn't go back to the house, not after what's happened. I just wanted to clear my head.'

'So you haven't been trying to avoid us?'

'Why would I want to do that?'

She was brazen, Alex thought. Even now, there wasn't the slightest glimmer of remorse for any of the things she had been responsible for. Getting the truth from this girl would be an excavation project; one that involved the type of patience Alex sometimes lacked. Despite that, she couldn't help hearing Leah's accusations against Isobel Matthews repeating in her mind. What if she was telling the truth? Had Isobel been behind the wheel of that car?

Was it Isobel that Leighton had been trying to protect, and not his wife after all?

'Amy Barker's out of her coma,' Alex said, pulling her chair closer to Leah's bedside. 'Thought you might be interested, seeing as you're the one who put her there.'

Leah's reaction suggested she had no idea what Alex was talking about. Either her stab wound had somehow caused her short-term memory loss, or she was an extremely convincing actress. They now knew enough about her to know the latter to be true.

'Heard from Tom at all?' Alex asked.

There it was: a telltale flicker in her eye. Leah knew that Tom was dead.

'No.'

Alex held eye contact, knowing Leah would break first. 'Amy's made a positive identification of you as the person who sold her the drugs. So don't think about doing another disappearing act, will you?'

Leah pressed the buzzer that rested on her bed. By the time a nurse arrived in the room moments later, tears had formed on the girl's face and her expression had morphed from stubborn defiance to that of a persecuted victim, helpless at the hands of these two detectives who were so mercilessly hounding her. She really was a calculating little cow, Alex thought.

'I think that's probably enough for one day,' the nurse said, reaching to the wall to cut short the sound of the buzzer still beeping out in the corridor.

'You're right,' Alex said, giving Leah a false smile. 'There's nothing that can't wait until tomorrow.'

She and Chloe left the room, leaving Leah in the hands of the fretting nurse.

'How the hell did she fall for that?' Chloe said, her voice laced with contempt. 'My God, that girl is one of a kind.'

Alex said nothing, too busy trying to unravel the jumble of thoughts that knotted her brain. As despicable as Leah was, it seemed her sister wasn't far behind.

CHAPTER SIXTY-FOUR

Alex and Chloe sat at the kitchen table drinking tea. They should both have gone to bed by now, but it seemed they had worked their way past the point of tiredness. It was a state with which Alex was becoming increasingly familiar.

'Let me know if you need any help with this,' Chloe said, gesturing to the pile of papers sitting by the microwave. They were all to do with arrangements for Gillian's funeral. Once the death certificate was issued, Alex would be assaulted with a barrage of decisions she didn't want to have to face. She would have to read through the endless documents that awaited her and make contact with the funeral home, but despite having known for months that its arrival would be imminent, a funeral was still something she felt unprepared for.

'Thanks. I think I'm on top of things,' she lied. 'Look … I know you think my reaction to all this has been a bit weird.'

'I don't think anything,' Chloe said, sipping her tea.

Alex raised an eyebrow. 'We didn't have the best relationship. We hadn't for a long time. And when you've watched someone dying for as long as I did … I don't know. It changes your response to it.'

'I get that,' Chloe told her. 'She's not suffering any more. That's a good thing.'

Alex stared at her tea, not sure why she'd bothered to make it. She didn't really like the taste. Like so many other things, it had become a mindless habit. 'There's something I want to tell you. I think I owe it to you – things will probably make a bit more sense. Years ago, about six years back, I had a miscarriage.'

Chloe's face fell. 'God, Alex, I'm so sorry. I didn't realise … I thought you …'

'It's fine,' Alex told her, feeling guilty now for having made her so clearly uncomfortable. 'I mean, it happens a lot. It happens all the time. Anyway, the reason I'm telling you this is more to do with what happened afterwards. My mother was quick to tell me I'd been too old to try and that my body probably couldn't handle it – that I should have thought about it sooner. I was fourteen weeks when it happened, so I needed a D and C.'

Chloe looked at her blankly.

'It's a procedure where … Don't worry about what it is. The point is, when we got back from the hospital – and I'll never forget it as long as I live – my mother stood there in the doorway of the living room and told me that it wasn't a proper baby anyway.'

'She actually said that?'

Alex nodded. 'I thought years later, you know, after the dementia diagnosis, that maybe it wasn't really her speaking. Maybe the illness had already taken a grip by then and she didn't have a hold over the things that were coming out of her mouth. But other times I don't think so … I think it was just her. Anyway, it *was* a proper baby – that's the point I'm making. When you've had IVF, you get an early scan. We saw a heartbeat at less than eight weeks, this little pulsing on the screen. And that's all I could think about when Keira North's post-mortem came back … that two lives had been lost.'

Chloe sat back in her chair and looked away for a moment. Things made so much more sense now. Alex had reacted almost personally to Keira's death; so much more so when the superintendent had suggested that it should be deemed an accident. This went a long way towards explaining that reaction, although Chloe knew that

Alex's desire for justice would have been just as strong had Keira not been pregnant.

'Harry knows about this, doesn't he?' she asked.

Alex nodded. 'But he's the only person at the station who does. No one else knew about it at the time.'

Chloe stared at the surface of her untouched tea, unsure of what to say. 'Do you think Leah's telling the truth? About Isobel driving that car?'

'I don't know. It makes sense, though, and it works alongside your theory – that someone pushed Keira thinking she was Leah. If Isobel had made the same assumption as us and thought that Leah was having an affair with her father, then perhaps it all adds up. She went to that party knowing she'd find Leah there, thought she'd found her and just reacted on impulse. It's tragic.'

'It's even more tragic – if you're right – when you think about how wrong she got it. Same as we did.'

Alex nodded. 'Look, Chloe, there's another reason why I've told you all this, and believe me, it's been awkward as hell and I'd appreciate it if we never mention this conversation again, OK? After the miscarriage, Rob and I never tried again. We just couldn't get past what it had done to us, and I never really got over the things my mother had said. I was thirty-eight years old and I let her treat me as though I was still thirteen. I kept that nagging voice in my head and it never switched off and I let it beat me.' She paused. 'I suppose the point I'm trying to make is that you can't let other people dictate your life. You've got to do what's right for you, while the chance is there.'

She stood and went to one of the kitchen drawers, opening it to retrieve a brochure. Chloe's cheeks coloured as Alex put it on the table in front of her.

'Don't let anyone or anything keep you from doing what's best for you.'

The brochure was one Chloe had picked up from an estate agent's a couple of weeks earlier. It advertised rental properties in South Wales. She had been thinking for a while that Alex needed her home back, her own space, and the longer she stayed there, the harder it was going to be for her to regain her independence.

'How did you …'

'I heard you talking with Scott a couple of weeks back,' Alex admitted. 'I wasn't eavesdropping, I promise. I popped back here for something and I just overheard.'

Chloe closed her eyes for a moment, worried how much Alex had heard. She and Scott had talked about her plans to move, but events of the past couple of weeks had changed everything. She couldn't leave Alex now. She hoped Alex hadn't heard her talking about just how vulnerable she believed the older woman to be.

'I'm sorry,' she said.

'What are you apologising for? Look, I appreciate you thinking of me and it's kind of you and everything, but there's such a thing as being too kind sometimes. When I asked you to stay here, it was about getting you back on your feet and away from that flat, and now those things are done, I don't expect you to stay here drinking crap tea with me every evening, watching life pass by without you.'

Chloe nodded, the colour in her cheeks fading. 'I'm grateful for everything you've done for me; you know that, don't you?'

Alex nodded.

'Do you think it's too soon?'

'Do you?'

'It feels like the right time.'

Alex smiled. 'Then you've answered your own question. Right,' she said, standing from the table and taking her unfinished tea to the sink. 'We should get some sleep or we'll be good for nothing tomorrow.' She rinsed out her cup and stood it upside down on the draining board. 'See you in the morning.'

CHAPTER SIXTY-FIVE

The whole team assembled that morning in the central incident room. The place had been a buzzing hive of rumour, news of the incident involving Leah Cross and Isobel Matthews having filtered through the station.

'Right,' Alex said, bringing the murmur of whispers and gossip to a hush. 'Quite a lot to go through this morning, as I'm sure you're all now well aware. Leah Cross has been found, though not under the kind of circumstances any of us might have anticipated. There are probably various versions of the incident doing the rounds, so let me put you all straight on what happened last night. Leah Cross went to a house on Broadway yesterday evening, having received a text message from the pay-as-you-go mobile phone Leighton used to contact her with. The house is one of Leighton's rental properties, so she went there thinking she was going to meet with him, presumably to discuss what happened when he was here talking to us about the hit-and-run. When she got to the house, it wasn't Leighton she found there but his daughter, Isobel.'

She gestured to a new photograph that had been pinned to the gallery of faces: a pretty young blonde woman, a younger version of Melissa Matthews.

'Isobel Matthews is twenty years old, just a few months older than Leah Cross. We now know that in the summer of 1996, Leighton had a two-week affair with a woman called Carol Chambers, who he met during a trip to Cornwall. A writing retreat, apparently,' she added, eyebrows raised. 'The result of that affair,' she traced her finger to the photograph of Leah Cross, 'was this young lady. We have yet to find out the details of how Leah discovered her father's whereabouts, but it seems increasingly apparent that her doing so was the catalyst for a number of incidents that followed, the most significant being the death of Keira North.'

Chloe caught Alex's eye and offered her an encouraging smile.

'Leah Cross, as we all know, is a compulsive liar, yet she's made an allegation against Isobel Matthews that might hold some weight. She claims it was Isobel driving the car that hit her. We know Leighton Matthews has been lying to protect someone, and until now we'd all assumed that someone to be his wife. What if he's been lying to protect his daughter? If Isobel made the same assumption we did and believed Leah to be having an affair with her father, Chloe's theory of mistaken identity becomes even more of a possibility. It seems entirely plausible Isobel might have gone to that party with the intention of confronting Leah. Was last night an attempt to correct the mistake she'd made? We need to speak again to these people,' Alex swept a hand across the array of faces surrounding the people who remained central to the investigation, 'and see if we can get anyone to identify Isobel Matthews as having been at the party that evening.'

'So Isobel Matthews pushes Keira thinking she's Leah,' Dan said.

Alex nodded. 'That's the theory at the moment. As soon as news of Keira's death hit the press, Isobel would have realised her mistake. This could have had a number of effects – she might have felt guilt at what she'd done to Keira, but equally she may have been angry that Leah had walked away from it all. It could have been a mixture of both. Perhaps she thought it was Leah's fault that Keira died, not hers.'

'So she stabs Leah after failing to kill her with the car,' DC Jake Sullivan said.

'Did she, though?' Alex questioned. 'I don't believe it for a second. Last night, Isobel Matthews was in such a state we were unable to speak with her for long. She was a bloody mess according to the first officers who attended the scene. Leah claims to have attacked Isobel after Isobel stabbed her. Really? She managed to beat the girl black and blue having just been stabbed in the stomach?'

'So what are you suggesting?' DC Daniel Mason asked. 'Leah beat her up first and Isobel stabbed her in self-defence?'

'More likely,' Alex said. 'We need to speak with Melissa again, see if she sticks with her recently changed version of events. If Leighton's covering for Isobel, it's likely Melissa will know about it.'

'And neither woman knows yet that Leah is Leighton's daughter?' one of the other DCs asked.

Alex shook her head. 'So far we've given him room to break that news himself. He's obviously still reluctant to, so perhaps we'll have to do it for him.'

'How did Isobel Matthews know about Leah?' Dan asked. 'I mean, there must have been something to link Leighton to her, or vice versa.'

'Something else we need to find out,' Alex said. 'These theories remain just that until we find proof. We also need to consider where Tom Stoddard comes into all this. There's the drug dealing to bear in mind. In his interview with us, Tom claimed Leah was involved in the dealing. Did she kill him to keep him quiet and keep herself out of trouble?

'Chloe, we're going back to the hospital to speak with Leah. Dan, I'd like you to pay another visit to Melissa Matthews this morning. The rest of you, we need to speak again with people we know were at the party that night. Let's see if we can get an ID on Isobel Matthews. And keep working your way through this CCTV, please – I know it's tedious, but perhaps now we have another face to look for, we might be able to find it. The footage from outside the shop on Railway Terrace might have picked up Isobel on the night of the party.'

She glanced at Harry Blake, who had been watching her throughout. 'Let's not forget that whatever else Leah Cross might have got away with so far, Amy Barker has identified her as having sold her the drugs at Fusion nightclub the Monday before last. It's not enough to secure a conviction, so let's make sure we find something else.'

CHAPTER SIXTY-SIX

Alex sat at her desk, waiting for someone to answer her call. She was trying to match up Leighton's story with any possible reason why Carol Brooks might have denied knowledge of Leah, but attempts to do so without first speaking again to the woman were likely to prove pointless.

Was Carol's refusal to even acknowledge Leah the reason why the girl hadn't left the area after the hit-and-run? It seemed odd to Alex that she had stayed in South Wales knowing the police wanted to speak with her. She must have known she would be suspected of involvement in Tom's death. Alex thought of what Leighton had told them following his last interview: that Leah had tried to kiss him. Alex had attempted to make sense of it, but it remained difficult to comprehend. When had the parameters of their relationship become blurred? Had Leah been looking for a father figure or was all this, as Leighton suggested, merely a way to blackmail him?

Whatever the truth, one thing seemed certain: Leah was a deeply troubled young woman.

The call was finally answered.

'Hello?'

Alex was sure it was the same woman she had spoken to previously. 'Mrs Brooks? This is Detective Inspector Alex King – we spoke briefly last week.'

There was a silence during which she thought the woman might hang up on her. She didn't.

'I told you before,' Carol said, her tone immediately defensive, 'I don't know a Leah Cross.'

Alex paused for a moment, weighing up how best to approach what was obviously a difficult subject. Why was Carol Brooks denying knowledge of her own daughter? What could possibly have happened between them for her to react in such a way at the mere mention of the girl's name?

'Mrs Brooks,' she said, deciding upon a different approach, 'Leah is currently in hospital, recovering from a stab wound. She gave your address to the University of South Wales's admin department – it's the only contact detail she's provided.'

There was a silence while Carol processed this new information. 'Is she OK?' she finally asked. 'What happened?'

'She'll be fine,' Alex told her. 'So you do know her, then?'

There was a sigh at the other end of the line. 'I assumed when you called before that she'd got herself into some sort of trouble. It wouldn't be the first time, and I doubt it'll be the last. I'm not an unreasonable woman, but that girl has brought nothing but misery to this house. She's her own worst enemy.' Carol was silent again for a moment, as though considering whether she might have said too much. 'Who stabbed her?' she finally asked.

'I'm afraid I can't go into any details at the moment, not while we're investigating the incident. I did wonder if perhaps you'd be intending to visit Leah. There are a few more things I'd like to speak to you about which would probably be best discussed in person, if that's at all possible.'

'I don't know,' Carol said quickly. 'I don't think that's my place. I'm sorry this has happened to her, I really am, but she's not my responsibility any more. I did plenty enough for her and it was thrown back in my face.'

'OK,' Alex said, keen to calm the situation and keep the woman on the phone. 'Look, I appreciate that whatever's gone on between the two of you is something fairly significant, and I wouldn't want to ask you to go over old ground unless I had reason to believe that

doing so might help us with investigations into a current case. I
don't want to speak out of turn, but whatever Leah has done, this
is probably the time she needs her mother most—'

'Mother?' Carol interrupted her. She laughed; a hard, brittle
sound. 'You've got something wrong somewhere. Leah's not my
daughter, thank God.'

CHAPTER SIXTY-SEVEN

Despite the protestations of the nurse they'd spoken with on their arrival at the hospital, the interview with Leah Cross was going ahead. It was impossible to feel any sympathy for the girl, though she continued with her vulnerable victim act with a professional precision.

'There's an unusually large amount of money in your bank account, Leah,' Alex said, gesturing for Chloe to take a seat while she herself remained standing at the foot of the bed. 'We assume you've got more stashed away in cash somewhere – you must have had something to live on over the past few days. Like to explain where that money came from?'

Leah looked from one woman to the other. She shrugged. 'Savings.'

'That's quite a substantial amount of savings for a student,' Chloe said. 'Especially considering you don't have a job.'

'Not in the traditional sense,' Alex added, her lip curling with the implication. 'Amy Barker has identified you as the person who sold her the drugs. The street outside the club has plenty of CCTV, so it's only a matter of time before we find one that picked you up there that night.' This was a lie. The CCTV from the club had been scrutinised; Leah was nowhere to be seen. The girl obviously knew where the cameras were. 'Tom Stoddard claimed you were involved in dealing drugs. You know what's happened to him, don't you, Leah?'

Leah turned her head towards Alex, her face masked with a look of feigned ignorance. God, she was good, Alex thought.

'What do you mean?'

'Tom's been killed.'

She held the detective's gaze, putting on her best show of surprise. She even managed to force tears to her eyes. How much practice had she had at all this pretence?

'Seems convenient for you that he's no longer able to incriminate you.'

'What happened to him?' Leah said, the question asked out of duty rather than concern.

'He was stabbed. Probably best you start telling us the truth, don't you think?'

The girl turned away and looked out of the window at the blank square of sky that stretched into the distance. 'I've been stabbed too,' she said flatly. 'I'm the victim here.'

Chloe shot Alex a look, rolling her eyes at the girl's self-pity. It seemed that Leah Cross and Tom Stoddard had been two of a kind: both careless to anyone else's suffering.

'You went back to the house,' Chloe said. 'Your mobile phone was there. Did you see Tom while you were there?'

Leah shook her head. Chloe and Alex exchanged another look; they were never going to get the truth from this girl.

'Isobel Matthews has been discharged,' Alex told her, 'but she's still in quite a state. Her face is black and blue, she's got a broken nose and two cracked ribs. I'm finding it difficult to believe you were able to inflict that level of injury after receiving a stab wound to the stomach, on top of the injuries you'd already sustained in the hit-and-run.'

'Believe what you want,' Leah said flippantly.

'I'll tell you what I believe. I believe that Isobel wanted to stab you and had every intention of doing so, but you managed to overpower her. She didn't get a chance to hurt you, did she? I believe you attacked her first and then stabbed yourself in an attempt to make Isobel's injuries look like self-defence.'

Leah said nothing, her face still turned to the window.

'Assault, blackmail, drug dealing … not looking good for you, is it?'

Alex crossed the room and stood in front of the window, blocking Leah's view of the outside world. The girl looked away, determined not to make eye contact.

'We know all about the money Leighton Matthews was transferring to your bank account, Leah. He's told us everything. His daughter and his wife are still under the impression the two of you were having an affair. Don't you think it's time they knew the truth?'

'I've told the truth.'

Alex wondered whether part of Leah believed that. Had her lies spread so wide – had her story become so elaborate – that she'd started to live the life of the person she pretended to be rather than the one she was? Had she told so many lies she'd come to forget what the truth was?

'I've spoken to your mother.'

For the first time, Leah looked directly at Alex. Her face was set in a grimace; her eyes questioning whether Alex was telling the truth.

'Your real mother,' Alex added. 'Not Carol Brooks … Carol Chambers … whichever you prefer to refer to her by.'

Leah looked to Chloe as though for sympathy or support, but it was evident she wasn't going to get either. She slid further beneath the hospital blanket, wincing at the pain caused by the movement.

'You're not going to ask how she is?'

'No.'

'OK.' Alex folded her arms across her chest and stepped away from the window. 'It's quite a story I heard this morning, Leah. Troubled young girl having difficulties at home, arguing with her mother; mother can't cope, despite her best efforts, so someone else steps in, the parents of one of the girl's friends. They offer to let the girl stay with them for a while, so she and her mother can resolve their differences. Very kind of them, don't you think? Unusually generous. You'd think the girl would be grateful that someone else cared enough to do something like that for her. But not this girl. This girl takes and takes until they've nothing left to give.'

Leah was crying. They were silent tears, fat and steady on her paled cheeks.

'Keira was your friend, wasn't she?'

Leah ran a hand over her face before turning to Alex. 'Of course she was my friend,' she snapped.

'Must be difficult for you now,' Alex said, 'knowing your lies might have killed her.'

A guttural sob escaped Leah's chest. She shook her head, trying to deny the words.

'Carol's daughter Kirsty was your friend too, wasn't she?'

The mention of the girl's name was enough to confirm Leah's guilt: a guilt that stamped itself upon her face with the force of a slap. She shifted beneath the sheet and winced again, turning her head to the side in an attempt to hide her tears.

'She trusted you with her secrets like a sister would and you listened like a good friend, storing away all the details. She had no idea you were going to use them for your own gain, did she?'

Leah was shaking her head. 'You think you get it,' she said, 'but you don't understand anything. You should be talking to Isobel, not me. She hit me with Leighton's car. She's the one in the wrong here, not me.'

'Telling yourself that must make everything so much easier,' Chloe said.

Leah shot her a glance of contempt. 'Look at you,' she said with a sneer. 'Just like the rest of them. Spoilt little rich girls. Why haven't you arrested Isobel? Because she looks better than I do. Because she has more money and her family is more respectable. She talks better than I do, so she can't possibly be bad, can she? She's going to walk away from all this because you lot are too stupid to get anything right. And I'll get the blame, just like always.'

'Is that what this is all about?' Alex asked. 'Money? Is that why you resented Kirsty – why you thought it would be acceptable to use her past to line your own pockets? Is that why you befriended Keira? I don't think either girl was really your friend, Leah. I think you used them for what you could get, and when you were done with them you ditched them. Other people are just a means to an end to you, aren't they?'

Leah pressed her face against the pillow. 'You can keep talking if you want, but I'm done now.'

'There was only one more thing anyway,' Alex said. 'Leah Cross, I'm arresting you for the supply of a class A substance. You do not have to say anything …'

As she read Leah her rights, Alex returned to stand at the foot of the bed. The girl's silent tears had returned, absorbed into the stiff cotton of the hospital pillowcase. Alex didn't believe for a moment that any of the tears she shed were for the people she had caused harm: for Kirsty Brooks, whose past she had stolen; for Amy Barker, whose life been jeopardised; for Keira, whose life had been taken. Leah Cross's tears were for herself.

CHAPTER SIXTY-EIGHT

Dan, Chloe and Alex sat in Alex's office discussing the morning's events. As requested, Dan had been to visit Melissa Matthews, but the woman's story had remained the same: Leighton had been out the evening Leah had been hit by his car and had come home during the early hours of the following morning. 'She's not shifting,' he told them. 'It was like getting blood from a stone.'

'She's protecting Isobel,' Alex said. She ran a hand through her hair, pushing it back from her face. 'Unless we get something concrete against her, Isobel Matthews is going to walk out of here.'

She sat back in her chair and tilted her face to the ceiling, focusing on the glare of the strip light above. Leah Cross was also likely to walk free, despite the fact that she'd been arrested for supplying the drugs that had landed Amy Barker in hospital. All they had was Amy's statement and the claims Tom had made during his interview, with nothing substantial to support either. They couldn't afford to have anyone else escape justice.

Isobel Matthews was downstairs in one of the interview rooms with a duty solicitor. So far, she had said little. She seemed to know exactly what to do. Presumably she'd already been briefed by her father and was now getting a second helping from the lawyer.

'How are we getting on with the other people from the party? Any updates?'

Dan shook his head. 'A few people have been spoken to, but no one remembers seeing Isobel there. There are quite a lot more still to get through.'

Alex admired Dan's optimism, but she couldn't share it. An ID on Isobel Matthews wouldn't be enough to secure a conviction against her; it would be laughed out of the courtroom. At this rate, they were going to look incompetent at best.

'Isobel wouldn't have needed to be at the party that long,' Chloe said, echoing Alex's concerns. 'She only needed to look for Keira – or Leah, as she thought she was – and if she acted on impulse like you think,' she looked at Alex, 'the whole thing would have been over in moments. The panic was coming from outside by then – that's where everyone's attention would have been. Isobel just needed to slip back downstairs and out through the front door and she was gone.'

'How did she know where to find her, though?' Dan asked. 'Upstairs on the top floor doesn't seem the most obvious place to start.'

'Seems too much of a coincidence that she just chanced on her there,' Chloe agreed.

They sat in silence for a moment, puzzling over the possibilities.

'She asked someone,' Alex said. 'It's the only thing that makes sense. She asked someone where Leah was and someone pointed her in the direction of upstairs.'

'But Leah was in the garden,' Chloe said, blowing the theory apart. 'According to all the housemates' statements, that's where she'd been for most of the night.'

'True.' Alex stood and gestured to Chloe. 'Come on … let's find out what she's got to say for herself.'

Despite her injuries and the events of the past forty-eight hours, Isobel Matthews had found the time and energy to go home, change her clothes and apply make-up. It wasn't enough to conceal the vivid bruising that marked her face and hung in heavy shadows beneath her eyes; if anything, it seemed to draw greater attention to it.

'Could you confirm for the recording that your name is Isobel Matthews; address Flat 24b, Waterview Apartments, Cardiff Bay.'

'Yes.'

'Tell us about what happened at the house on Broadway, please, Miss Matthews.'

'I already told you,' Isobel said. 'I met Leah there. I knew she'd come because she'd think it was my father.'

'Why did you want to meet her?'

'That girl has been sleeping with my father,' Isobel said angrily, a flare of red erupting behind the bruising on her cheeks.

'So you were angry with her?' Alex asked. 'You wanted to confront her about it? You weren't angry with your father too?'

Isobel's jaw tensed. 'I hate him. Everything he's put us through.' She stopped for a moment and sat back in her seat.

'You told us that Leah attacked you.'

Isobel nodded. 'She went crazy, like some wild animal. She just lost it. And then she stabbed herself in the stomach.' She looked to the duty solicitor in disbelief. 'She had the knife in her hand and I thought she was going to attack me with it. Instead, she just stabbed herself. She's a lunatic.'

'How did you find out there was something going on between your father and Leah Cross?'

Isobel hesitated, choosing her words carefully. 'You arrested him for hitting her with his car,' she said, as though they needed reminding of this. 'It didn't take much working out, not with his track record.'

Alex studied Isobel's face, searching for visual indications of her lies. The girl had gone out that evening knowing exactly what she intended to do. She had wanted to hurt Leah, and she had wanted her father to take the blame. Leighton had needed to suffer for everything he had done to his family.

'I think you knew about it before then. Quite a while before then.'

Isobel said nothing.

'Leah was blackmailing your father,' Alex told her. 'You probably already knew that too. How did you find out?'

The girl faced Alex defiantly, but again refused to speak.

'Here's what I think,' Alex said. 'I think you found evidence of Leah's blackmail – a bank statement, perhaps, or an overheard conversation – and you put two and two together. I think you've probably been looking for a while for evidence of another affair. You and your mother have had quite a lot to put up with over the past few years.'

The girl had clammed up now, seeming to realise that anything further she might say could incriminate her. She wore the same resilient look they'd seen stamped on the face of her mother: a calm, determined expression that implied a resolve not to be caught off balance. Where Melissa Matthews was concerned, that resilience appeared to apply to her marriage. It seemed that until now – until her daughter had become involved in such an incriminating way – Melissa had been willing to accept her husband's behaviour, facing each affair with the same headstrong defiance with which she dealt with everything else.

Isobel's resilience told a different story. For her, this seemed a chance for revenge. Her father had made the family suffer. Now she was going to repay the favour. With no evidence against her, everything pointed towards him. She was clearly hoping he would be arrested and charged with the hit-and-run. She must have known that neither of her parents would correct the police in their assumption that it had been Leighton who was responsible.

'Do you go to your father's office regularly?' Alex asked.

Across the table, Isobel's eyes narrowed. 'Why are you asking that?'

'We know that Keira North delivered an essay there for Leah Cross. That essay never made it to Leighton – he claims never to have seen it.'

'Perhaps he's lying,' Isobel said. 'He makes quite a habit of it, haven't you noticed? I don't see what relevance this essay has to anything anyway.'

'Do you want to tell us what you did with it?'

Isobel looked at her lap. 'I don't know what you're talking about.'

'I think you do,' Alex said. 'I think you were there that day, at Leighton's office. Keira wrote an email to your father telling him she'd left the essay on his desk. In that email, she mentioned having spoken briefly with a member of staff there, someone who told her it was fine for her to leave it there. I think that was you. You'd already found out by this point that your father had some sort of involvement with a woman called Leah Cross. You picked up that essay, saw the name, and made the mistake of assuming Keira was Leah.'

Alex sat back for a moment, continuing to study Isobel. The girl's resilience was still firmly stamped in place.

'You probably checked out her Facebook page,' Alex continued. 'You wouldn't have seen much – Leah's account is set to private. But her profile picture is a photograph of her and Keira together.'

Still Isobel said nothing.

'You went to that party with the intention of confronting the girl you thought was Leah Cross about her relationship with your father. What did you hope to do, Isobel? Humiliate her in front of her friends? Or did you set out with the intention of hurting her?' Alex paused, waited a moment, but the young woman's silence was defiant. 'You found her sitting upstairs on the ledge outside her bedroom window. Did she see you come in? Or was her back turned to you, unsuspecting?'

'This is a very elaborate theory, DI King,' the duty solicitor said, 'but have you proof of any of it?'

'I think you reacted impulsively,' Alex continued, ignoring the solicitor. 'All the anger you felt at your father and his behaviour over the years was released for a moment when you pushed her. You went away thinking that some sort of justice had been served. But what then? You saw Keira on the news, realised she wasn't Leah – that you'd made a mistake. You found out she'd been pregnant. Did you feel guilty when you realised what you'd done? Or did it cause a whole wave of fresh anger? It was Leah's fault that Keira died. She needed to pay for it, didn't she?'

Isobel Matthews still refused to respond, but the truth was there. It was in her eyes; in the glazed, watery mist that had filled them and that she now fought back, almost concealing it behind the defiance she wore so well.

Leah Cross and Isobel Matthews might have led very different lives, Alex thought, but in many ways the two girls were so similar. It seemed almost ironic now that they weren't related after all.

'Interview paused at 14.37,' she said, reaching across and stopping the tape recorder. 'You might be interested to know,' she added, standing from her chair, 'that Leah has never been involved with your father. Not in the way you thought. So all this has been for nothing.'

CHAPTER SIXTY-NINE

Alex and Chloe sat in the incident room looking once more at the gallery of faces pinned to the evidence board. They were out of time, and with nothing substantial with which to charge Isobel Matthews, they'd had to let her go. The knowledge smarted. The team was working at maximum capacity to make contact with the people who'd been at the party that night and reassess the CCTV footage from the area, but hope of finding any evidence that way was wearing thin. It was impossible for them to account for every person who might have been at the house at some point during the evening on the night Keira North died.

'What was she like when you spoke to her?' Chloe asked. 'Leah's mother?'

Alex had spoken with Kimberley Cross after her phone conversation with Carol Brooks. Kimberley had been able to fill in the missing details of Leah's past, citing behaviour Alex found entirely believable given the nature of the young woman they had encountered.

'She didn't sound surprised by what's happened. Do you think she had any idea what her daughter was up to, pretending to be another woman's child?'

Alex shook her head. 'Seems she washed her hands of her a while back. By all accounts, Kimberley did everything she could for her after Leah's father died. By the time she hit her teens, her mother was already struggling to handle her.'

'If she was so difficult to manage, why would Carol Brooks offer to have her stay with her family?'

'I wondered the same,' Alex said. 'According to both mothers, Carol's daughter Kirsty and Leah were close throughout secondary school and Leah was very convincing when it came to her version of events. She told people she was neglected, that her mother drank too much and didn't care about her. She played the innocent victim very convincingly.'

'Not difficult to believe. We've seen how good she is at that.'

'Exactly. Kimberley admits she had her problems. Her husband died when Leah was seven – he was killed in an accident at work. She told me she didn't cope well after his death; said she never really recovered from it. She said Leah seemed to resent her and the relationship just got worse over time. Apparently after her husband's death a tribunal decided that the accident had been avoidable and had been caused by personal error, so the company never had to pay out any compensation. The couple were young and he had no life insurance. Kimberley worked two jobs to try to keep afloat, but being out so often meant Leah had free rein to run off the rails. By the time Leah went to stay with Carol, Kimberley was getting therapy for depression and addiction to prescription medication. She admitted all this freely. She said Carol was trying to help her. Carol told me she'd done some fostering in the past, but she bit off more than she could chew with Leah.'

Chloe shook her head. It was difficult to comprehend how such kindness had been repaid with such deceit. 'How did Leah find out so much about the relationship between Carol and Leighton?'

Alex shrugged. 'Both mothers said how close the girls were, so I suppose they talked a lot. They had the fact that they were both missing their fathers in common. Kirsty's stepfather, Jonathan, has been in her life since she was five, but Carol told me she'd always been honest with her about how she was conceived and why she didn't know her real father. Let's remember that Leah was living in the house too – it was easy for her to gain access to photographs of Carol with Kirsty as a baby.'

Chloe shook her head again and studied the image of Leah pinned on to the evidence board. 'Clever,' she mused. 'Very clever.'

'Not so clever she didn't get caught out.'

'Think the same will apply to Isobel?'

'Our best option at the moment is to keep applying the pressure. We get someone who claims to have seen her at the party and we bring her back in. She'll cave in eventually. There's also the knife to consider. It's still with forensics, but once we get it back, we can make a start on finding out where it came from.'

Chloe stretched her legs in front of her and stifled a yawn. 'Do you think Leighton ever questioned Leah's surname? Surely he must have wondered why it wasn't Chambers, or Brooks?'

Alex shrugged. 'She's an expert liar. She knew enough to convince him, I suppose. He knew what he'd done all those years ago; he wasn't prepared to risk losing everything.'

'What do you make of Leah trying to kiss Leighton? No wonder that was a shock for him, given that he still believed she was his daughter.'

'I don't know. The boundaries have all become so blurred, I doubt she knows why she did it. Maybe she's attracted to him. Maybe she felt a different kind of bond developing. I think she came to South Wales with a cash cow in mind, but Leighton perhaps became something more. He seems to have some inexplicable appeal to younger women, though God knows why. Whatever happened, Leah is one very troubled girl.'

'What was the final straw then?' Chloe asked. 'What happened that made Carol Brooks so reluctant to even acknowledge Leah?'

'She stole Kirsty's university savings,' Alex said, standing from her chair. 'Over three thousand pounds, apparently.' She tilted her head to one side, easing the tension in her neck. 'Come on, let's call it a day. We're not going to achieve anything by sitting here wondering what's gone on in the mind of that girl. We'd be here until Christmas.'

'How soon do you reckon we can get Isobel back in?'

Alex glanced at her watch. 'We'll try again tomorrow, but we'll need to be careful. If the Matthewses start shouting harassment, Harry's going to be straight on to us. I still think if we keep pushing hard enough, Isobel will break. Right – home time.'

Alex headed back to her office to retrieve her things, arranging to meet Chloe in the car park. When she got to reception, however, she was intercepted by a flustered-looking desk sergeant, accompanied by a couple of the night-shift officers and a civilian dressed in a supermarket uniform.

'This lady says she's just witnessed an attack out on the street.' The sergeant gestured to the woman in the supermarket uniform. 'Apparently a man hit a woman and bundled her into his car.'

'There's no apparently about it,' the woman said defensively, as though the desk sergeant thought her drunk or mad. She waved an arm in the direction of the main doors. 'I just watched him doing it.'

'Thing is,' one of the officers said to Alex, 'this woman … it sounds as though it might have been Isobel Matthews.'

CHAPTER SEVENTY

'How long ago did Isobel leave here?' Alex asked the desk sergeant.

'By the time she'd been signed out,' he said, glancing back at the clock, 'about ten minutes ago.'

Alex turned her attention to the woman, who had told them her name was Nicola. 'And when did you see this happen?'

'About ten minutes ago; that's what I've been trying to tell him.' She glanced at the desk sergeant exasperatedly before looking back to Alex. 'It would've been less if he'd bloody listened to me. I'd just got off the bus by the park,' she explained. 'I go past here on my walk home; that was when I saw him. He was pacing the street outside, waiting by a car. I should have realised he looked a bit dodgy. She came out of there,' she pointed to the main doors of the station, 'and, I don't know, everything happened so quickly. He called to her, then hit her with something and dragged her into the car.'

Alex looked to the two officers waiting alongside her. 'Has anyone been sent out yet?'

'We've let one of the cars know – they're looking for him now.'

Alex heard the door sound behind her and turned to see Chloe heading towards them, clearly wondering why everyone was gathered in reception.

'Everything all right?' she asked.

'Not quite. This man,' Alex said to Nicola. 'What did he look like?'

'Young. Short hair, dark blonde. He looked on edge, restless, you know? He was definitely waiting for that girl to come out of here.'

'And the car?'

'Light blue,' Nicola said. 'Small. I don't know what make it was … I'm useless with cars.'

It didn't matter: Alex already knew who the young man was. 'Jamie Bateman,' she said, turning to Chloe. 'He's taken Isobel.'

'What? Why?'

'He was the father of Keira's baby,' Alex reminded her. 'Somehow he's found out she was here and now he's making up for what we've been unable to do.'

She turned away for a moment, racking her brain. She had realised how upset Jamie had been over Keira's death, but she would never have anticipated that he might do something like this. She realised that had been an error of judgement. Nobody's behaviour could be predicted.

'All his details are on the database,' she said. 'He drives a blue Fiat – the registration is on file along with the rest of the information. One of you get straight on to a car already out and tell them to go to his address. Could you also take Nicola to one of the interview rooms and take a full statement.' She looked to Nicola. 'You're happy to do that?'

The woman nodded almost too eagerly, pleased that someone was finally taking her seriously.

Alex turned to Chloe. 'There's no one else at the house in Railway Terrace. He might be headed that way.'

'It's the first place we'd look for him,' Chloe said. 'Would he be that reckless?'

Alex pulled a face. 'He's waited outside the station for Isobel and abducted her in the car park. I don't think he's planned this thoroughly, do you? CCTV from the car park,' she said to the desk sergeant. 'Let's check it out, please – confirm it's him.' She looked back to Chloe. 'Is Dan still here?'

Chloe shook her head. 'Left about half an hour ago.'

'We need a call for backup,' Alex said, thinking aloud. 'Wherever he's taking her, he isn't thinking straight. He might have been drinking … he had been when I saw him at Keira's funeral. We need a trace on his mobile. His number's on file too. Meet me back down here.'

She watched Chloe head back upstairs. Wherever Jamie had taken Isobel, she prayed they made it to them in time. She had underestimated how volatile he was; how unpredictable. Jamie seemed to spend his life in the shadow of others. Perhaps he had finally had enough of being underestimated.

She was snapped from her thoughts by the click of the main entrance's double doors as they slid open. A familiar figure entered reception, face set in its trademark grimace.

'Have you released my daughter yet?' Leighton Matthews demanded.

CHAPTER SEVENTY-ONE

Alex pressed her foot further to the accelerator, narrowly missing an amber light turning to red. She had just ended a call to the station, where tracking on Jamie's mobile phone had been run via his service provider. So far they were no closer to finding out where he might have taken Isobel. The officers that had already been out had gone to the house on Railway Terrace, but there was no one there and Jamie's car wasn't anywhere to be seen.

'Do you know what he said, the cheeky bastard?' Alex said, referring to her earlier run-in with Leighton Matthews. 'He said none of this would have happened if we'd done our job properly and arrested Leah earlier.'

'Right,' Chloe said, giving the word three syllables. 'Didn't consider that none of this would have happened if he'd kept his dick in his pants, then?'

Alex shook her head, exasperated. 'Do you know, I'd almost let him take the fall for the hit-and-run just to see him suffer. No wonder his own daughter can't stand him.'

'Do you feel sorry for her at all?'

Alex glanced at Chloe. 'Sorry for Isobel? Christ, no. She may have been through a bit as a kid, but that doesn't give her a green light to take matters into her own hands. There's only so long you can go on blaming your parents for your own decisions. No one made her push Keira from that roof. Leighton didn't make her drive that car at Leah.'

For a moment, the irony of what she'd said rang around her in the confines of the car. Wasn't blaming her mother exactly what she'd done during that embarrassing conversation with Chloe at the kitchen table just a few evenings ago? She had more or less admitted that she'd stopped trying for a family because of her mother's words; that she had allowed Gillian's irrational behaviour to shape her own. She couldn't go on blaming her. She had made a decision, and it had been hers alone. Now she had to live with it.

'Do you, then?' she asked. 'Feel sorry for Isobel?'

Chloe exhaled loudly. 'No, not now. I think there was a moment when I could have, but it was quickly lost during that interview. What she did was calculated, the same as Leah really. Ironic in a way … If they had been sisters, it would have been entirely believable.'

The Bluetooth screen on the dash of Alex's Audi lit up; it was the station.

'We've got a track, but not through Jamie's phone,' the officer at the other end of the line told her. 'We've picked up Isobel's mobile … they're in Porth. Where are you now?'

'Bypass on the way to Llantrisant,' Alex told him. 'We'll turn back and head up there now. Anything more specific?'

'Yeah … we think they're on an industrial estate just off the new road past the bridge. Place should be quiet this time of night; probably why he's there. There's a carpet warehouse next to a vet's clinic on the main road – you need to take the next right into the estate.'

Alex left the roundabout at the last exit, heading back the way they'd just come. 'We'll be about ten minutes,' she said. 'Anyone else closer?'

'There's a car a few minutes away.'

Alex requested to be put through to the other car; within moments she was transferred and was speaking to one of the officers who had earlier been to the house on Railway Terrace.

'Do not approach him until we get there,' she warned him, 'not unless you can see that Isobel is in immediate danger. I don't think he's going to hurt her any more than he already has, but he'll be panicked now, and if he sees us barging in, that might makes things worse. Just hang back for now … we won't be long.'

'How badly hurt is she already?' Chloe asked as Alex ended the call. 'Do we know?'

Alex shook her head. 'The woman who saw it happen said Isobel was hit with something, but she was also pretty certain that when he dragged her to the car she was fighting back. So she was conscious then, at least.'

'Didn't the witness try to intervene?'

'She was across the other side of the main road. She said that by the time she ran over, the car was already pulling out of the car park. There were no other pedestrians about, apparently, only people in vehicles, and none of them bothered to bloody stop and help.'

'Wouldn't have had him down as the type,' Chloe mused, looking out of the passenger window as the A470 rushed past in a blur of concrete.

'That's the point,' Alex said. 'There doesn't seem to be a type.'

CHAPTER SEVENTY-TWO

As they pulled into the entrance of the industrial estate, Alex and Chloe could see the flashing blue light of the police car up ahead, stopped in front of a closed-up garage. There was only one other car in the car park: Jamie's. He was standing by the boot, an officer just a few metres away from him. Jamie was holding a petrol can in one hand, brandishing it in front of him like a sword.

'Shit.' Alex cut the engine and approached the other officer. 'Is backup on the way?'

The man nodded. 'He's covered the car in petrol. We can hear the girl in the boot.'

'Stay there,' Alex warned Chloe, gesturing to the waiting officer. She approached the second officer, who was trying to talk Jamie into stepping away from the car. Isobel's cries could be heard from inside the boot. Intermittent bangs against the metal frame signalled her desperate attempts at escape.

'Jamie,' Alex said softly. 'You don't want to do this.'

She raised a hand to him, palm opened, showing him she was unarmed. As she took a step towards him, she saw the lighter in his other hand, gripped tightly between his fingers.

'I know why you're doing this,' she said, 'but I know that if you go through with it, you'll spend the rest of your life regretting it. This isn't the way, Jamie.'

'What is the way then?' he challenged. 'You just let her go. If you won't do anything, who will?'

'You know when I gave you a lift home from Keira's funeral?' Alex said, taking another tentative step towards him. She reached an arm behind her, the palm of her hand stretched flat to ward back the other officers. 'Know what I was thinking?'

The boy shook his head. His eyes were raw with old tears and wet with fresh ones. It was the sadness that Alex feared the most at that moment. In the midst of his grief, this young man could destroy someone else's life and ruin the rest of his own.

'I was thinking what a nice young man you are. What a shame it is that there aren't more people like you about. Gentle. Kind. The world is full of bad men, Jamie. And bad women … there are plenty of them, too. But it's the people like you that keep the place afloat, isn't it? The honest people – the ones who try their best and don't tell lies and don't cause harm to others. Not knowingly, anyway. Not intentionally. Not like this.'

She stood her ground, not stepping any closer. She looked at the lighter gripped between Jamie's thumb and finger, his hand shaking with the possibility of what it might be capable of.

'Don't be one of the bad guys, Jamie.'

'Why not?' he said, his voice shaking on further tears. 'What do the good guys get? Shitty jobs in glorified call centres. So-called mates who sleep with the girls you like. Kids you never get to meet.'

His voice cracked, his tears now allowed to fall freely. Alex saw his grip around the lighter tighten. The sounds of Isobel Matthews fighting to get the boot of the car open pierced the unnerving silence that had fallen over the car park.

'You let her walk away,' Jamie said, his voice trembling across every syllable. 'She killed Keira and she murdered my baby and you let her walk away. So that's what the bad guys get. That's justice, is it?'

Alex shook her head. Where had he got this from? Who had he spoken to? Someone must have told him that Isobel was suspected of pushing Keira from the window.

Leah. She'd already mentioned Isobel in connection with Keira. Whatever else the girl might have been, she was far from stupid. Even from her hospital bed, she was continuing to wreak mayhem.

'We need time, Jamie, that's all. We'll find the evidence we need, I promise you we will.'

She hated the sound of her own words: lies, all of them. Any evidence that might have been retrieved from the house had been lost; she would never forgive the first attending officers for that. She would never forgive herself. Too many mistakes had been made; too many of them were now culpable for the repercussions. They would need a confession, and there was no reason to believe Isobel would offer them that.

Jamie was shaking his head; he wasn't fooled. 'You won't,' he said. 'If you could, you'd have already done it.'

He raised his hand and thrust the lighter towards the car.

'Jamie,' Alex said, taking another step forward. 'Listen to me. David North lost a daughter too. He could be here now, the same as you – don't you think he feels exactly the way you do? But that's not what Keira would want. She wouldn't want her father to end up in prison because of something someone else was responsible for. And neither would your child.'

Jamie met her eye, his arm still outstretched towards the car; his hand still shaking around the lighter.

'Do the right thing, Jamie, please. This isn't you ... you know it's not.'

The lighter fell from his hand and the young man dropped against the car before sinking to the ground, his body weighted down by his grief.

As the other officers rushed to handcuff him and retrieve the lighter, Alex hurried to the boot of the car. She released the lid and looked down at Isobel, curled into a foetal position and poised to kick out her legs again. Her black eye make-up ran in thick smears down her bruised cheeks and there was blood at her temple where Jamie had hit her.

Chloe's words echoed, and for the briefest of moments – so fleeting it might have been easy to miss it – Alex felt pity for the girl. Then she remembered everything she'd done, and the moment passed, lost to the sudden stillness of the night air.

CHAPTER SEVENTY-THREE

Two days later, Alex and Chloe sat opposite Isobel Matthews in one of the station's interview rooms. This time, she had been formally arrested. By the end of the interview, Alex thought, as she pressed a button on the tape recorder, the girl would be charged with two counts of murder.

'You've had quite an ordeal these past few days,' she noted, after Isobel had confirmed her name and address for the recording. The girl said nothing. They were back to this; the silent treatment and the blank stares that Isobel obviously hoped would be enough to save her skin.

But not this time.

'Where were you on the evening of Sunday 11th June?' Alex asked.

Isobel Matthews glanced at her solicitor. She didn't look as self-assured as she had during the last interview, as though she knew that this time the police had secured the evidence they had previously been lacking.

'I don't know,' she answered. 'At home, probably.'

'Would anyone else be able to confirm that?'

'I live alone.'

Alex nodded. 'Nice flat for someone your age. Cardiff Bay, overlooking the water … must have cost a fair bit. So let's get this right. You hate your father for what he's put your family through over the past few years, that much is obvious. The affairs with his students, the allegations of sexual harassment – that must all have been pretty distressing for you, as well as embarrassing. But you were happy enough to have him buy you a flat.'

Isobel pursed her lips. 'It was a deposit,' she corrected. 'Plenty of people get help from their parents with that. And it was my mother's money anyway.'

Isobel Matthews – along with her mother, Melissa, and younger sister, Olivia – now knew about the affair her father had had when Melissa had been pregnant with her first child. They knew of Leah's deception, and also of the fact that a real half-sister existed: Kirsty Brooks, who maintained she wanted nothing to do with Leighton or his family. Kirsty was now at university in Reading. The news of Leah's deception had apparently come as little surprise to her, though it must have smarted to realise how she had been used and manipulated by a girl she had regarded as a friend and trusted with her secrets.

By all accounts, Melissa had finally told Leighton to leave. Wherever he was staying, he had decided to keep a low profile. Alex had been half expecting him to turn up at the station in a bid to find someone else to blame for his new-found homeless status, but perhaps he was finally taking responsibility for his decisions and actions.

Although she doubted it.

'Had you ever been to that student house before the night of the party?' she asked.

'I've never been to that house,' Isobel said. 'Not on the night of the party … not ever before it.'

'Other than the night you went to Railway Terrace with the intention of hitting Leah with your father's car,' Chloe said.

'What's being done about that man?' Isobel asked, ignoring Chloe's comment. 'I get hit on the head, abducted, nearly set fire to, but I'm the one here being questioned.'

'It was water,' Alex said, sitting back and folding her arms across her chest.

'What?'

'The petrol can. He covered the car in water. He wasn't going to set fire to anything, Isobel; he just wanted you to think you were going to suffer. He wanted you to know what fear feels like.'

Alex sat forward again and reached for the file that sat on the desk in front of her, retrieving a photograph from its contents. Jamie Bateman had been charged with assault and abduction; Alex wished the outcome could have been different for him.

'Do you recognise this?' she asked Isobel, pushing the photograph across the table.

Isobel glanced briefly at it. 'No.'

'You didn't take a very close look.'

'I don't need to. I don't recognise it.'

Alex slipped a hand into the file again and produced another photograph. This time, Isobel's reaction was obvious. It was a photograph of her taken on a night out with friends; an old profile photo retrieved from her Facebook page just the previous day.

Alex turned the image so that it was facing Isobel. She placed a finger on it, pointing out the necklace hanging at Isobel's throat. 'Doesn't the charm on the necklace you're wearing there look very much like the one in the first photograph I showed you?'

Isobel shifted in her seat. 'So? There's probably loads of them about.'

'I notice you're wearing a similar gold chain today. No charm hanging from it, though.'

'It's never had one.'

'When you provide us with that chain you're wearing at the end of this interview, Isobel, a professional jeweller will be able to identify whether this charm,' Alex gestured to the first image she had shown her, 'is a match and was indeed once part of that necklace. Gold has identifying features … it's not a difficult process, apparently.'

Isobel's expression had changed, the colour draining from her cheeks. Her eyes looked grey with the bruising that still remained from Leah's beating; that greyness was now beginning to stain the rest of her features.

'This charm,' Alex said, tapping a finger on the photograph, 'was found by Keira's parents when they went to the house to clear her things from her bedroom. It was lying by the skirting board just inside the bedroom doorway. Keira didn't wear gold jewellery; it irritated her skin. Her parents assumed it belonged to Leah and left it on the chest of drawers. It belongs to you, doesn't it, Isobel?'

The young woman said nothing. She didn't bother now to look at the solicitor, who had fallen silent in the seat beside her.

'One of the other people who attended the party that night has identified you as being there,' Alex continued. 'She said she saw you on the first-floor landing not long before Keira fell. What do you think ... has this person made a mistake?'

For the first time, there was a reaction. A single tear was now tracking its way down Isobel's cheek. As with Leah Cross, Alex doubted whether the tear was for Keira.

'Perhaps this is a mistake as well.' Alex placed two clear bags on the desk between them. 'For the purposes of the recording, I'm showing Miss Matthews exhibit N17 and exhibit T12. You recognise both these, Isobel?'

The young woman's face became ashen as she stared at the knives encased in the plastic bags. She must have known that evidence against her would be found. It seemed the deeper she had fallen into her mission for revenge, the more careless she had become.

'This knife,' Alex said, gesturing to the first of the two bags, 'is the one Leah Cross used to stab herself in the stomach with. The knife that you took with you to the house on Broadway.'

Isobel said nothing, her attention still fixed on the desk in front of her. The solicitor was looking at her with increasing doubt.

'This,' Alex continued, pointing to the second bag, 'is the knife that was used to kill Tom Stoddard. You know who he is, don't you?'

'No,' Isobel said quickly.

'These knives are part of the same set. They were bought at a DIY shop in Cardiff. Guess whose debit card was used?'

For the first time, Isobel dragged her attention from the knives. She focused instead on her hands in her lap; anything to avoid Alex's penetrating stare pressing upon her from the other side of the desk.

'Did you think your father would end up taking the blame for this as well?' Chloe asked. 'The store has provided CCTV footage from its car park, Isobel. There's footage of you leaving the shop after purchasing the knives.'

Alex reached into the file and took a photograph from it: a still from a CCTV camera on the main road four streets from Railway Terrace. She placed it beside the two evidence bags on the table and waited for some sort of reaction from Isobel. DC Jake Sullivan had proven his worth finding this one.

'Something wasn't adding up. We know you killed Tom, but we couldn't work out why. This,' she said, tapping the photograph, 'might explain everything. Again, for the purposes of the tape, I'm showing Miss Matthews exhibit T20. This is Tom Stoddard, walking south along Broadway in Treforest shortly before midnight on the same evening on which Leah Cross was hit by your father's car on Railway Terrace. It would have taken him approximately three minutes to get home from here, by which time it's very likely he would have met up with Leah Cross, who was also making her way home. He saw you hit her, didn't he? Or at the very least, you feared he might have? Tom needed to be silenced.'

Isobel remained silent, a fresh stream of tears now falling. The self-pity was strangely reminiscent of Leah Cross.

'Isobel Matthews. I'm arresting you for the murders of Keira North and Tom Stoddard. You do not have to say anything …'

Alex watched the girl as she cried, unable to feel anything towards her but revulsion. 'Your bitterness towards your father has taken two lives,' she told her. 'Three, in fact. I assume you've not forgotten Keira's daughter?' The scraping of her chair pierced the uncomfortable silence as Alex stood. 'It's cost you your future too, Isobel.'

CHAPTER SEVENTY-FOUR

Chloe followed Alex out of the interview room. 'She's guilty as hell,' she said once the door had closed behind them.

Alex gave her a smile, but there was nothing behind it. She couldn't feel triumphant about this arrest, not this time. Too many people had been dragged into Leah's lies. Until she saw that girl take her day in court, little would feel like a victory. And Leah might still walk away from all this. They had only Amy's identification as evidence. Whether it would be enough to hold up in court remained to be seen. It was one of the unfortunate realities of the job.

The superintendent appeared from the next room, from where he'd been watching the interview play out on a video recording. 'Excellent job,' he said, giving Alex a smile. She knew it was difficult for him to admit, considering all the doubt he had shown during the previous week.

'There's something you should know,' he told them both. 'There's been a raid on a property in Cardiff and three local men have been arrested. The police have been able to make links to who they think is bringing that bloody junk into the country. Irish import, by all accounts.'

'Where does this leave us with Leah Cross?'

'Cardiff has her details and they've been made aware of her possible involvement in the dealing, but unless one of these men now gives police her name, we've got nothing to follow up on, at least not where the drugs are concerned. Amy Barker's ID won't be enough to make it to court, not without evidence.'

'So Leah walks away,' Chloe said.

'Not from everything,' Alex said. 'We can still get her on a blackmail charge, surely?'

Harry nodded. 'It's frustrating, I know, but at the moment that's the best we can hope for. Are you OK?'

The question was aimed at Alex. Her reaction to the prospect of Leah walking away scot-free was evident in the tightening of her jaw. 'No. That girl's still to blame for all of this. A conviction for blackmail will get her, what – a suspended sentence at best?'

'Not necessarily,' Harry told her. 'The amount of money she's had from Leighton will definitely go against her. She could be looking at a custodial sentence.' He shrugged. 'Unfortunately, we can't charge her with being a liar.'

Alex closed her eyes for a moment and exhaled loudly. 'I realise that. It's just … bloody hell, it seems so unfair. That girl's got nine lives.'

Harry offered her a sad smile. 'She'll get her comeuppance eventually. We've met plenty of cases like hers before. In the end, something or someone will catch up with her. I owe you an apology,' he added, unabashed at having to offer it in front of Chloe. 'I doubted you and I was wrong.'

'No you don't,' Alex said quickly. 'Not at all. We got there in the end. I suppose that's all that matters.'

CHAPTER SEVENTY-FIVE

There were few people in the cold hall of the crematorium that afternoon: a couple of the neighbours who had come to pay their last respects and one of the carers from the nursing home who had not-so-secretly always been Gillian's favourite, despite her protestations to the contrary. There was Chloe and Scott, who had kept Alex company all morning, trying to distract her with talk of everyday, mundane topics. Then there was Harry, who sat at the back of the room but whose presence alone was enough to confirm to Alex that the friendship between them was fully restored. Despite the tensions of the previous few weeks, she would be sad to see him go.

Listening to the words of the sermon as they rose from the front of the room like hazy smoke that blurred her vision, Alex thought it strange that after death a person seemed to gain a new character. She almost didn't recognise the woman being described by the white-collared man who had never even known her. Gillian hadn't been the loving, patient woman the priest portrayed with his well-rehearsed words; he made her sound like some sort of Mother Teresa figure. She hadn't been a bad woman either. She had just been normal.

But no one wanted to celebrate normal. No one wanted to mourn its loss.

The crematorium was a depressing place, though Alex realised that was the point. The hard wooden benches, the cold stone floor; the black curtains that hung around her mother's coffin like the Grim Reaper's cloak, enveloping Gillian in an irreversible fate: here, there was no distraction from the harsh realities of death.

'Take comfort from the knowledge that our dear friend Gillian is no longer in pain. Her suffering has been eased by her passing, though we may for some time to come feel as though that pain has been transferred to us in our grief.'

From a distance, the words probably sounded quite nice. There, at the front of the room, their insincerity felt tangible. Alex wondered for a moment whether she might stand up and say something, to contradict the priest, but acceptance had suddenly become a far preferable option. She accepted that this was the right way to say goodbye to her mother. The only way she would find peace with their relationship was to forgive her.

She wondered if – before it had been too late – her mother had also found it in herself to forgive her.

The readings ended and the congregation watched as Gillian's coffin was lowered before disappearing from view. She felt a hand on hers, cold despite the heat outside the hall, and Chloe's fingers closed gently around her own. 'I'm OK,' she told her.

Outside, they gathered in awkward clusters at the side of the small building. The next funeral party had already arrived, a growing sea of short-sleeved black shirts and sombre summer dresses spilling through the gates and flooding the car park. This new group eyed Alex's as though they had invaded their mourning; as though their grief couldn't possibly match up, given how few of them there were.

There was no wake to attend. No warm beer and barely filled sandwiches with curled-up corners. Death didn't seem something to be celebrated, so Alex stood there politely accepting well-intended platitudes from the handful of people who had taken the day off work – cancelling their daily routines in order to be there – while longing for the comfort of her own living room; her own bed.

Embarrassment crept into the faces of some of the people her mother had once known but who had lost touch since her move into the nursing home, as though not knowing what to say was a cause for shame. But what could you possibly say to someone who had watched a person slowly and painfully disintegrate before them, everything they once were becoming the mere echoes of a life left behind?

Alex watched them filter away one by one until only four remained.

'If you need anything …' Harry said, wrapping his broad arms around her in an awkward embrace. 'And I mean that.'

'I know you do. Thanks. Now go on – your kids have waited long enough to have their dad back.'

Harry offered her a smile before saying goodbye to Scott and Chloe, leaving the three of them alone outside the crematorium. They headed to Scott's car.

'You should eat,' Chloe told Alex. 'Shall we pick something up on the way back?'

Alex nodded. She couldn't really think about food yet, but if it kept Chloe happy for five minutes, she'd have agreed to anything. She opened the door when Scott unlocked the car and got into the back seat.

'Have you told Scott yet?' she asked, pulling her handbag on to her lap.

'Told me what?' Scott asked, meeting her eye in the rear-view mirror. He gave Chloe a sideways glance before pulling out onto the main road.

Chloe turned in the passenger seat, her eyebrows raised questioningly. 'No idea,' she said.

'Her contract has come to an end,' Alex said. 'I'm kicking her out.'

Chloe shot her a look, her lips turned up in a knowing smirk, then shook her head. 'God, you're a nightmare,' she said with a smile. 'You know very well I'm not going to argue with you today of all days.'

Alex sat back and rested her head against the window as she watched the crematorium grounds slip from view. Maybe, she thought, Chloe wasn't the only one who needed to move forward.

THEN

The two girls sat on the single bed, their backs resting against the pink patterned wallpaper. Leah drank from the bottle of rosé wine she was clutching before passing it to her friend. 'Haven't you ever wanted to know who he is then, your dad?'

The question was met with a shrug. 'I know who he is. My mother's never kept it from me.'

'But you don't want to see him?'

Kirsty shook her head. 'Not much point now, is there?'

'Don't you feel as though you've missed out by not having a father?'

Kirsty studied Leah for a moment, her friend's face made soft by the blur of alcohol flooding her system. Leah asked a lot of questions. She supposed that was what good friends did, and Leah was even closer than a friend; more like a sister really.

'Not especially. I mean, I've got one. Jonathan's my father. Do *you* feel like you've missed out? I mean, I get that you miss your dad – you can probably remember him, or certain things about him anyway. I never knew mine. You can't miss something you've never had, can you?'

Leah wasn't sure this was true. Growing up, she'd often gone without. She and her mother had never had any money and everything had always been managed on the tightest of budgets. She had missed out on school trips, birthday parties and treats – all the things the other kids in her class seemed to have in abundance. She had grown up seeing what everyone else had and silently loathing them for it.

She had missed out on everything.

How was it possible for her to have never known money and yet miss it so intensely?

'My dad's dead, so it takes away the option. Yours, though … don't you think he owes you something?'

Kirsty gave a wry smile, took another sip of the wine and passed the bottle back to Leah. 'No. He didn't want to stick around – my mother didn't want him around anyway. It would never have worked, us keeping in touch.'

Leah looked around her friend's bedroom and a familiar flood of envy coursed through her. Nice clothes, expensive perfumes lined up on the dressing table; laptop and iPad and the latest smartphone. Kirsty didn't need her real father.

She took a long gulp of wine. It burned the back of her throat before warming her insides. It filled her with a growing confidence. 'Tell me what you know about your dad.'

Her friend looked at her sceptically. 'What do you want to know?'

Leah gave her a smile and shrugged. 'Everything.'

AUTHOR LETTER

Dear Reader

I want to say a huge thank you for choosing to read *The First One to Die*. If you did enjoy it, and want to keep up to date with all my latest releases, just sign up at the following link. Your email address will never be shared and you can unsubscribe at any time.

www.bookouture.com/victoria-jenkins

Writing this book was a very different experience from writing the first in the King and Lane series, and knowing there were readers who enjoyed the first story and wanted to read more of Alex and Chloe gave me a great boost in confidence. I am so grateful for your positive reviews and responses and I hope the characters will continue to provide you with enjoyment and entertainment as their stories progress.

I hope you loved *The First One to Die*; if you did, I would be very grateful if you could write a review. I'd love to hear what you think, and it makes such a difference helping new readers to discover one of my books for the first time.

I love hearing from my readers – you can get in touch on my Facebook page, through Twitter, Goodreads or my website.

Best wishes
Victoria Jenkins

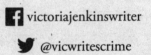

victoriajenkinswriter

@vicwritescrime

ACKNOWLEDGEMENTS

As always, a massive thanks to my editor Jenny Geras and to my agent Anne Williams – it has been a pleasure working with you both on this second book. Thank you to all the Bookouture team – staff and fellow writers – who have made me feel so welcome and have made this whole process a dream come true. Special thanks to Kim Nash and Noelle Holton for promoting my work with such enthusiasm.

Lecturers aren't portrayed in the most positive light in this novel, but that is purely for the sake of the story. My own experience has been far different, and there is one person in particular who has remained in my thoughts while writing: lecturer and poet Nigel Jenkins, a brilliant teacher and a lovely man. I wish I'd thanked you while there was still time.

Thank you to Dad, for always asking how the writing's going and for always telling me to get a move on; I wish you were still able to read this. Thanks to Steve and Kate – my dream team – for keeping me sane; you both know I'd get nothing done without you.

And finally, this book is for a very special little girl: Mia Jenkins, who has already made the world a brighter place. What amazing stories lie ahead of us.

ACKNOWLEDGEMENTS